She awakened and saw his face . . .

Walking across to the bed, Preston saw that Bridget still slept. She lay on her side, her chocolate-brown hair spilling across the pillow. In repose, she looked positively angelic and perfectly harmless. But, of course, he knew better.

He reached down and shook her shoulder. He had not previously noticed how long and thick her eyelashes were, but as they fluttered upon her pale cheeks, Preston once again thought that the girl showed promise. If only she would do something with her hair and wash the grime from her face.

Bridget yawned, stretching her slender arms overhead. Her eyes opened and focused on Preston, her lips slowly curving in apparent appreciation.

Preston frowned, disconcerted by the utterly seductive and feminine smile transforming her features. As she came fully awake, however, the smile disappeared, replaced by a wide-eyed expression of panic. Preston watched in bemusement as Bridget frantically groped beneath the covers. Bolting upright in bed, she suddenly pulled the gun out of concealment, leveling it toward him.

She barely saw his hand as it whipped forward, whisking the gun away. "Give that back!" she demanded.

"You won't be needing it," he answered coolly. "I will abide by my pledge. And you're damned lucky you didn't blow off your foot," he added in rebuke . . .

Also by Casey Claybourne

THE DEVIL'S DARLING

My Lucky Lady

Casey Claybourne

JOVE BOOKS, NEW YORK

MY LUCKY LADY

A Jove Book / published by arrangement with
the author

PRINTING HISTORY
Jove edition / December 1994

ISBN: 0-515-11504-5

A JOVE BOOK®
Jove Books are published by The Berkley Publishing Group,
200 Madison Avenue, New York, New York 10016.
JOVE and the "J" design are trademarks
belonging to Jove Publications, Inc.

PRINTED IN THE UNITED STATES OF AMERICA

10 9 8 7 6 5 4 3 2 1

For my spiritual sister, Judith—
thank you for your love, your support,
and your generous friendship

PROLOGUE

The moonlight glittered on the calm waters of Dunbriggan Bay. All was shadowed in gray and ebony as the filmy clouds danced back and forth in front of the glowing crescent in the sky. Suddenly, from the darkness, appeared a figure, flying wildly across the cool sands. The small being sped down the beach, long hair sailing about her like a ship's banner in the wind. Her joyful laughter carried easily in the night air.

On the cliff above, an old Irishman chuckled to himself as he watched the elfin form race by. 'Twas truly a lucky man who spied a leprechaun, legend said.

CHAPTER
1

The loud, rippling crack shattered the midday quiet only seconds before the traveling coach lurched heavily to one side, tossing its sole occupant forcefully against the far wall.

"Damn and blast!" growled Lord Preston Campton, second Baron of Grenville, as he crashed painfully into the carriage's sturdy wooden frame. The unfortunate baron let loose a descriptive stream of epithets while, all around him, the papers he had been examining floated willy-nilly throughout the coach's interior. The whinnying of the frightened horses and the sudden clap of thunder contributed to the sense of chaos reigning about the toppled carriage.

Gritting his teeth against the sharp pain in his shoulder, Preston pushed himself up and began to climb toward the coach door. Before he reached the top, however, the door was pulled open by his concerned-looking coachman.

"My lord, we've got a bit of bad business," the man advised, extending a helping hand to hoist his employer out of the listing vehicle. "The rear wheel broke coming through a gully. Musta been washed out with the new rain." He gestured to the rut in the road behind them, and Preston sighed, recognizing that his hopes of reaching Sorrelby Hall this evening had been shattered with the wheel.

"Well," muttered Preston in resignation, "at least the next posting inn should be just up around the bend. Phillips, take a horse and have them send a wagon around. We'll have to stay over until the wheel is repaired."

"Aye, my lord." The man scurried off to see to his master's bidding.

Spying his trunk, which had fallen loose during the accident, Preston gingerly walked over and seated himself. He cast a glance to the darkening clouds above him, thinking it only fitting, in light of his recent run of bad luck, that he should get a thorough drenching while awaiting Phillips's return. What with the foul weather that had plagued his trip and the inconclusive documents he had obtained, Preston was beginning to believe his entire mission ill-fated.

The long voyage to Wales had been made with a variety of purposes, foremost of which had been Preston's desire to leave London. The enigmatically aloof baron had grown weary of Society's endless rounds of balls and fetes to which his rather demanding mistress, the widow Chelsea Chesterhaven, had insisted he escort her. Despite his initial attraction to Chelsea's voluptuous charms, those charms had waned the last few months in direct proportion to Preston's increasing boredom.

Therefore, when it came to his attention that a friend of his, Thomas Jamison, had possibly been defrauded by one Lord Frances Pitham into purchasing a racing horse of questionable bloodlines, Preston had made a few discreet inquiries into Pitham's activities. After learning that Lord Pitham had been making a number of sales from his own stables, many of which Preston believed to be suspect, he had decided to verify the papers on Jamison's animal. A visit to the Welsh horse farm had appeared most welcome.

Preston had been reviewing those documents at the time of the accident and, unfortunately, had been unable to find any hard evidence supporting his suspicions. That fact alone had soured Preston's mood, and then the damned accident . . . The jingling of a harness interrupted his musings, and Preston allowed himself a relieved smile as he saw Phillips approaching.

Just a short while later, after having instructed the coachman to see to the carriage's repairs, Preston limped up the stairs of the posting inn to his room. Upon his arrival, he had requested a hot bath be sent up. His shoulder pained him terribly, and he hoped the warm water might ease his discomfort.

Stepping through the doorway, he briefly appraised the accommodations, thankful that despite the accident, he would be spending the night in a warm bed. Although he had been eagerly anticipating a visit to Sorrelby Hall, home to his friends, Colin and Olivia Forster, one more evening on the road would not unduly burden him. After the long trip to Wales, Preston had grown accustomed to living out of a trunk.

Avidly eyeing the steaming bathwater, he quickly stripped off his rumpled clothing and tossed them carelessly to the floor. He stood naked in the middle of the room and flexed his aching muscles, rolling his broad shoulders and rotating his stiff neck.

The mirror across the room reflected the image of an unusually tall and heavily-muscled man whose intimidating size was alleviated by sparkling turquoise eyes and a thick shock of light blond hair. He was certainly a striking specimen of the male of the species, a fact which Preston disregarded due to lack of vanity.

Favoring his bruised knee, Preston crossed the room to his trunk to get out a fresh set of clothes. He stooped and noted with a frown the battering the chest had suffered when it had been flung from the coach during the accident. His long fingers struggled with the bent latch until finally the unwieldy fastening came free.

He threw back the lid to discover a pair of dazed sapphire eyes staring back at him in horror.

Bridget Flannery was in shock. Her enormous blue eyes grew wider and wider, until they threatened to overtake her small face. Crouching before her, as naked as the day he was born, was a man. Not just any man, but a godlike creature molded of rock-hard muscle and golden plains of flesh. One whose muscles rippled like liquid steel as he slowly unbent from his position over the trunk.

"What the bloody hell!"

Bridget started visibly, looking up at the tall stranger now towering far above her. Unfortunately for her sensibilities, her eyes came level with . . . She swallowed convulsively. Her first view of a man was certainly an awesome one, she judged, even as she felt fire begin to burn in her cheeks. Unaware that she had been holding her breath while gaping at this Adonis, Bridget's vision began to blur, reminding her of her need for air. With a gasp, she heaved in a deep, ragged breath. Her sharp intake broke the brief stillness, apparently provoking the handsome stranger. Thick, golden eyebrows drew together in an ominous glower.

"What the hell are you doing in my trunk?" he growled again, the very rafters seeming to quake with the force of his words.

Bridget opened her mouth to answer, but her voice stuck in her parched throat.

She had awoken only a few moments earlier after having been knocked unconscious when the trunk had tumbled from the coach. At least, Bridget presumed some accident had befallen her temporary quarters, for her last memory was one of weightlessness as she felt herself flying through the air and then—darkness.

The man placed his fists upon his hips, his anger becoming more apparent at her lack of response.

"Are you perhaps feeble-minded and incapable of speech?" His voice cut with the keenness of a well-honed blade.

Dry throat notwithstanding, Bridget's rising ire at his slight to her intelligence summoned her voice while her fascination with his nudity gave way to her temper.

"I'm no half-wit, you . . . you hulking exhibitionist!" she shot back at him, blue eyes flashing. "I imagine that certain females might be entertained by you parading your wares

like any wharfside doxy, but I would appreciate you clothing yourself!"

The man's menacing glower became less pronounced as
he tore his eyes from Bridget and hazarded a glance at
his naked form. Bridget thought that perhaps, for a brief
second, humor might have flickered behind those aqua eyes
before the stranger answered her in arctic tones.

"I cannot avail myself of my dressing gown for your bum
is planted squarely upon it."

Bridget followed his gaze to a heap of crushed burgundy
silk. "Oh," she stated evenly, her anger slightly deflated.

She then attempted to rise to remedy the situation only
to discover that her legs had lost all sensation. As her limbs
bore weight, her knees unexpectedly crumpled beneath her,
and she pitched headlong over the side of the trunk.

The floor rushed up to meet her, a forceful collision
imminent. Suddenly Bridget felt herself roughly grabbed
beneath the armpits and swiftly pulled to safety. She blinked
in astonishment as she looked directly into the stranger's
impassive face. Albeit begrudgingly, she had to appreciate
his lightning reaction.

Hanging limply from his outstretched arms, her feet
dangling nearly a foot from the ground, Bridget thought
she knew how a rag doll must feel. Her proximity to his
unclothed body might have unnerved her if not for the
acute onset of pins and needles shooting painfully through
her reawakening limbs.

She squeezed shut her eyes, biting down on her lower lip
to stifle the cries of pain. A tiny drop of blood blossomed
against her pale lips.

"Here now, child, are you all right?" The man shook her,
unintentionally doubling Bridget's discomfort.

Her eyes popped open, and despite the softening she saw
in his features, she snapped, "Dammit, do I *look* all right?"

Still holding her at arm's length, he stared at her curiously for a long moment while she met his gaze with a
belligerent glare, the agony easing in her legs. She was
on the verge of barking at him again regarding his naked

condition, when he pivoted on his heel, wordlessly marched over to the bed, and then unceremoniously dumped her onto the mattress. He paid no heed to her grunt of protest or the thrashing of her tangled limbs as he stalked back to the open trunk to recover his maltreated robe.

Bridget huffed to herself, muttering beneath her breath, as she rolled over onto her back. Coming up on her elbows, she watched him from beneath lowered lashes, galled by her fascination but incapable of averting her gaze. Although she was irritated, she could not help but admire the flexing contours of his lightly furred chest as he shrugged into the silky dressing gown. His muscled shoulders bunched and rolled smoothly, their masculine power fascinating the virginal lass.

While belting the sash, he suddenly looked up, catching Bridget off guard, and she guiltily dropped her eyes.

Annoyed both with herself, for her unbridled interest, and with him, for his bothersome effect upon her, Bridget finally raised her head when she was certain that the embarrassed flush had left her cheeks. She noted with surprise that the man no longer stood in front of the trunk but had moved noiselessly across the room to the bedside chair. Their eyes clashed.

Back home in Ireland, Bridget had developed a somewhat ambiguous celebrity. From an early age she had discovered that she possessed a gift for reading people: an expression, a shift of the body, a certain tone of voice. Through simple observation, she often could ascertain much more of a person than they intended to disclose.

However, at this moment, Bridget found her talents useless, for the stranger's cool gaze and shuttered expression proved completely inaccessible. Loath to surrender him the upper hand in their confrontation, she attempted to school her own features into a similarly stoic mask.

The man's deep voice splintered the silence. "Let us begin at the beginning," he calmly suggested, folding his arms across his broad chest. "I am Lord Preston Campton. Of London. And you are?"

"I don't think I should say."

One brow lifted in mild surprise. "Why is that?"

"I don't trust you."

He obviously found the statement amusing, for a hint of a smile formed at the corners of his generous mouth. "Well," he reminded her, "you trusted me enough to stow away in my trunk."

Bridget sat up on the bed, jamming her hands into the pockets of the old pinafore that she had donned for her escape. "I had no choice," she haughtily retorted.

"No choice of trunks, you mean?"

Bridget glared at the man. He was plainly mocking her. "That's right. No choice of trunks."

"Rather an unconventional mode of travel," he pointed out. "Have you considered a coach?"

"Yes, I have considered a coach," she bit out between clenched teeth. "However, circumstances being what they were, I had to be inventive."

"Well, I'll certainly give you that." His condescending smile rankled Bridget to no end.

"I do regret that I have dragged you into this affair, but—"

"Affair?" he questioned in mock horror.

Bridget bit her tongue to smother an oath. "But," she continued, "it was a truly horrific tangle I was in, and I simply had to do something!"

"Like stow away in a strange man's trunk?"

Oooh, Bridget seethed. *How I'd love to wipe that smarmy smirk off his handsome face!* But she also knew that this Campton fellow held her future in his hands. As of yesterday, she had been only a day's travel from Sorrelby Hall, so even with today's hours on the road, she knew she was still dangerously close. Dangerously close to a Court debut, a forced marriage, and a lifetime as the chattel of some pompous English bore!

"I had hoped that you might help me," she pleaded. Her hands clenched and unclenched in the pocket's folds while she valiantly attempted to muster up a sufficiently forlorn look to gain this man's sympathies. However, Bridget was no expert in the pitiful waif imposture, and her wide eyes and exaggerated sigh only produced a bark of laughter from her audience.

"Dashed, but you're the sly-boots." He chuckled. "Batting those long eyelashes so innocently when what you really yearn to do is scratch my eyes out."

Bridget scowled back at him, piqued that her pretense had not succeeded. "Oh, stop your guffawing. If you were even half a gentleman, you'd hear me out!"

Preston's chuckles subsided as he studied the bedraggled girl. In a slightly more sober tone, he prodded, "All right, let's have it."

Leery of his sudden compliance, Bridget slanted him a suspicious look. He sat placidly with arms folded, a patient, if somewhat doubting, expression on his handsome face.

"Well, you might have noticed that I'm Irish."

Preston nodded, acknowledging the fact.

"At any rate, I'm in the most dire straits. I was tricked into coming to England—I shan't bother you with the details—after having no intention of ever leaving Ireland, only to just discover that I've been brought here—under false pretenses, mind you—to be married off!"

She concluded her speech with an emphatic bob of her head, assuring him, yes, unbelievable as it might seem, it was all quite true.

Preston surveyed her dubiously, his eyes taking in her small form with one swift glance: the freckles, her unbound hair, the voluminous pinafore. "Come now, dear girl. Have you had a row with your governess?"

"Governess?" Bridget echoed, perplexed, following his gaze. With sudden clarity, she understood. *He thinks me a mere child!* So accustomed was she to her diminutive size that she had not fully recognized how she might appear to a stranger, dressed as she was in her old tattered apron. The childlike attire, coupled with her disheveled appearance, most likely stole a few years from her, she thought.

She worried her lower lip, wondering if it might not prove to her advantage should he believe her younger than her nearly nineteen years. He might feel more compassionate to her plight.

"No, truly," she argued, her voice sincere. "They intend to marry me off as soon as possible, and I'm positively terrified."

Preston frowned. "So what do you expect me to do?"

Bridget hopped to her knees, an animated glow enlivening her face. "Please. You must take me back to Ireland, back home."

"Won't you still be in the same predicament?" he questioned darkly.

"Oh, no," Bridget answered, fudging the truth a bit. "You see, my father was away when these other people made their plans for me. But once he returns home, he would never allow anyone to force me into such a decision."

Preston massaged the bridge of his nose with his thumb and forefinger. He felt a headache burgeoning behind his temples, and he was certain it had something to do with this feisty elf.

"I cannot think on an empty stomach. I would imagine you're on the peckish side yourself, hmm?"

The mention of food caused Bridget's stomach to growl most indelicately, and she clamped a palm over the offensive area. With an engaging moue, she answered, "I guess I am."

Preston arose from the chair, tightening the sash about his waist. "I'm going to have a meal sent up." He gestured to the bathtub. "You look as if you are in greater need of a bath than am I, so if you wish to avail yourself, I'll give you ten minutes, no more."

Bridget looked mutely over at the tub and then back to the handsome lord. "You're going out like that?"

Preston smiled wryly as he pulled the robe more firmly across his chest. "It seems as if I have little choice." Then, with an admonishing wag of his finger, he added, "Already, you begin to see the difficulties of traveling with a gentleman, little . . . ?"

"Bridget," she supplied helpfully. She flashed him a captivating grin, which momentarily gave Preston pause.

"Bridget," he softly repeated before quitting the room.

CHAPTER 2

Bridget flopped back onto the bed, releasing an enormous sigh. She had done it! She had escaped!

Not that it had been easy. Fustian, but it had been deuced uncomfortable in that trunk, Bridget reflected irritably, rubbing her backside as she recollected the many hours she had spent curled up like a snail in an undersize shell. Truly, she had been fortunate that the London lord had stopped so early, for she might have been forced to spend a full day in such tight quarters.

As she stared up at the beamed ceiling, Bridget recalled the shocking revelation of only a week ago that had set this catastrophic chain of events into motion.

"*Cousin? I have no cousin!*" she had nearly shouted at the frowning Elspeth.

"Well, the letter said differently, lass," the fractious housekeeper had argued. "The Countess of Sorrelby claims that she's been looking for her mother's family and, according to her, ye are all that remain of her McClellan kin. So, she wants ye to come to England."

"You know that I cannot leave Dunbriggan," Bridget had protested. "If Da were to come home . . ."

Elspeth had rolled her eyes expressively, but she had refrained from launching into her usual litany regarding the futility of Bridget's hopes.

Four years ago Bridget's father had disappeared without a trace. Incapacitated with grief by the untimely death of his young wife, Patrick Flannery had succumbed to the lure of the bottle. So when one evening he mysteriously vanished, the authorities assumed him the victim of a drunken accident. Bridget, however, refused to believe him dead and had clung staunchly to her belief that someday her father would return.

"Don't you see, lass. 'Tis your dream come true," Elspeth had argued impatiently. "This wealthy relative of yours—a countess, no less—is searchin' for her missin' family. With her help," Elspeth had cunningly added, "ye might be able to find yer father."

Prepared to refuse the summons outright, Bridget's mouth had snapped closed once Elspeth invoked the memory of Da. She stood silent, deliberating the housekeeper's words before warily demanding, "Let me see the letter."

Elspeth had claimed the letter had accidentally fallen into the fire. "But, see here, Bridget," she had said, pulling from her pocket a sizable sum. "Here's the money the courier brought for the trip."

Although Bridget had always distrusted the acerbic housekeeper, the sight of such wealth convinced her that Elspeth's tale must be true. Especially since Bridget and Elspeth had been scraping along these past years on the most meager of coin. The possibility of locating her father, combined with Bridget's own nagging restlessness, had eventually swayed her. With mixed emotions, she had broken her self-imposed vow not to leave Dunbriggan until her father's return and had consented to travel to Sorrelby Hall.

Then last night, on the eve of arriving at their destination, she had made a frightening discovery. While Elspeth engaged in her nightly habit of drowning herself in ale at the inn's pub, Bridget had retired to their room. Searching for a handkerchief to use as earplugs against Elspeth's snoring, Bridget had accidentally stumbled upon the letter.

My dear Bridget—

Kindly allow me to introduce myself. I am Olivia Forster, Countess of Sorrelby. My grandmother, Ann Fitzsimmons, was older sister to your mother, Maire. Therefore, we are cousins.

This might not seem of great import to you; however, due to the fact that my mother died when I was but a child, I knew nothing of her ancestry. For years I have yearned to find members of my Irish family, and at last I have found you!

Naturally, I am eager to meet you and pray that you will accept my invitation to come to us at Sorrelby Hall. To this end, I have transmitted the sum of 100 pounds for your traveling expenses.

Lord Sorrelby and I enthusiastically await your arrival. Unfortunately, it is too late to present you this Season, but we have already petitioned for a Court presentation, and I assure you that yours will be a smashing debut! If you don't receive at least a dozen offers, I will be truly shocked!

Have no fear, Bridget, that you will be welcome in our home. Lord Sorrelby and I feel honored to have you join our family, and we shall attend to your every desire. I pray that your journey is a pleasant one, and I hope that you anticipate our meeting as keenly as do I.

> Your cousin,
> Olivia

Faith, but Bridget had been overset! Presented at Court? Married off to some idiot English fop? Leave Dunbriggan forever, abandoning her hopes of Da's return? Not bloody likely, she had told herself.

Now, lying on Lord Campton's bed, Bridget allowed herself a few moments to assess Elspeth's motives. Last night she had been too panicked and too overwrought to think of anything but her escape.

Six years ago, when Bridget's mother had died and Bridget's father had taken to drink, Elspeth had abruptly been saddled not only with the household duties but also with the care of young Bridget. The housekeeper had grown bitter and intractable, especially so after Patrick's disappearance, and Bridget had often wondered why the woman remained with her. Certainly, no love was lost between the two. Bridget had instinctively felt Elspeth's resentment, but since she was alone, she had chosen not to dismiss the housekeeper. Nevertheless, this unshakable evidence of Elspeth's perfidy had unsettled the young woman.

There was no mistaking the fact that Elspeth had lied to her and deceived her. She had purposefully concealed Olivia Forster's missive. But for what reason? The one hundred pounds? A fortune, certainly. When Elspeth had revealed the funds brought by the courier, she had obviously withheld a goodly portion.

But if the money was her objective, why even bother making the trip? Elspeth could have kept the one hundred pounds, disposed of the letter, and never breathed a word to Bridget of Cousin Olivia. Evidently, Elspeth had known that Bridget would not consent to traveling to England once reading Olivia's letter. And, for her own reasons, whatever they may be, Elspeth wanted Bridget to go to Sorrelby.

Bridget rolled onto her stomach, resting her stubborn chin in the palm of her hand. Little matter the purpose for Elspeth's duplicity, wild horses could not drag her to Sorrelby Hall now. The mere idea of being fobbed off to some snuff-snorting, monocle-peering London twit sent shudders of revulsion racing up Bridget's spine.

Ironically, the capricious Fates had provided Bridget a London lord—precisely what she had hoped to escape—as a savior. The only question that remained was said lord's willingness to save her.

When Preston had appeared downstairs in his dressing gown, the innkeeper had quickly ushered him to a private dining room, his sallow face revealing none of his astonishment. He'd been in the business long enough to know that the gentry were prone to queer ways and that silence usually bought one a fat tip.

Alone in the dining room, Preston drummed his fingertips atop the trestle table, contemplating his dilemma. Naturally, he realized that the chit would have to be returned to her guardian immediately. A mere slip of a child could not go gadding about the English countryside unescorted. Preston vaguely recalled having seen a woman of a certain age dining with a small companion last evening at the previous inn. He had paid them scant attention at the time, so eager was he to escape from the rain. But now his mind's eye struggled to reproduce a picture of the woman, whom he assumed to be Bridget's governess.

There had been nothing truly remarkable about the woman, Preston mused. An older woman, she had appeared drawn and pale, thin with light hair. He frowned to himself, dismayed that he could remember nothing more of her. No matter. He had already asked the innkeeper to send a messenger to the Blue Rock Inn with his hastily penned note, advising the governess of Bridget's whereabouts. The poor woman was probably already suffering a severe case of the vapors, having discovered her charge missing.

Preston shook his head with quiet laughter as he pictured Bridget, that naughty minx, stuffing herself into his luggage. Then a chuckle escaped him, echoing loudly in the empty room, with the memory of her flabbergasted expression when he had raised the trunk's lid. His laughter escalated as he silently wondered which of them had suffered the greater shock at her unveiling. The urchin had certainly gotten more than she had bargained for, he thought, now roaring out loud.

"Excuse me, my lord," the innkeeper interrupted from the doorway. "The tray you requested."

Preston's laughter died instantly as the landlord gingerly placed the covered tray at one end of the table. Obviously reluctant to come too near the lunatic lord, the man backed cautiously out the door, a polite smile frozen on his face.

A smile lifted at one corner of Preston's mouth. He hadn't laughed that hard since his wild days up at Oxford! Sadly, the antics of his salad days seemed long past, overshadowed by the more jaded activities of London's social world.

Preston had not always found life in the capital arduous in its artificiality. On the contrary, as a young man he had zealously embraced the freewheeling social license afforded a young, wealthy, attractive member of the nobility. Soon, however, he had seen through the glittering illusion and had decided on a change of pace by embarking on a military stint.

Upon his return, London had seemed even more lacking. Frustrated by this sense of emptiness in his life, Preston had seized upon feminine companionship to fill the void. Although she was a legendary beauty, Chelsea Chesterhaven had proved to be a remarkably poor choice. Spoiled and demanding, she had merely echoed the shallowness he had sought to escape. No, Preston mused, some other element was missing in his life. Something indefinable. He only hoped that this elusive something, his long-awaited epiphany, would soon occur.

Although perhaps not an epiphany, discovering a stowaway in one's luggage certainly qualified as a startling event, Preston reflected with a wry grin. His thoughts returned to the young girl awaiting him upstairs.

He considered her story, questioning its veracity. Marriage. By Jove, that was hard to swallow. The lass could hardly be out of the schoolroom! She couldn't be a day over thirteen, he figured, or, envisioning that dazzling smile right before he quit the room, perhaps fourteen. Fifteen at the outside? Checking his pocket watch, he noted that three minutes remained of the ten allotted.

If luck was with him, he calculated, Bridget's governess should arrive late this evening to retrieve her rebellious ward. At the very least, tomorrow morning should herald the woman's arrival should she decide not to attempt night travel. Preston's mission, therefore, would be to mollify the lass until that time he could hand her over.

Unexpectedly a twinge of regret threaded through his wandering thoughts. Should Bridget's story be more than a Banbury tale, and her fate truly tied to London's marriage mart, Preston knew that the spirited girl would be in for a difficult time. Regardless of her sentiments, she would eventually be bartered and traded to the highest bidder, her future decided for her. Preston shook his head regretfully, believing it nearly criminal to sell a girl, barely out of the nursery, into a loveless marriage.

An unwelcome wave of pity washed over him, and Preston scowled darkly. He could hardly be bothered with every reluctant young miss pushed to the altar before she was ready, he reasoned with his protesting conscience.

Vexed with himself and the predicament forced upon him, he picked up the tray and strode upstairs. Knocking upon the door, he waited for Bridget's summons before pushing open the portal. Instantly his eyes flew to the glinting barrel of the pistol pointed directly at his heart.

CHAPTER 3

Bridget held the heavy pistol with two trembling hands, clamping her jaw tightly to disguise the quivering of her lips. Judging by the expression on Preston's face, her trepidation was far from unwarranted.

Following his initial look of shock, an expression of pure fury compressed Preston's lips into a harsh, rigid line while his turquoise eyes hardened dangerously. Bridget met those glittering blue-green shards, cringing inwardly.

After Preston had left the room, Bridget had replayed their conversation in her mind, eventually concluding it unlikely that the pompous Lord Campton would agree to escort her home. Recalling his arrogant attitude and his somewhat flippant response to her predicament, Bridget had surmised that more forceful persuasion would be necessary to secure Lord Campton's compliance. Once determined to strong-arm the handsome lord, a swift rifling through his belongings had produced the pistol.

Now, as the lethal weapon grew heavy in her hands, Bridget considered the alternative. While the penalty for kidnapping a member of the peerage would be stiff, she would prefer Newgate over a forced marriage. Her resolve strengthened and she steadied her aim.

Slowly Preston leaned over, placing the dinner tray upon the floor. His eyes never left Bridget as he righted himself.

"What are you doing?" His voice lashed her with its controlled rage.

"I'm ensuring your cooperation," she answered him defiantly, thrusting her chin a notch higher into the air.

Bridget watched him carefully as the seconds ticked by, gauging the extent of his anger as he glared threateningly down the nose of the pistol. To her surprise, he suddenly seemed to relax. His broad shoulders dropped with the release of tension, and the anger slipped away from his features. She frowned in consternation.

"Now, Bridget," he began in soothing tones, advancing toward her.

"Stop!" she warned, her voice hoarse with panic. "Not a step closer."

Preston froze as Bridget's finger twitched nervously upon the trigger.

"Do not be so foolish as to believe I will not shoot you, Lord Campton. I am a desperate woma—er, girl. I do not relish the idea of putting a bullet through you, but I would rather kill the both of us than to be taken to London and leg-shackled to some English fribble."

Cautiously Preston lowered his outstretched hand, his gaze riveted to the weapon.

"Give me the gun," he softly ordered.

"I certainly will not!" she burst out, waggling the pistol at him. "You," she ordered, "are going to take me back to Ireland!"

"Of course I will," Preston replied easily, his wary eyes belying the calm tone.

A frown creased Bridget's forehead. "You will?"

"Certainly. I had already planned to do so," he said. "Your little melodrama was totally unnecessary."

Bridget regarded him suspiciously, hopeful that her instincts would assist her in determining his truthfulness.

Unmoving, he reminded her of the statues of the Greek gods she had once studied; his face could have been carved in granite for all the emotion it betrayed. And yet, despite his stillness, Bridget sensed the leashed power pulsating beneath the stony facade. She imagined that at any moment the raw force of him might explode through that seemingly impervious veneer, shattering the man to pieces. But he remained chillingly and masterfully controlled.

Silently, Bridget questioned whether she could ever trust such an enigmatic, yet magnetic, man. She did not know what to make of him for he was unlike anyone she had ever known; the Irish were not renowned for their cool heads, and this Preston Campton brought new meaning to the word *composure*. Unsettling as this might be, Bridget had to make a decision before her fatiguing hand faltered in its grasp of the pistol. Flustered by the havoc his masculinity wreaked on her senses, Bridget doubted whether she could put faith in her usually infallible intuition. Dare she trust him?

Narrowing her eyes, she demanded, "Swear to me on your word of honor—your word as a gentleman—that you will escort me home."

Frigidly Preston returned her stare. "I give you my word as a gentleman that I shall accompany you back to Ireland," he solemnly vowed.

Her stance still cautious, Bridget stepped back. Her stomach ached, either with nerves or hunger, she did not know which. The decision made, she motioned him to the small table with a wave of the pistol. "Very well, then, Lord Campton. Let us eat."

Over the rim of his wineglass Preston studied the audacious little baggage who had dared threaten him with his own pistol. She ate ravenously, her dinner etiquette not quite up to snuff, her concentration solely on the meal. To the side of her plate rested his firearm.

An unbidden smile quirked Preston's lips. Lord, but the lass had nerve! Although he could have overpowered her at any moment and wrested the pistol from her, he had surprised himself by playing along with her. Though loath to admit it, the girl's temerity had earned his grudging respect. He could not name another man of his acquaintance, and certainly no woman, brave enough to pull a weapon on him.

Of course, that was due, in part, to his reputation as a duelist of the first caliber. The bold Irish chit had not the benefit of that knowledge before undertaking her foolhardy stunt.

The girl looked up from her plate. "Aren't you going to eat?"

Preston glanced to his own half-eaten meal. "Yes. I, however, prefer to *savor* my food," he commented pointedly.

Bridget's jaw slowed its chewing as she took his meaning. Deliberately she placed her fork on her plate and picked up her wineglass. She thirstily gulped the expensive claret.

Across the table Preston frowned. "Easy now," he scolded. "Too much of that stuff will stunt your growth."

Bridget shot him a quizzical stare before emitting a bell-like tinkle of laughter. "Is that a joke, Lord Campton? I wouldn't have believed you capable of such levity."

Preston's scowl deepened. "Precocious little minx, aren't you? I only meant that if you ever hoped to fill out that tent you're wearing, you should refrain from drinking spirits."

Bridget examined her oversize garment with a jaundiced eye. Addressing Preston once again, she explained, "I sincerely doubt that I will be doing any more growing, nor is there the slightest chance I shall ever 'fill out' this pinafore."

"Are you the runt of the family, then?"

Preston noted with surprise the flash of vulnerability that crossed her face before she dropped her eyes. Astonished, he realized that his pint-size, gun-toting hellion harbored a weakness. Apparently, in regard to her family.

"I guess I am," she answered him quietly and once again reached for her wine.

Preston assessed Bridget's somber countenance, trying to envision her without the dirt-smudged face and the lanky fall of hair obscuring her features. Truly, he thought, the child might be pretty once cleaned up. Not, he reproached himself, that he ever dallied with underage girls, but if she were as old as fifteen, it wouldn't be so very shocking should her family wish to see her wed.

And what of the pledge he had sworn? He had promised to return her to Ireland. However, he had *not* specified the time. It might very well come to pass that he would escort her home as a married woman. After meeting with Bridget's governess and determining the family's plans for the lass, then Preston could decide how to fulfill his vow.

Glancing over at the girl who was smacking her lips in obvious enjoyment of her repast, Preston thought it improbable she would be married off right away. A touch of London refinement would not be amiss in her case. Clearly, the lass needed a few more lessons in etiquette, and she obviously lacked any regard for the proprieties.

As to proprieties, Preston ruefully considered his own attire. He still had not found the opportunity to clothe himself, and he was beginning to feel a trifle conspicuous in his dressing gown.

"Bridget—may I call you Bridget?"

She bobbed her head in agreement while tearing into a crust of bread.

"I am not *au courant* with kidnapping protocol, but I would like the opportunity to bathe and dress. Since you have the pistol, I would assume that I'll need your . . . approval."

Bridget's gaze slanted to the now ice-cold tub that she had purposefully not availed herself of earlier, having concluded that her unkempt state contributed to her more youthful appearance.

"Well," she considered, noisily swallowing her bread, "I suggest, my lord, that when you request another hot bath, you inquire about a privacy screen."

"Ah." Preston's brow arched in amusement. "So you plan to remain in the room while I bathe?"

Bridget hoisted the pistol from the table, shrugging her shoulders nonchalantly. "I'm afraid we have no choice . . . Preston," she added with a wicked smile.

"And how, pray tell, shall we explain your presence to the innkeeper?" He returned her fiendish smile in kind. "The proprieties of the situation are lax to say the least."

"I will hide."

"In the trunk again?" he inquired hopefully, appearing delighted by the possibility.

"No," Bridget sharply retorted. "Behind the door. With the pistol," she emphasized.

Preston nodded, his disappointment plain. The idea of cramming the urchin into his traveling case had, at least momentarily, enthralled him. He could easily anticipate his satisfaction of dropping the lid upon that mischievous grin.

Elspeth Brady awoke with an atrocious headache and a mouth that felt as if she had eaten cotton for dinner. Groaning, she rationalized her excessive drinking by telling herself that last night represented a celebration. Only one day separated them from Sorrelby Hall . . . and the answer to all her prayers.

Laboriously pushing herself upright, Elspeth established that she was alone in the room. Unconcerned by Bridget's absence, she assumed the lass had gone downstairs for breakfast, or perhaps nuncheon, as the sunshine suggested the hour was late. When her bleary eyes finally focused, a stab of alarm cleared the remaining cobwebs from Elspeth's pickled brain.

The room was in chaos. Having fallen into bed last night in a drunken stupor, she had failed to note either Bridget's absence or the chamber's untidiness. Now the light of day brought both these issues into startling clarity. Especially as Elspeth's gaze fell upon the letter.

Frantically, the woman scrambled out of bed, her heart pounding in her ears. *No, please, no,* she whispered to herself. But grabbing the piece of parchment from the pile of clothing confirmed the housekeeper's worst fears. Bridget had found the letter from Olivia Forster.

"Aagh!" Elspeth wailed, crumpling the incriminating paper in her fist. "Ye stupid girl, ye're going to spoil everything."

For four long years Elspeth had waited. Waited and watched until it came time to collect for her patience and self-perceived sacrifice. While the villagers had pitied, some even mocking, the scrawny Flannery orphan, Elspeth had seen the promise of beauty in the lanky waif. She recognized how the creamy skin and cerulean eyes, although unremarkable on the filthy urchin who ran wild through Dunbriggan, would serve to highlight the girl's lovely features once time softened her sharp angles. And at last these past few months had wrought the changes Elspeth knew were to come. Dunbriggan's little leprechaun had metamorphosed into a breathtaking young woman.

The Flannerys's housekeeper had also been privy to a piece of information that would have greatly shocked young Bridget. The lass was the granddaughter of an Irish duke. Of course, as the daughter of his daughter, Bridget was not in line for any inheritance or title, but her bloodlines were impeccable, the finest to be had.

Since the day Patrick Flannery disappeared, Elspeth had been banking on a marriage settlement for the girl. A young virgin of noble birth, with Bridget's unusual loveliness, would bring Elspeth a tidy sum. Although not a blood relative, after all these years, she considered herself Bridget's guardian and thus, in a position to negotiate on the girl's behalf.

In many ways repulsed by the high-spirited lass whose keen eyes and intuition seemed to cut directly through to Elspeth's avarice, the housekeeper, nevertheless, stuck to her post. She had come to think of Bridget as a marketable commodity, forgetting that a sensitive nature lay beneath the girl's brash demeanor. So, when Lady Sorrelby's letter had arrived, the housekeeper had nearly wept with joy, believing at last to cash in at Bridget's expense.

Surely, Elspeth had conjectured, the extremely wealthy Earl and Countess of Sorrelby would settle a comfortable pension on Bridget's devoted custodian. Especially when Elspeth detailed the many sacrifices she had made, refusing even to marry so as to care for her young ward.

Of course, if Elspeth were forced to admit the truth of the matter, she had deliberately chosen not to marry her beau, James, until he abandoned his career as a high-wayman. As the mistress of Meath County's most notorious thief, Elspeth had even, on occasion, joined James in his criminal activities. Patrick Flannery's monies had expired over a year earlier, in part due to Elspeth's excessive whiskey expenses, so she had augmented their income with ill-gotten gains. Much to Elspeth's relief, Bridget had remained ignorant of her housekeeper's nefarious enterprise.

Sitting upon the cold floor, Elspeth determined that she had to find Bridget. She could not possibly continue to Sorrelby Hall claiming that the lass had run away. However, to hunt the girl down, she would need help. The kind of help that only James could provide. Tossing her articles into her valise, Elspeth silently thanked Olivia Forster for her generous traveling fund. She would need it for her trip back to Ireland.

An hour and a half later a knock sounded at the door heralding the arrival of yet another hot bath. Bridget quickly scurried to the side of the door, admonishing Preston with a finger to her lips to remain silent about her presence. He curtly acknowledged her instruction as he motioned for her to back farther into the wall. Satisfied with her compliance, he grabbed hold of the knob and swung open the portal. Sidestepping around the opening, Preston's body further shielded Bridget from view.

"Another bath for ye, milord," one of the two servants announced as they hefted pails of hot water over the threshold. "And 'ere's the screen ye asked for."

As the man addressed him, Preston inched backward slightly to ensure Bridget's complete concealment. Between his shoulder blades, he could feel her warm breath penetrating the thin silk fabric of his robe, a not altogether unpleasant sensation.

Obviously unable to resist the jibe, the other servant commented with a twinkle in his eye, "Ye're certainly a fastidious one, eh, milord?"

Preston heard a quiet hiccup of laughter behind him and, suppressing an overwhelming desire to thrash one small Irish imp, he smiled unctuously at the pair. "You know what the good book says: Cleanliness is next to godliness."

Shaking their heads at the eccentricities of the upper class, the servants shuffled out the door, mumbling to themselves.

When the latch clicked shut behind them, Preston irritably pivoted about. Bridget stood only a few inches away, her animated face alive with mirth. He watched with absorption as her ginger-colored freckles appeared to dance across the top of her nose with her laughter.

Further aggravated by his sudden interest in her speckled complexion, he warned, "You are fast becoming a thorn in my side, little one."

His ominous tone sobered Bridget somewhat, but still she taunted, "Better a thorn than the barrel of this pistol."

Briefly Preston glanced down at the weapon in her hand, sorely tempted to bring this farce to an end. In a matter of seconds he could disarm her. He reasoned, however, that as long as she believed herself in control, he could more easily maintain his surveillance of her until the governess's arrival. So, Preston took a deep, calming breath and counted to ten.

He had only reached seven when Bridget blithely interrupted, "Unless you wish to order your third bath of the day, I would suggest you hop to it."

"Are you always such a managing baggage, or is it merely when you're packing a pistol?" he gruffly demanded.

Bridget smirked in reply, a dimple materializing to the left of her mouth. To avoid throttling the smugness from her grimy countenance, Preston stalked over to the screen and stepped behind to the tub.

With ill-feigned insouciance, Bridget strolled to the bed, her eyes following his progress. The robe was tossed over the top of the screen, succeeded by the splashing of hot water being added to the tub. A soft groan of pleasure wafted across the chamber when Preston lowered himself into the waters, and it was all Bridget could do not to echo the sultry moan as she envisioned once again that muscled frame. She could not explain her wanton reaction, but there was no denying it. Simply by imagining that wondrous anatomy, Bridget felt her pulse begin to race and her cheeks flush with emotion.

Both enjoying and despising her unchaste preoccupation, her attention was suddenly caught by a note being slipped beneath the bedroom door. Frowning, she cast a glance in Preston's direction, although the muffled splashings assured her he had not seen the note's mysterious appearance. Quietly Bridget hopped off the bed to investigate.

The letter, addressed to Lord Preston Campton, Second Baron of Grenville was sealed. Under the circumstances, however, as his temporary abductor, Bridget felt no compunction in breaking the seal.

Regret to inform you that the lady you sought, Elspeth Brady, departed earlier today without leaving her direction. By your leave, we will retain your letter in the eventuality of her return.

The Blue Rock Inn

The unsuspecting Lord Campton ought to have been grateful for the protection of the privacy screen because the blistering glare Bridget leveled in his direction would certainly have set him afire.

CHAPTER 4

"Bridget," Preston called from the bathtub. "Be a good little girl and fetch me a towel. Just toss it over the screen, will you?"

Her irritation fueled by Preston's unconsciously condescending manner, Bridget narrowed her eyes. What was she now? His handmaiden?

Still clutching the note in her small hand, she answered him, her tone falsely sugar-coated, "Sorry, Preston, dear, but I left your linens at the Blue Rock Inn. I'm afraid that certain items had to be jettisoned in order to accommodate yours truly."

Preston grunted ill-naturedly, his mutterings lamenting the lack of a towel and the other "items" abandoned by the troublesome stowaway. Before he could improvise on a drying device, however, Bridget sauntered around the edge of the screen, waving a piece of parchment above her head.

"But perhaps you could use this instead," she mockingly offered.

Hurriedly Preston strategically positioned the bathing sponge in a futile effort to preserve a modicum of modesty.

"Damnation, girl!" he protested loudly, chagrined to feel his color rising. "This isn't the least bit proper."

But his lecture was cut short as Bridget, holding the paper

between thumb and forefinger, suddenly released the note, and it began slowly wafting toward the bathwater.

Automatically Preston rescued the parchment before it could meet a watery end. His eyes quickly scanned the message, and when he raised his gaze to Bridget, he suffered the scorching blast of her full-blown outrage.

"Word of a gentleman, a rat's ass!" she swore, her Irish lilt fully audible in her anger. "Ye had every intention of turning me over to Elspeth, did ye not?" Azure eyes flamed as she acidly mimicked his earlier words. " 'I had already planned to escort you home. No need for melodrama, Bridget.'

"Ha!" she spat, her hands fisted on her hips. "You London prigs are beneath contempt. Why, you're nothing more than a lying cheat!" Drawing herself up proudly, she righteously proclaimed, "Now, an Irishman's word means something. 'Tis a matter of honor. Nothing *you* could understand, Lord Campton."

Momentarily confounded by the note's contents, Preston was slow in reacting to Bridget's attack. Her final words, nevertheless, captured his full and immediate attention for not once, in his twenty-eight years, had anyone dared to challenge his honor.

Notorious for his rigid composure, Preston nearly choked on her slanderous reference to his integrity. His jaw worked convulsively as he struggled to contain himself. He would be damned if he'd allow some half-pint chit to provoke him to the heights of emotion that even the horrors of the Peninsula War had failed to elicit!

As he battled his indignation, Preston could feel the muscle at his cheekbone spasming, its pulsing appearing to mesmerize Bridget. Her comical, slack-jawed expression revealed both fascination and trepidation.

When finally Preston was able to force words through his clenched jaw, icicles might have dripped from his frosty tone.

"You dare speak of honor. You who have stolen my own weapon in your hare-brained plot to kidnap me so that I may play nurse to a slovenly, tantrum-prone brat!"

Bridget's sharp intake of breath softened Preston not one iota.

"Regardless of what you may think, my word is of value. We leave for Ireland at daybreak. But I give you fair warning, Bridget," he threatened with deadly promise, "should you ever be so foolhardy as to pitch a like fit again, I shall turn you over my knee and give you the sound thrashing that you so richly deserve."

Enormous blue saucers stared back at him, shock and confusion warring in their depths. Preston took advantage of her temporary tongue-tied condition.

"Now, I strongly advise you retire to the other side of the room before I make good on that beating."

Visibly dazed, Bridget hurriedly backed away from the tub, leaving Preston in peace. In peace, he scoffed to himself. He would know no such luxury until he had unloaded this Irish chit. The devil, but the girl swore like a sailor! Her family honestly believed that they would be able to pawn off this undersize shrew on a man of breeding?

Stepping from the tub, Preston shook like a rain-soaked hound before wrapping himself back into the robe. Ruefully he contemplated the reasons for his acquiescence. By all rights, he should be shipped off to Bedlam, he thought. If he had his wits about him, he would deposit the girl on the steps of the first orphanage he could find and then run like hell!

But, dammit, he admired her spunk. Perversely he was drawn to the very characteristic that lay at the root of her pugnacious temperament. She was a handful, by God, but for the time being, his handful. If only due to the fact that she had hidden in his trunk, he felt responsible for her. After all, no gentleman worthy of the title could abandon a lost child in the far corners of England.

And then, of course, there remained Preston's personal reasons for playing along with her half-baked scheme in the first place. Oddly dissatisfied with his life of late, he had been desperately seeking relief from the monotony of his *haute society* existence. Arguably he had not been searching for anything quite as unusual as Bridget, but Providence had tossed him the Irish imp, so he would see his mission complete. He only prayed that he would be able to resist strangling the impudent girl before safely delivering her to Dunbriggan.

Morning dawned all too soon for Preston. Rubbing the base of his spine, he arched his thickly muscled back in an attempt to stretch out the kinks his makeshift bed of hay had produced. Lord, what a night! His restless sleep had been interspersed with nightmares of blue-eyed she-devils leaping from pockets, desk drawers, and coin purses. Especially disturbing, his dreams had held an erotic flavor, usually ending with him making passionate love to these fiendish apparitions.

Grimacing as he recalled his nocturnal fantasies, Preston wondered with horror if he were developing a perverted proclivity for children. No, he staunchly assured himself. 'Twas only that he had been too many weeks without a woman.

Strolling from the stable into the dusky morning light, Preston hoped he would not encounter the innkeeper while sneaking back up to his room. The man already questioned his titled guest's mental condition, and should he discover that although having paid for the best room at the inn, Preston had chosen to sleep in the stables, well . . . Preston shuddered to think.

Luckily all was silent as he crept upstairs and knocked softly upon the door of his chamber. There was no answer, and Preston tapped again. While his knuckles rapped gently, he caught a movement at the corner of his eye and turned to find the landlord watching him bug-eyed from the top of the stairs.

Preston cleared his throat awkwardly, running his hand across the portal's surface. "Solid," he roughly declared. "Nice solid wood." And without further ado, he let himself into the chamber.

Rubbing his hand across his forehead, he decided that he would forgo the morning meal. His stomach growled in protest, but Preston deemed it preferable to skip breakfast rather than to face the innkeeper's leery scrutiny.

Walking across to the bed, Preston saw that Bridget still slept. Curled into a tight ball, she lay on her side, her chocolate-brown hair spilling across the pillow. In repose, she looked positively angelic and perfectly harmless. But, of course, he knew better.

He reached down and shook her shoulder. He had not previously noticed how long and thick her eyelashes were, but as they fluttered upon her pale cheeks, Preston once again thought that the girl showed promise. If only she would do something with her hair and wash the grime from her face.

Bridget yawned, stretching her slender arms overhead. Her eyes opened and focused on Preston, her lips slowly curving in apparent appreciation.

Preston frowned, disconcerted by the utterly seductive and feminine smile transforming her features. As she appeared to come fully awake, however, the smile disappeared, to be replaced by a wide-eyed expression of panic. Preston watched in bemusement as Bridget frantically began groping beneath the covers. Bolting upright in the bed, she suddenly pulled the gun out of concealment, leveling it toward Preston.

Bridget barely even saw Preston's hand as it whipped forward, whisking the gun from her unsuspecting fingers. He glared at her, flagrantly discounting her cry of protest.

"Give that back!" she demanded.

"You won't be needing it," he answered coolly. "I will abide by my pledge. And you're damned lucky you didn't blow off your foot," he added in rebuke.

Bridget's gaze flickered to the pistol, then back to Preston. "I can take care of myself," she belligerently rejoined.

After pocketing the weapon, Preston folded his arms across his chest, a lazy grin forming around his response. "If that is true, then why am I being abducted to protect you?"

Bridget's clear, blue eyes sparkled with indignation. "You're not to protect me! You're to . . . act as facilitator." She frowned. "No innkeeper will let a room to a woma—girl," she hastily corrected, "traveling alone. We will claim that you are my brother, and it will all seem quite respectable."

Preston cocked a disbelieving brow. "Aside from the fact that, physically, we could not be more disparate, I cannot relish even the pretense of such a relationship. Your brother? I would have to be a candidate for canonization, surely."

Ignoring his barb, Bridget conceded, "Well, if anyone asks, we can say that you're my half brother."

Preston smiled crookedly. "Well, I am glad to see that you have some respect for the conventions. I had begun to believe you nothing short of a barbarian. Barging in on a man while he's bathing?" he queried, his amusement evident in his deep voice.

Wrinkling her nose, Bridget scowled at him. "Occasionally, when miffed, I act impulsively. You seem especially gifted at getting my dander up, so you must suffer the consequences. Besides," she added loftily, "a true gentleman would refrain from further mentioning that unfortunate incident."

Preston subdued a laugh, doubting that the little spitfire had known many "true" gentlemen. He could not help but be curious as to the environment in which the lass had been raised to produce such outlandish conduct. Bridget had remained steadfastly close-mouthed regarding her background. Truly, her outrageous behavior would suggest that she had been born in the wilds of the colonies or the jungles of India. Only her refined English accent convinced Preston otherwise.

Bridget glanced to the window impatiently. "Shouldn't we be on our way?"

Preston followed her eyes, noting that the day was indeed growing brighter. Secretly he had hoped to receive a last-minute message from Elspeth the governess—a type of royal reprieve, as it were. He could barely credit that the woman was not frantically searching the countryside for her ward. But the fact that she had failed to leave her direction at the Blue Rock, in the case of Bridget's reappearance, confused him greatly.

He sighed. "Yes, the hour is here."

Bridget looked puzzled by his dramatic tone as she scampered off the bed. "You sound as if you're bound for the gallows."

Preston could hardly confess that her observation was close to the mark.

Shrugging into his coat, he outlined the plan. "I will precede you downstairs and divert the landlord. You will need to creep downstairs, undetected, and slip into the carriage awaiting you in front of the inn. I have already advised my coachman, Phillips, of your . . . er, arrival. He will assist you into the coach. Wait there with the curtains drawn until I join you. Understood?"

Bridget nodded her head vigorously. "What is our first destination?"

"Bristol, a full day's ride. I have my own vessel docked there. The captain, no doubt, will be surprised to see us, but he's a capable man and should have us out of port tomorrow."

"Your own ship?" Bridget queried.

"Yes," Preston drawled. "Propitious, is it not?"

Preston was not surprised to see that she heartily agreed with him as she flashed a self-satisfied grin.

Bridget literally bounced up and down on the luxurious leather squabs, her excitement uncontainable. She was feeling rather full of herself, overwhelmed by the success of her "kidnapping."

Not only had she coerced the laconic Lord Campton into taking her home to Ireland, but the wealthy lord had his own carriage and ship in which she could travel in style. And notwithstanding his unarguable arrogance, the handsome baron made a most pleasant companion with whom to while away the hours of travel. Yes, indeed, Bridget considered herself quite clever in her selection of abductees.

The lush, verdant English landscape appeared even more vibrant this morning in the light of Bridget's good fortune. She admired the emerald valleys and crisp sky, happily whistling an Irish jig.

"Are you always this energetic in the morning?" Preston asked with a hint of irritation as he studied her from across the carriage confines.

"I guess so," she cheerfully returned, swinging her legs back and forth. "I'm certainly not a laze-abed like you London types. I like to keep moving."

Preston crossed his arms across his broad chest. "You have spent a great deal of time in London?"

Gazing out the carriage window, Bridget retorted, "Never been."

"In your studies, then," Preston persisted, "you have learned of the English capital?"

"Good gracious, no," she laughingly returned, wrinkling her pert nose. "Geography always left me cold."

"Then how, pray tell, do you know so much about us 'London types'?"

Bridget swiveled her gaze to his. "Umm," she mumbled, strangely intimidated by the censure she saw in his eyes. "I just figured, well, um . . . that is . . ."

She suddenly felt like the child she was pretending to be, suffering the wrath of a displeased tutor.

Piercing her with a rebuking stare, Preston counseled, "A word of advice, Bridget. Hasty judgment can prove costly."

Softening his tone, he asked, "If you disliked geography, tell me which other subjects interested you."

"Well, I haven't really been at my studies in some time," Bridget scoffed without thinking. Preston's inquiring brow alerted her to her gaffe.

"What I mean to say," she hastily amended, "is that I've studied a wide variety of subjects lately. Geography was in the past."

"What areas are you pursuing now?"

Blast the man, Bridget silently cursed. If he questioned her specifically on a subject, she would undoubtedly reveal her ignorance. Not since before her mother's death had she sat down to proper study. During these past six years, her education had consisted of surreptitious "borrowing" from the vicar's library. Although lately she had suspected that the vicar knew of her unauthorized use of his archive for the door had always been conveniently left unbolted.

"Well," Bridget hedged, "there's been botany and horticulture."

After all, she reasoned, she did tend the garden at home.

"And zoology." She truly loved to fish and had kept a pet cat since she was a child.

"But," Bridget added unconsciously chewing on a fingernail, "the prospect of becoming a bluestocking has kept me primarily involved in household management."

Now, that was certainly the truth, Bridget nervously consoled herself. Elspeth spent the days deep in her cups, never bothering to lift a hand in the household chores, so, naturally, Bridget had been forced to take over the care of their domicile.

"Have you brothers or sisters?"

"None."

"And what of your mother? Is she in favor of your taking an English husband?"

Bridget swiftly turned to the panorama of the rolling countryside, not wishing Preston to glimpse the flash of pain that his question had provoked.

"My mother's dead."

Silence reigned for a long moment.

"I am sorry, Bridget."

The sympathetic rumble in his deep voice unaccountably assuaged the hurtful memory.

"So, that left only you and your father. Tell me about him."

Although his voice was kind, Bridget abruptly became conscious of the trap Preston laid for her. She pivoted her

head around to stare into those knowing blue-green eyes.
A distinctively astute man, Bridget knew that he might
refuse to take her to Dunbriggan should she accidentally
divulge too much information. If he discovered that she
was orphaned, as well as apparently deserted by Elspeth,
he would foil her plans to return.

"Oh, no, you don't," she warily declared. "You have all
you need to know. Just get me back to Dunbriggan."

Preston smiled softly. For one so young, her mental
faculties seemed unusually sharp. Not having known many
children, Preston wondered if Bridget's intellect conformed
to the norm or if, as he suspected, she was possessed of an
especially keen mind.

"Dunbriggan," Preston persevered. "What is it like?"

"Just a fishing village. Nothing but people and fish."

Faint though it was, Preston ascertained a note of melancholy in her voice. "Do you miss it?" he gently asked.

Bridget lowered her dark lashes to shutter her eyes. "I
don't know." She shrugged. "Not really. The villagers think
me odd. They call me the leprechaun."

Preston half-smiled. "The leprechaun?"

"Aye," Bridget answered, unconsciously slipping into her
brogue. "I've never exactly fit in. The villagers—"

Her eyes flashing, Bridget suddenly cut short her words
while casting an accusing glare at Preston. "I positively do
not want to talk about them," she asserted with a fierce
scowl.

Preston masked his disappointment at his failure to glean
more information from the young girl. Instead, he lightly
inquired, "If you don't choose to talk about yourself, your
family, or your home, what would you like to discuss?"

The scowl melted away and Bridget tossed him a saucy
glance. Once again, Preston wondered at her age. Surely,
he thought, she must be at least fourteen. The natural,
unpracticed flirtatious mannerisms suggested a young woman approaching her maturity. And yet again, that filthy,
muslin pinafore she insisted on wearing would be more
suitable for a child half her age.

"Since you say I know nothing of the real London," she answered, folding her hands upon her lap, "why do you not educate me? I would like to hear of your experiences."

His experiences? Preston cringed as myriad images flitted through his mind, primarily involving drink and women. Hardly appropriate subjects for a young girl's ears.

So, disregarding his own forms of entertainment, Preston described the fireworks at Vauxhall and ice-skating in St. James Park. Whenever he exhausted a topic, Bridget shot another question at him, and so they passed the morning in an exhaustive discussion of London and its charms.

CHAPTER
5

Standing on deck of the *Circe*, Bridget rested her hands upon the railing, gazing wistfully at the bloodred sun setting on Bristol Channel. Preston had ordered her to stay below until they set sail in the morning, but the crisp, salty air was too inviting for her to deny. The pungent aroma of the sea reminded her of Dunbriggan, coaxing her from her cabin.

She breathed deeply, desperately wishing that she could run free. Back home, whenever her emotions overcame her, she would send her feet flying down the Irish shores until her heart felt as if it would burst through her chest. Exhausted, she would then fall to the sand, her anger or melancholy spent.

Staring out at the waters, Bridget felt the overpowering need to release her frustration this evening. Simply stated, Preston Campton was driving her mad. Mad with wanting.

He had ridden with her in the coach until their first change of horses, but then he had hired a mount to ride alongside. Left to her own devices, Bridget had spent the remainder of the day fantasizing about her devastatingly handsome escort.

The previous night she had been hard-pressed to fall asleep, envisioning over and over again the magnificence of his nakedness. Tossing and turning, she had tortured herself, wondering if his bronzed muscles would feel as warm to the touch as they appeared.

Although the man rankled and unnerved her, constantly sparking her volatile temper, she could not banish him from her mind. In fact, whenever she consciously tried to put thoughts of him aside, his turquoise eyes and silver-blond hair snuck back into her daydreams, both annoying and pleasing her.

Never before had Bridget experienced the thrill of attraction for a man. The quickening of her pulse when he looked directly into her eyes or the sudden tightening in her stomach when he inadvertently touched her amazed the naive girl. Preston had unknowingly awakened the most thrilling feelings deep within her; feelings Bridget had not even known herself capable of.

Galling, however, was the indisputable fact that he treated her like a child. Of course, Bridget had encouraged the misconception in order to gain Preston's sympathies, so she had only herself to blame for her current predicament. Yet now that her whole body vibrated in response to his masculinity, she desperately wanted him to see her as a woman.

Although more than ready to throw off the childish masquerade, Bridget judged it wise to wait until they had left port. She would maintain her guise for now, but then . . . An impish smile graced her fair face.

Leaning her elbows upon the railing, she dropped her chin into her hands. At times like this, Bridget's thoughts invariably turned to the mother she had lost six years ago. It had been precisely when Bridget had needed her most, as she ventured onto the baffling path of womanhood, that her mother had died. Perhaps if she had lived, Bridget lamented, her mum might have been able to explain these chaotic sensations that Preston invoked in her. No doubt her mother could have advised her in the ways to attract such a man's interest.

Naive as she might be, Bridget recognized that Preston was not your run-of-the-mill male. To her, he seemed to be the knight in shining armor of the fairy tales her mother had read to her as a child.

She sighed despondently. Alas, the fairy tales called for the gallant prince to rescue a lovely princess, and Bridget knew herself to be far from princesslike. No, she was the unruly ragamuffin nobody wanted. The orphaned hoyden running unfettered through the Irish hills, the subject of jokes by the more callous Dunbrigganers.

How dare she hope for someone like Preston when even her own father had not loved her enough to return to her? Bridget dug her nails into her palms, desperately determined to deny the traitorous thought. Of course, Da loved her, she repeated over and over again like a comforting prayer. She had to believe that. She simply had to. For deep down she knew that if she did not, she might believe herself totally unworthy of anyone's love.

A tap at her shoulder startled her, and her heart leaped in anticipation. However, as she pivoted about, she saw only the cabin boy.

"If ye please, dinner is to be served in His Lordship's cabin in ten minutes. He'd like fer ye to join him."

Bridget nodded her acquiescence, and the boy hastened away.

As the sun sunk a little lower into the horizon, Bridget did not allow her spirits to descend with it. Instead, with her unique Irish determination and her inborn resilience, she stubbornly resolved to muddle her way through this foreign experience of feeling like a woman. And, she vowed, to make damn sure that Preston saw her as one!

"What are you reading?"

Preston raised his gaze from the documents he was reviewing for the fifth time in as many minutes. His eyes rested upon the person guilty of all these interruptions, and he repressed an impatient sigh.

Bridget sat in his special chair, the overstuffed Chesterfield; although not quite the thing for sea travel, Preston had insisted on bringing it aboard, as he had grown accustomed to the chair's leathered luxury. Ruefully he surveyed Bridget's filthy skirts draped across the expensive

Cordovan, secretly hoping that the grimy lass was not des-ecrating his throne.

With her legs crossed and tucked under her pinafore, Bridget appeared a mere speck against the massive piece of furniture, the tufted leather seeming to engulf her tiny frame. She watched him curiously while idly twirling a lock of hair about her forefinger.

"I am reviewing bloodlines on a number of horses," he explained, returning his attention to the papers.

"Do you like horses?" she asked.

Oh, God, Preston silently groaned, *here we go again.* Since setting sail that morning, Bridget had investigated every nook and cranny of the ship, inquiring about every-thing from square knots to bilgewater. Preston's throat was raw from the unending dissertations he had expounded on to satisfy the lass's never-ending thirst for knowledge. He would wager that she now knew more about the *Circe* than half his crew!

Closing his eyes, Preston took a deep breath, reminding himself that patience was a virtue.

"Yes," he finally answered. "I take great pride in my stables."

"I wish I had learned to ride," Bridget replied, her voice unmistakably wistful.

"You cannot?"

Bridget shook her head. "I've never even been on a horse. Dunbriggan, you see, is a fishing village and hardly any of us could afford to keep an animal for sport."

"What a pity." Preston reflectively smiled. "There is nothing like the blast of cool air whistling past your ears as you race headlong into the wind."

Preston opened his mouth with the intention of offering to teach her, then quickly snapped it shut. What was he thinking? He would deposit the girl at home in a matter of days, and God willing, that would be the last he'd see of her!

"Oh, I know what *that* feels like," Bridget smugly returned. "I run."

"I beg your pardon?"

"I run. You know, walking, only faster."

Preston's brows met in confusion. "Run from what?"

"I don't run from anything. I just run. Seamus told me that one can lose their sorrows in the Irish wind."

"Seamus?"

Bridget sketched a reminiscent smile. "Ah, he's a bit like me. He's Dunbriggan's local hermit. Older than the fairies, they say." She shook her head as if letting go the memories. "Anyway,'tis just as he said. The wind roaring in your ears, your heart pounding. All you can think of is drawing your next breath."

"Huh," Preston grunted, not entirely sure that he understood. "Interesting."

He picked up the next sheaf of documents, attempting to concentrate.

"Are you thinking of buying those horses?"

That sigh finally escaped him. "No. They've already been purchased." Preston refused to look up from his work.

"If they've already been bought—"

"Bridget!" He cut short his aggravated roar, nearly biting his tongue. Striving for a more pleasant tone, Preston asked, "Would you like me to explain?"

"Yes." Bridget settled more deeply into the chair.

"When you and I met, I was returning from a trip to Wales. A friend of mine, Lord Jamison, had recently purchased a horse from a man whom I believe falsified the animal's papers. I traveled to Wales hoping to find evidence of the fraud."

"Jiminy," Bridget breathed, eyes wide. "Did you?"

Preston distractedly tapped his pen across the corner of the worktable. "Frankly, I cannot tell. I had thought that the forgery would be clear, but it seems I will need to compare these papers to those of the animals in question once I return to London."

Bridget contemplatively chewed on her lower lip.

"Odd that you'd travel all the way to Wales," she observed. "Why shouldn't your friend have gone?"

Preston shrugged with studied nonchalance. "I was not adverse to leaving London at the time."

An inquisitive pair of dark brows arched skyward. "Why was that?"

"I . . . was eager for a change."

"A change of what?" the minx persisted.

"A change of scenery."

Bridget rubbed her cheek speculatively. "That's funny. Your description of London made it seem rather pretty. Is that not so?"

Preston glared at his papers. London reminded him of Chelsea, his vain, self-centered, voluptuous ex-mistress, half the reason he had left the capital. Little Bridget was the last person in the world with whom he wished to discuss Lady Chesterhaven.

"London can be very pretty, yes," he conceded.

"So if it wasn't London itself . . ."

Exasperated, Preston spun about, tired of the question-and-answer game. "Isn't it time for you to go to bed?"

"What?!"

"You've had a busy day poking about the ship," he argued, "and the first day at sea can be quite draining. I think you could use a good night's rest."

"Faith, I don't believe it! I have not been ordered to bed since . . ." Frowning, Bridget lapsed into silence.

"Go on." Preston shooed her away. "We'll be at least another three or four days to Dublin. I promise that you'll have ample time to pester me into an early grave."

As she leaped from the chair, Bridget scowled. "Aren't you going to read me a bedtime story?"

Preston's face darkened at her taunt, the erotic dreams of two nights past flashing into his mind. "I don't think that's a good idea," he succinctly pronounced.

Pouting, Bridget made her exit.

The following afternoon Bridget acquainted herself with the crew, especially Captain Mac, the soft-spoken Scotsman with the glowing red hair. His paternal demeanor reminded

Bridget of her own father, and she happily trotted after him as he regaled her with seafaring tales. As a Scot, like the Irish, he, too, had a great love of folklore, and Bridget forgot all her worries, whiling away the hours in his pleasant company.

However, when she found herself alone again in her cabin that evening, the bothersome images of Preston slunk back into her troubled mind. Yesterday she had chosen to postpone her campaign to attract the captivating baron. She had decided it prudent to wait until they were well at sea before unmasking herself, since Bridget dared not guess how Preston might react to the revelation. God forbid, he might turn about and head back for England!

Now, a full day's sail away, she was ready to mount her attack. She squashed any hint of trepidation, remembering the past two sleepless nights she had suffered. She could not go on like this, fiercely desiring a man who patted her head with a "Good girl" when she produced a clever observation. She wanted that hand to touch her in a different manner, not as if she were an obedient puppy dog!

Having requested a bath be sent to her cabin, Bridget placed her hands upon her hips. *First things first,* she thought firmly. Her eyes scornfully raked the tattered pinafore while wishing that she had taken her new amethyst gown with her when she had fled Elspeth. Frowning, Bridget recalled the attention she had garnered wearing that particular dress during her trip to England. More than one masculine head had turned in her direction, and Bridget did not doubt that the lovely gown had been the reason.

Suddenly her eyes alit on the captain's trunk nailed to the floor. Should she pry? After all, this was her temporary home. Wasn't she entitled to take a peek? Surely, she reasoned, there must be something in there she could use; even a tablecloth would be more attractive than this infantile apron.

Forcefully, Bridget threw open the lid with a clatter, gasping with delight as she saw that her fondest hopes had been miraculously realized. Jewel-toned satins, silks, and velvets created a vivid rainbow of fabrics, shimmering in the dusk's rosy light. Her modest amethyst gown would pale into insignificance compared to the extravagance of this dazzling wardrobe.

Every item a lady of quality might desire lay within the trunk's treasures. Gloves, slippers, bonnets, nightrails, and—Bridget blinked—a mind-boggling selection of silk, lace and cotton unmentionables. Bridget laughed self-consciously, thinking that she wouldn't even know how to put on some of the articles obviously designed for intimate wear.

Sighing with amazement at her good fortune, her eyes returned to the luxurious gowns. Bridget's fingers caressed a bottle-green Florence satin, trimmed in the finest, most delicate lace, and impulsively she pulled the dress from the trunk. Bridget marveled that such finery could be crafted by human hands. 'Twas a dress from a fairy tale, she thought with delight, remembering her daydreams yesterday of gallant knights and fair princesses.

Skipping over to the mirror, the elegant garment draped in front of her, Bridget smiled mysteriously at her reflection. Preston was in for a surprise.

After meeting with the captain to review the sailing orders, Preston settled into his own comfortably appointed cabin with a cigar and a brandy. Truly, it had been a remarkable day, he reflected. Only twice had he been tempted to throttle his diminutive traveling companion, a number he considered phenomenally low in light of her abrasive temperament. Of course, much of that was due to Captain Mac acting as nursemaid throughout the greater portion of the day, leaving Preston a few hours of much needed quiet.

Sipping at the aged brandy, Preston confessed to himself that the hours of quiet had seemed almost too peaceful. He had missed the excited chatter and sparkling eyes, the unique *joie de vivre* with which the girl was blessed. She was as changeable as the sea and as active; one moment rolling easily along, the next pitching and storming. Although she had been dubbed a leprechaun by her townspeople, Preston thought that perhaps a sea nymph might be a more appropriate appellation. She certainly made one feel alive, he thought with a smile.

Glancing to the clock, he noted that dinner was to be served shortly. He hoped that the cabin boy had remembered to advise Bridget early of the appointed dinner time so that tonight, just possibly, she might consider washing up. The girl obviously held no fondness for water, Preston mused, and then laughed to himself, deciding that Bridget could not possibly be a sea nymph.

A tap sounded at the door, and Preston called out his permission to enter. The door swung open so slowly that he wondered if the cabin boy was having difficulty with the dinner trays. To his surprise, no red-cheeked boy entered, but a woman!

Although the fading sun shone at her back, rendering it difficult for Preston to clearly see the outline of her features, the curvaceous silhouette suggested an extraordinarily lovely woman.

Preston quickly sprung from his chair. *By God,* he muttered beneath his breath, *not another stowaway!*

"What is the meaning of this?" he gruffly demanded, advancing menacingly upon the unexpected visitor.

Her answering soft laughter arrested Preston's steps, and he gazed into the woman's face, his own a comical mask of astonishment.

CHAPTER
6

By Jove, the girl was breathtaking! Granted, he had believed his mistress, Chelsea, to be a beautiful woman, and certainly, his dear friend Olivia Forster was renowned for her loveliness, but Bridget . . . Cleansed of the camouflaging soot, her ivory skin glowed like the rarest Chinese silk. And, good God, those lips! How had he previously failed to note their irresistible rosy fullness?

Preston's glazed eyes moved down to the enticing cleft between her creamy breasts. He was dumbfounded to discover the womanly treasures the ridiculous pinafore had been able to conceal. Further inspection revealed a waist so tiny that his hands could easily span its circumference and, to his chagrin, he sensed an impulsive, almost irresistible, itching in his fingertips to do just that.

When at last he remembered to speak, his voice sounded strangled even to his own ears. "You put up your hair?" he hoarsely questioned, in gross understatement of her recent transformation.

Bridget smiled beguilingly. "I did it myself. Do you like it?"

Frankly, Preston had not yet even noticed the upswept curls gently brushing her softly rounded shoulders, but he did so now. Yes, he whispered to himself, he did like her hair.

Dazed, he told himself that this could not possibly be the same ragshag girl he had left tying hitch knots on the foredeck only a few hours earlier. Not the same dirty elf who had, only yesterday, disdainfully scorned his offer of assistance at boarding, instead scrambling agilely up the rope ladder and vaulting over the railing with all the grace and dexterity of a circus monkey. However, his eyes convinced him that it was indeed one and the same.

As he stared unblinking at the pulse beating at the base of her neck, Preston's stupefaction slowly began to recede, giving way to a growing sense of embarrassment. How could he have been so blind! The girl—no, the woman— had taken him for a rube, and he had fallen hook, line, and sinker! Lord, but he had made an absolute fool of himself!

After a long moment of silence Preston inquired in a deceptively soft tone, "Exactly how old are you?"

Bridget cocked her head to one side, her eyes twinkling mischievously. "I will turn nineteen the last day of this year."

"Eighteen years old. Nigh on to nineteen," he stated more to himself than to her. His eyes narrowed imperceptibly. "And why, pray tell, did you allow me to believe you a schoolroom chit?"

Obviously detecting the hint of anger in his deep voice, Bridget shifted uncomfortably.

"Well," she began with ill-feigned innocence, "if you assumed me to be younger than eighteen, 'tis no fault of mine."

"Do not trifle with me, Bridget," he cautioned her. His voice, as well as his expression, were both tightly controlled. "You dressed in that childish monstrosity of an apron merely to dupe me into believing you younger, is that not correct?"

"It most certainly is not," Bridget indignantly huffed. "I always wear that pinafore at home. It allows me more freedom of movement than this sort of thing." She waved disparagingly to the fashionably cut gown that had so pleased her but a moment earlier.

Preston's gaze automatically followed her gesture. His eyes fell upon her bosom, so enticingly displayed by the gown's low décolletage that he momentarily lost all cogent reasoning. Damn, but the brilliant green of the gown contrasted well against her white skin.

He shook himself. What *had* he been saying? He frowned in aggravation, his fingers unconsciously rubbing his temple as if to stimulate the sluggish organ. Fortunately for him, Bridget resumed the line of conversation where Preston had so absentmindedly dropped it.

"I certainly had not intended to deceive you," she defended herself. "There just didn't seem much reason in clearing up your misunderstanding."

Not much reason, Preston wryly repeated to himself, recalling his torrid nocturnal fantasies. He had hardly dared sleep these past nights, he had been so disturbed by his arousing dreams of a certain blue-eyed waif. At any rate, he was vastly relieved to discover that his unconscious lust had been directed toward a woman and not a child.

"Anyway," Bridget continued cheerfully, "I was pleased to discover your sister's gowns." She spread out her skirts, displaying the shimmering fabric. "Of course, I had to pin up the hem, but do you think she'll mind me borrowing just this one dress?"

"Sister?" Preston echoed unthinkingly, confused by the abrupt change of topic.

"I assumed . . ." Bridget brought herself up short, her winged brows meeting in consternation. "You don't have a sister, do you?"

Preston ran a large, bronzed hand through his silver-blond locks. "Well, no, but—"

"To whom do these dresses belong?" she interrupted him, her imperious tone demanding an explanation.

"They belong to me."

Bridget pursed her lips, her raised eyebrows scornfully questioning such an outrageous claim. "They're *not* your size."

"I didn't mean—" Preston blustered. "You know perfectly well that I didn't mean . . . The gowns were purchased for female guests," he finally spat out angrily.

"Oh, no, you don't," he growled, disgruntled to realize that she had neatly turned the tables on him, managing to place *him* on the defensive. "Let's return to the subject at hand: your willful deception. While I'm sure you found it entertaining to hoodwink me so successfully, I am far from pleased to be the butt of your joke. Furthermore, I—"

A loud knock sounded at the door, and Preston whirled around, his face a study in frustrated control. The door swung open, and the cabin boy blundered into the tense scene, his gangly arms laden with the dinner trays. Preston, sensing a disaster about to happen, steadied the lad's elbow when the boy nearly dropped the meal, his awestruck gaze alighting on Bridget.

"M-m-milord," the boy stuttered, addressing Preston although his round eyes were fixed on Bridget. "Th-the cook only sent up dinner for two. I d-didn't know we 'ad another guest on board."

Apparently, the lad did not recognize Bridget, either, Preston deduced. Unaccountably irritated, he regarded the gawking stripling while fighting a startling compulsion to drape a shawl around Bridget's exposed shoulders.

"Only two will be dining this evening, Johnny. Close your mouth and set the table before the dinner grows cold."

"B-but what about Miss Bridget, sir? Should I take a tray to 'er room?"

"That won't be necessary," Preston declared, ignoring Bridget's grin. "Now step to it, boy."

Prodded from his bemused absorption, the boy nervously hastened to his task. As he laid out the dinner, he continually slanted doe-eyed looks at Bridget, who merely returned his adoration with a soft smile. The assignment complete, Johnny stood beside the table, his hands hanging at his sides, his lovesick expression inexplicably souring Preston's stomach.

"You're excused," he barked, more harshly than he

intended. Startled by his master's reprimand, Johnny flushed beet-red and obediently scurried out the door.

"You needn't have shouted at the lad, Preston," Bridget chastised as the door slammed shut and she took the seat he held out for her.

Preston, leaning over her chair, breathed in her floral, freshly bathed scent. This unexpected reminder of her womanliness, and his own galling gullibility, further baited his poor humor.

"I'll speak to my employees any damn way I see fit," he coldly returned, pushing her chair to the table a tad too forcefully. He heard her sharp intake of breath.

"And you needn't shout at me, either, you ill-mannered boor," she snapped.

Seating himself, Preston offered her a supercilious smile. "It's so reassuring to see that although your appearance has changed, your disagreeable temperament remains unaltered."

"*My* disagreeable—" Bridget sputtered. "Why, you practically bit off the poor boy's head!"

"I told you. He works for me and he's paid to have his head bitten off if it suits my purposes."

"What a perfectly hateful attitude," she scoffed, heedless of the warning implicit in Preston's frosty expression. "You London aristocrats actually believe you own people simply because they're on your payroll. My God, to think I had almost believed you human!"

Preston watched her from beneath lowered brows, annoyed to note that Bridget's temper heightened her beauty, bringing a flush to her pale cheeks and turning the blue of her eyes a deep indigo.

"I hasten to remind you that you know nothing of London or its 'hateful' aristocrats."

"Well, I'm learning fast!"

Bridget heaved a deep, indignant breath, causing her bosom to quiver and Preston to spill the wine he was pouring into his glass.

"You still have a lot to learn," he acidly returned, glaring at the burgundy stain expanding upon the white damask cloth.

"And what is that supposed to imply?" she angrily asked, spearing a pea on her fork.

"I mean that although you may dress in a woman's clothes, beneath them, you are still nothing more than a spoiled brat!"

Bridget opened her mouth but no sound came forth. Her fork clattered noisily to her plate as a wounded, lost expression flashed across her face. Roughly she shoved away from the table and ran from the room. *cabin.*

Preston ruefully watched the twitch of her skirts as she fled. Damn, but he had behaved badly. For some unaccountable reason, he had allowed her to pierce his usually impenetrable thick skin. The hurt he had seen in her eyes when he had tossed that last barb had pained him as well. What on earth was the matter with him?

After pouring himself another glass of wine, Preston leaned back in his chair and attempted to rationalize his rare display of ungentlemanly behavior. No man enjoyed being made the fool, he argued to himself. He had every right to be piqued by her outrageous duplicity. Or, a niggling inner voice questioned, was it is his own gullibility that rankled him so?

Of course, he reasoned, her abrupt transformation had taken him completely off guard. For a man accustomed to controlling his environment, including the people within it, he had found Bridget to be less than manageable. And that was when he had believed her to be a child. The "mature" Bridget would probably thoroughly unhinge him if he did not take care.

Preston still found it difficult to grasp how he had failed to notice those feminine curves. Admittedly, she was significantly smaller in stature than most women, but there was certainly nothing meager about her bountiful proportions. No, indeed.

Preston unconsciously sighed, mentally picturing the lush fullness of her mouth. Lord, but that rosebud called out for a

man to taste its nectar! With a regretful smile and a shake of
his head, he mused that only the bravest of men would dare
venture past those curving lips, for although they lured one
with their promise of honey, surely only nettles would be
found on the end of that spitfire's rapier tongue!

Bridget slammed shut the cabin door with a resounding
and satisfying bang. She turned and nodded spiritedly to the
closed portal, mentally shouting "so there" to the imaginary
Lord Campton on the opposite side. Of course, Bridget's
Pyrrhic victory over Preston's smug, lopsided smirk did
little to relieve the grumbling of her empty stomach. While
he dined on lobster, peas, and plum pudding in the comfort
of his cabin, she suffered from both hunger and . . . dare she
admit, heartache?

Unwittingly Preston's jibe had rekindled painful memories of another time when Bridget had tried to be something
she was not.

She had just turned sixteen, and spring had arrived
in Dunbriggan. All around her, Bridget saw the rebirth
of nature and the inevitable pairings as Dunbriggan's
youth succumbed to young love. Disregarding Elspeth's
snickering, Bridget had retrieved one of her mother's old
gowns, scrubbed herself clean, and walked into town. Proud
of her finery, she had not seen how the outdated dress had
hung from her skinny frame like a sack upon an understuffed
scarecrow.

The cobbler's son, a couple years older than herself, had
been the first to note her altered state. His mocking laughter had drawn a crowd until Bridget had been surrounded
by taunting, leering faces. Humiliated, she had run away,
hiding for days in the hills outside of town. When she
finally returned to the cottage, she had changed into her
old pinafore. The woman inside Bridget had hidden behind
that pinafore until now.

Pacing back and forth within the confines of her cabin,
her hands linked behind her, Bridget shrugged away the
bitter memory. She had changed a great deal since then,

if not emotionally, certainly physically. The mirror told her that she was no longer a scrawny child.

Preston, however, had failed to appreciate this change. Bridget scowled, thinking that the disastrous evening had not gone as she had hoped.

She had taken such pains with her hair, jabbing pins hither and thither in her struggle to create some semblance of a fashionable coiffure. And heaven knows 'twas only by the grace of God that she had finally succeeded in shortening the borrowed gown for, once she had buttoned herself into the contraption, she had had no intention of removing the complicated garment. Therefore, she had been forced to pin up the hem while still wearing the dress, pricking her calves and ankles at least a dozen times in her clumsiness.

She had fully expected to bowl Preston over with her Cinderella-like transformation. But for all her efforts, rather than swoon at her feet as she had so naively anticipated, he had harshly berated her for her harmless masquerade. Bridget's sentimental hopes had instantly withered, and the subsequent disappointment had given seed to smoldering resentment. So, of course, at the very first provocation, she had flown into the boughs and ruined her plans for Preston to finally see her as a woman.

Bridget paused in her pacing to step over to the mirror. Critically studying her reflection, she saw nothing out of the ordinary. Bath, hair, and gown notwithstanding, she was still just Bridget Flannery, Dunbriggan's infamous leprechaun.

Reluctantly she recalled Preston's explanation regarding the feminine wardrobe he kept aboard for "female guests." Her heart contracted with an unfamiliar stab of jealousy as she wondered what type of woman Preston generally entertained on his ship. A sophisticated, worldly woman, no doubt, one whom he would not need to reprimand for her slovenly eating habits or her propensity for foul language. A lady, in every sense of the word; a title which Bridget could never aspire to lay claim to.

Turning away from the pensive face staring back at her,

Bridget crawled onto the bed, tucking her feet beneath her as she pondered her plight. Damn the infuriating man! Here she sat, brooding like some infatuated ninny, while he wouldn't give two figs for her! She had only to remember his wooden expression when she first entered his cabin this evening to realize as much.

In fact, she admitted, only twice had she been able to disrupt Preston's perpetual mask of stoicism: first, when she had leaped from his trunk and then, again, when she had barged into his bath. Really, she thought with exasperation, she could hardly hope to continually garner his attention by such outlandish methods!

A knock at the door startled her from her musings. Leaping hurriedly from the bed, Bridget's skirts tripped her up, and she crashed into a table before forcefully reminding herself to slow down and walk like a lady. Squaring her shoulders and smoothing her skirts, she continued sedately to the door.

As she pulled open the door, she schooled her features into what she hoped was a placid smile of welcome, scrupulously attempting to conceal her happiness at finding the object of her contemplation at the door. Preston leaned casually against the doorframe, a tray balanced upon his large palm.

Glancing curiously past her into the cabin, he asked, "Is everything all right?"

Anxiously Bridget pivoted about to follow his gaze then turned back to Preston. "Yes, of course."

"I thought I might have heard something fall," he explained, a slight frown between his aquamarine eyes. Bridget winced but made no comment.

Straightening away from the doorframe, Preston nodded toward the tray in his hand. "I brought you dinner," he offered. "I have seen your healthy appetite and . . ." He paused. "I felt ashamed that my display of temper drove you away from your meal. I was unnecessarily harsh, and I have come to apologize. I hope to persuade you to enjoy this fine repast."

Bridget wanted to shout with triumph but restrained herself. An apology! Would wonders never cease? Now, if she could only hold on to her own temper, this evening might not be a complete and utter failure after all, she thought.

Gracefully she bowed her head in acknowledgment of his statement. "Please, come in," she softly entreated, backing away from the door. Her downcast eyes failed to catch the glimmer of amusement in Preston's face as he marveled at her stately demeanor.

"Thank you," he answered, the corners of his mouth twitching as he walked into the cabin and closed the door.

Whispering to herself, Bridget tried to dredge up the lessons on etiquette her mother had endeavored to instill in her headstrong daughter so many years ago. She gnawed on her lip as she followed Preston to the small table. Was she supposed to curtsy before taking her seat?

Preston laid the tray down and moved away from the table as if ready to take his leave. "If you—" he began.

"Won't you join me?" Bridget blurted out. "I mean, I know that you already ate, but would you mind sitting with me?"

Bridget easily read the quizzical stare he leveled at her but offered no explanation for her sudden desire for his company.

He bowed slightly, answering her with a slight smile. "I would be honored."

Throughout the meal, Bridget studiously and daintily chewed her food, gently replaced her fork and knife upon her plate, and made prodigious use of her napkin, constantly dabbing and patting at invisible crumbs. Considering that lobster was the main course, she found herself truly challenged not to simply hoist up the creature by a claw and tear her teeth into the awkward crustacean.

From time to time she would glance up, certain that she glimpsed humor lurking behind Preston's opaque eyes, but a second look always found his aspect to be most somber.

For his part, Preston considered it an extraordinary achievement not to fall to the floor in hysterics. Never had he seen anyone consume an entire lobster with such unsoiled diligence. A messy affair, one was usually allowed certain liberties in the consumption of the delicacy, but Bridget's exactness was simply unparalleled. He could not help but wonder at her sudden fastidiousness since only this afternoon, at the midday meal, she had torn into a plate of roast partridge with the eagerness of a feral dog. His censorious regard had tempered her enthusiasm a tad, yet she had still consumed the enormous meal in what must have been record time. He stifled a chuckle at the memory.

Looking across the table, he theorized on his traveling companion's deliberate modifications of both appearance and behavior. What had so induced her to assume the identity of a lady when she had previously appeared quite content to be nothing more than a hot-tempered hoyden? Cynically he asked himself if perhaps Bridget were angling to compromise herself. She was, after all, traveling unaccompanied with a gentleman—a highly irregular circumstance.

If, however, she had marriage-minded designs, surely she would be more than eager to get to London, he debated. To the contrary, she had literally shanghaied him in her desire to return to Ireland.

Further, this metamorphosis shed an entirely different light on Preston's job as escort. Before, he had believed that he was transporting a runaway child home. Now, however, he accompanied an unattached young woman—a surefire route to a leg-shackle. Admittedly, Bridget had suggested that they travel as brother and sister, but that still did not exonerate her from scheming for a marriage license.

As Bridget delicately finished the plum pudding, Preston decided to maintain a watchful eye on his temporary charge. She had to be up to something.

CHAPTER
7

"James," the gray-faced woman called loudly as she approached the seemingly deserted cottage. "James, it's Elspeth. Where are ye, man?"

Exhausted from her traveling through the past two nights, Bridget's housekeeper dragged a weary hand across her brow while her colorless eyes nervously searched the perimeter of the dense thicket. She feared that she might collapse in despair should James have played his common trick of changing hideouts during this past week.

Suddenly a shifting form displaced the deep shadows of the forest and a burly man appeared through the concealing trees. He was as dark as the Irish woods from which he came, black-eyed, black-haired, and black-tempered. He glared at the thin woman as she slid thankfully from the horse's back.

"What're ye doin' 'ere in the light o'day, Elspeth?"

"Now, James, don't be gettin' riled, but I need yer help," she wheedled, her pale blue eyes beseeching. Her lank hair fell about her face, and a layer of dust covered her from head to toe, but her beau seemed not to mind overmuch.

The highwayman, his ire apparently forgotten, presented her with a licentious smile and, reaching forward, abruptly grabbed hold of Elspeth's wrist. None too gently, he pulled her against his broad chest.

"Why don't ye help me first, lass?" he cajoled, his dark eyes burning from weeks of unslaked lust. "Give us a kiss now."

Without hesitation, Elspeth complied, falling willingly into his lusty embrace. She did not protest when the big man swung her up into his arms and marched toward the cabin door, but she did wish to remind him that she had another purpose for coming. "James, don't forget. I do need to talk t'ye."

"Ye can talk after, woman. Right now I need ye."

The cottage reeked of mold, whiskey, and unbathed bodies. The aroma did not sit well on Elspeth's already queasy stomach, although she forgot her ailment in the throes of her lover's passion.

As usual, James did not embellish upon the basics, and it was only a few minutes later that Elspeth sat up, rearranging her skirts. She glanced over at her bedmate, who was still panting from his exertions, and decided that now was as good a time as any to bring up her request.

"James, Bridget has run away."

He snorted into the mattress. "Good riddance, I'd say. She always gave me the willies, that one did. Like she could see right through ye."

Elspeth frowned at her beau's muddy boots, which he had neglected to remove prior to their interlude. "Ye don't understand, James. I've got to find 'er."

The man rolled onto his side, his eyes half-closed. "What for? The scrawny li'l bit's old 'nough to take care of 'erself."

"Ye haven't seen her in a good six month's time, James. The lass isn't as scrawny as ye remember."

"So?" James scratched at his bushy mustache, obviously befuddled as to Elspeth's sudden concern for the girl.

"Well," Elspeth slowly began, resigning herself to the fact that she would have to share her spoils. "Remember that trip to England I was makin' with the lass?"

James grunted in response, and Elspeth proceeded to outline her plans to con a hefty settlement from the Earl and

Countess of Sorrelby. When she mentioned the sum that had been sent merely to cover traveling expenses, James sat up on the bed, his interest clearly piqued.

Unfortunately, not blessed with exceptionally quick wits, the highwayman still had difficulty piecing the plot together.

"But they plan to pay ye for bringing the girl to England, right?"

Elspeth nodded in agreement.

"Well, then, how d'ye plan to weasel more outa the earl and 'is lady?" He recommenced his confused scratching.

Sighing heavily, Elspeth tried again to explain. "When I make them understand how much I sacrificed for the lass"—she ignored James's derisive laugh—"and how I was countin' on a marriage settlement as a pension for my old age—"

"Which is just about on ye," James interrupted, sniggering.

Elspeth slapped his shoulder but proceeded, "—they'll surely wish to repay me for all that I've done for their sweet Irish cousin."

"But a marriage settlement?" James scoffed. "Come on, now, Elspeth. Ye'd have to be the one to pay to get that filthy dickens off yer hands," he mocked.

The housekeeper shook her head at her beau's mental deficiency. "I'm tellin' ye, man, the girl has changed."

James cocked a graying caterpillar-like eyebrow. "Faith, but she woulda 'ad to," he proclaimed.

Elspeth disregarded his comment. "Are ye comin' to England to help me find her or not?" she demanded.

"By all the saints, woman, what makes ye think we can even find 'er? By the time we cross the Channel again, she'll 'ave a good week's headstart."

"But the girl has not even a farthing. Nothin'. How far can she go?" At James's doubting expression, Elspeth coaxed, "And if we do find her, think of the money, love. Ye could retire off the pension." Prudently she did not add that upon his retirement, she planned for him to make an honest woman of her.

The highwayman rolled over to pluck a piece of straw from the floor. Picking his teeth with the dirty implement, he assumed a thoughtful expression.

"Well, Elspeth, me girl. I'll make ye a deal. I see how ye need to find the lass soon, but I cannot leave until tomorrow. There's a job lined up for t'night that's too good to pass up. But," he suggested, "if ye want to lend me a hand with t'night's work, I'll go with ye first thing in the morn."

Elspeth agreed, although she would have been happier leaving immediately. As tired as she felt from the trip, she was more than eager to get her hands on Bridget again, for she felt certain that the girl was the key to her fortune.

Due to favorable winds, the *Circe* spanned the waters of the Irish Channel in only four days time. Preston and Bridget had spent the final three days in a surreptitious game of masquerades. Bridget played the role of a gently bred woman, only occasionally allowing an oath to slip from her forgetful tongue. She was able to hold her volatile temper in check, mainly due to the fact that Preston said very little for the remainder of their voyage. He politely listened to her chatter about fishing and Irish folklore, but remained quietly reserved as he watched Bridget struggling with her guise of a lady. He made no attempts to bait her into one of her typical outbursts, although, perversely, he missed her high-spirited banter.

He had yet to unravel the mystery of her abrupt metamorphosis, but he felt confident that if he were patient, she would eventually reveal her motive. It was patently obvious that her upbringing was sadly deficient in certain areas, although her refined accent hinted of the upper class. Once or twice, he had tried to prod her into divulging something of her background, but she had astutely recognized his intent and deflected his queries.

On more than one occasion she had unconsciously revealed a vulnerability to the subject of family, the blue of her eyes clouding before she had turned away from Preston's keen scrutiny.

"You mentioned your father during our first meeting," Preston had subtly probed one quiet afternoon. "Will he be at home when we reach Dunbriggan?"

Intent on learning to knit—one of the sailors had offered to teach her—Bridget's eyes were on the pile of mangled yarn overflowing her lap. Preston noted that her fingers momentarily stilled while she measured her response.

"I cannot be certain," she had answered haltingly. "He is away a great deal of the time."

"Away on business?"

Bridget's fingers clenched around the knitting needles, her knuckles white. "I believe so."

In spite of his burning curiosity, Preston had let the subject pass since Bridget appeared so uncomfortable with his questioning.

He had not, however, completely abandoned his desire to learn more of the secretive young Irishwoman. If he had found her entertaining when posing as a child, the womanly Bridget was beginning to become an obsession. Preston found himself continually watching her movements, weighing her words, attempting to make sense of the numerous contradictions that constituted Miss Bridget Flannery.

She was unsophisticated, yet cultured; artless, yet naturally coquettish. And although she had a hot temper, Preston found her to be one of the most compassionate people he had known. But what most intrigued him about his mysterious traveling companion was the occasional glimpses of vulnerability she unknowingly afforded him. She had appeared so brash at their first meeting, wielding his firearm with admirable bravado, that Preston found her buried sensitivity to be in unforeseen contrast to his initial impression of her.

So, he studied her, while he and Bridget performed a strange dance of drawing close, then skittering apart when one or the other grew uncomfortable.

By the time they finally pulled into port, Preston felt as if they had both been on emotional tenterhooks. He had gleaned enough from Bridget to learn that her home lay only a day's ride from Dublin, and it was with ambivalent emotions that he steadied her hand as she stepped onto the dock. His mission was nearly complete.

Preston had sent Phillips ahead to seek out lodging for the night, and as they ambled into the inn, Preston nodded with satisfaction. He had specifically ordered the coachman to select a respectable lodging place not frequented by the aristocracy. Unlikely as it might seem, he would not want the misfortune of meeting someone of his acquaintance while traveling with a young woman. Bridget's reputation would be immediately ruined as he would not be able to claim her as his sister. And then, of course, he would be required to repair the damage done to her reputation. . . . His mind quickly shied away from the thoroughly unnerving consequences.

Solicitously cradling Bridget's elbow in his hand, he steered her into the inn's central room. Though not of the first caliber, the roaring fire in the hearth and the sheen from the freshly washed floors assured Preston that Phillips had chosen well.

The hour grew late, and he could hear the faint rumblings of Bridget's stomach as it called for its dinner. Lord, but the undersized wench had the appetite of a trencherman! With a shake of his head he appreciatively scanned her diminutive waist. He would swear that she had outeaten him at every meal they had shared. He could not imagine where she packed it away, but as the thought entered his head, he glanced down to her deep cleavage and felt that he had found his answer.

A movement to his far right caught Preston's eye, and he quickly glanced over to an oddly matched couple standing at the base of the staircase. A swarthy, bearlike man, a cap pulled low over his eyes, accompanied a frail, washed-out woman sporting a gown too young for her years. But what had captured Preston's attention was the woman's startled reaction as she clasped a shaky hand to her bosom, her pale gaze affixed to Bridget.

Preston immediately recognized Elspeth from the Blue
Rock Inn. The infamous governess. At last, he thought with
a spurt of anticipation, he would have some answers to the
mystery surrounding Bridget's flight from England and this
woman.

Apparently Bridget had not yet realized that she was the
focus of the stranger's attention, her own interest centered
on the aromatic trays being carried to the dining room.

"You have an admirer, Bridget," Preston advised her, his
voice subdued so as not to carry.

"What?" Bridget turned to Preston, but, in doing so,
Elspeth and James crossed into her line of vision. Preston
felt her startled jump beneath his hand.

"Is that not your governess?" he gently questioned. He
could sense the onset of her panic, but before she could
answer, the woman scurried over to them.

Throwing her arms around Bridget, she cried, "Oh,
Bridget, me dearest girl, I was so afeared for ye. 'Tis
glad I am that ye've found me, love."

Preston saw Bridget stiffen under the unfamiliar embrace,
and her eyes leaped to his in a silent, anguished plea.
Instinctively responding to the unspoken message, Preston
reached over and wrapped a protective arm around Bridget's
shoulders, pulling her away from the woman's embrace.

Upon having Bridget dragged from her arms, Elspeth
stepped back to look up into Preston's face. "And just who
might ye be?" she irritably demanded.

"I am Bridget's temporary guardian," he answered,
relishing the look of outrage forming on the older woman's
face. "And you are?"

"Why, I am Bridget's guardian!" Elspeth fiercely remonstrated. She opened her mouth to say something else, but
Preston brusquely forestalled her.

"Then we have much to discuss. Wait here for me while
I see that Bridget is settled comfortably in her room." He
spoke like a man accustomed to being obeyed, as well
he was, and Elspeth automatically complied with his curt
demand.

After procuring the keys to their rooms, Preston guided an unusually silent Bridget upstairs. Unlocking the door to her room, he almost pushed her inside. Suddenly she spun about to face Preston, her blue eyes enormous in her small face. "What are you going to do with me?"

As at the dock, Preston experienced a pang of regret at the thought of walking away from Bridget. Despite all her spunk and bluster, she remained refreshingly naive, and he felt an inexplicable need to protect that naivety.

"Do not fret," he consoled her, placing a warm hand upon her shoulder. "I will not go against your wishes."

He felt some of her tension dissipate as she looked searchingly into his face.

"Do you know my wishes, Preston?" she softly asked him.

Sensing that more lay beneath her whispered query than he perceived, he lowered his brows quizzically. "You wish to return to Dunbriggan," he stated almost as a question.

Bridget dropped her chin to her chest and nodded.

Frowning, certain that he had missed something in the exchange, he squeezed her shoulder reassuringly.

"I'm going to speak with Miss Brady, Bridget. I want you to stay right here until I get back," he ordered. "No sneaking off in strange men's trunks, understood?"

Again Bridget nodded and looked up at him so woefully that Preston barely resisted the urge to place a kiss upon her forehead. Instead, he whirled about, closing the door behind him. Pausing outside the door, he pulled her room key out of his pocket, then decisively turned it in the lock, ensuring that Bridget would be inside upon his return.

CHAPTER 8

Preston strolled across the main room, his hooded eyes missing none of the activity bustling about him. He was gratified to note that Elspeth stood alone, apparently having dismissed her behemoth bodyguard. Idly he wondered at the relationship between Bridget's guardian and the shady-looking character he had seen her with earlier. With the exception of Bridget, Preston generally considered himself an excellent judge of character, and he had immediately disliked the dark, burly man.

As he approached Elspeth, Preston came to a number of quick assumptions regarding the woman weaving skittishly from one foot to the other. Despite having referred to her as a governess, instinctively he knew that she lacked the appropriate breeding to assume such a post. If she had held a position in Bridget's household, he conjectured, it was most likely of a more menial nature.

He noticed how her colorless eyes flashed furtively around the room, continually assessing its occupants. Her wary manner intrigued Preston, for her attitude reminded him of a hunted animal when cornered by its pursuer. When her gaze alighted on him, Preston had the distinct impression that she wanted to flee, but something hardened behind her pale eyes, and she stood her ground.

"Preston Campton, at your service," he greeted her with

a slight nod, purposefully omitting his title.

"Elspeth Brady," she briskly introduced herself. Preston saw her clasp her fidgety hands together, obviously in an attempt to disguise her tension.

"I have taken the liberty of securing a parlor where we may speak privately," he informed her. With a wave of his arm, he indicated for her to proceed him down the hallway to an open door.

Following her down the passageway, Preston evaluated the woman's garish violet gown, her soiled gloves, and, in conspicuous contrast, the expensive diamond baubles hanging from her earlobes. How peculiar, he reflected with a frown, that she should possess such jewels.

As they approached the chamber, Preston saw Elspeth hesitate as she warily peeked inside. Coming up behind her while waiting for her to enter, Preston picked up the lingering scent of whiskey about her person. Another clue, he silently noted, before he followed her through the door.

Elspeth did not take a seat, however, but straightened her spine and turned about in the middle of the room to face him, her expression stiff.

"I want to thank ye for helpin' Bridget get back to me, and, of course, I'll repay ye for what ye spent. The lass is a bit headstrong, but she's not a bad girl." She frowned, adding, "I shouldna let 'er get away from me."

Preston strolled over and languidly dropped his tall form into a chair. "Yes," he drawled, "precisely the topic I wished to discuss. Why did she flee you, Miss Brady?" he asked pointedly.

Preston watched the woman's pallid eyes shift as she calculated her response. "What did she tell ye?"

"I'm afraid that she told me very little aside from her desire to return to Ireland."

"Oh," Elspeth responded breathlessly, and Preston almost laughed to see the woman sag with relief.

"After all she's been through, the poor dear, ye'd think she'd be beggin' to leave Dunbriggan," Elspeth began in patently false tones.

"What do you mean?"

"Well, Bridget was only a wee thing when she lost her mum and da. If it hadna been for me, she woulda been all alone. Ye see, her mum and da had run aways together, both banished by their kin, so there was no one fer the lass to go to—"

"She told me she had a father," Preston interjected.

"Ah, she'll never give up. Her da disappeared nigh on to four years now," Elspeth explained, her faint scorn detectable to Preston's keen ear. " 'Twas thought he drowned, but Bridget won't believe it. She thinks he'll be returnin' any day now." She shrugged indifferently. " 'Course they all laughed at her, they did."

"Who?" Preston queried, confused by the recitation.

"The villagers, of course. Bridget was like a wild animal. She ate and slept at home, but for the most part, she ran about like a heathen. But she'd never leave, waiting for her da, she said."

Pity surged in Preston's breast for the unfortunate child, and he began to understand the basis for some of Bridget's unorthodox behavior.

"Then the letter came." Elspeth heaved a dramatic sigh.

Preston wanted to ask "What letter?" but Elspeth garrulously continued her story.

"Ye'd think she'd a jumped at the chance to leave, but, ye see, at last, the lass had found love. Bein' forced to go to England and leave her newfound happiness 'twas too much for her. Ye know how it is, sir. A young lass pushed into a marriage she didn't care for. And though I sympathized with me dear girl, her cousin—an English countess, ye understand—insisted that she go." Elspeth grew more animated in her theatrics, crossing her arms across her bosom as if to still the pain therein. "But as much as I love me Bridget, ye see, sir, I have me instructions to follow. I knew it was killin' 'er to leave Ireland, but what could I do?"

Although Elspeth's tale coincided with Bridget's own, Preston easily discerned the counterfeit emotion behind the woman's narrative.

"What do you mean when you referred to Bridget 'at last finding love'?"

"Well, 'tis the reason she was so against leavin' Ireland. She's madly in love, sir."

Nary a flicker of surprise showed on Preston's face, although he felt as if the woman had just taken a pitchfork to his stomach. For the space of a few seconds, he held silent for fear that his voice would betray him.

"With whom is she in love, Miss Brady?" he asked her tonelessly.

"James," the woman blurted out. "James Kenney."

He could almost see the cogs whirling inside Elspeth's brain as she scrambled to lend credence to her outrageous claim.

"He's with me now, sir. Ye might have seen him when ye came in. He was so upset to hear of her disappearin' that he begged to come with me to help look for the lass."

To his credit, Preston disguised his shudder of revulsion.

She was lying. She had to be. Preston regarded the woman stonily. He could not—nor would not—countenance, for even a fraction of a second, that Bridget was enamored of that brooding giant. He knew her heart to be innocent, untouched by passion. She might have duped him regarding her age, but he would have sworn on his father's grave that Bridget was as pure as the day she was born.

Obviously eager to terminate the interview, Elspeth pulled a coin purse from her dress pocket. "So if ye could tell me what I owe ye and"—she shot him a speaking look—"hand over the key to Bridget's room, we'll be on our way to Sorrelby again in the mornin'."

Preston froze. If only Elspeth had known how much her nervous prattling had just cost her. *Sorrelby.* My God, it all clicked! Prior to embarking on his trip to Wales, Preston had received a letter from Olivia, relating the exciting news of her recently discovered cousin's impending visit. Her *Irish* cousin. Whom, as he now recalled, was named Bridget. The coincidence seemed nearly laughable.

If his coach had not cracked a wheel that fateful afternoon, he would have arrived at Sorrelby Hall that same evening with Bridget in his trunk!

Elspeth's "hrrmph" brought him back to the present.

"The debt, Mr. Campton. And the key." Her voice had taken on a querulous edge that grated Preston's ears.

"I think not, Miss Brady," he answered her coolly. Her gaping mouth leaked a few more whiskey-laced fumes that caused Preston to suppress a grimace of distaste. There was no way he was going to hand Bridget over to this liquor-loving schemer and her coarse-looking conspirator!

"Wh-what do ye mean?" she gasped.

Preston did not want to tip his hand, so he judiciously adopted a mollifying tone. "I only mean that I would like the opportunity to talk the situation over with Bridget before handing her over to your care."

"But ye know the lass will say anything to avoid goin' to England," Elspeth protested, a look of panic settling about her wan features.

"Of course, Miss Brady, I understand that," he soothed her. "I simply desire a farewell interview with Bridget. I believe that I may be able to put some of her fears to rest so that she will be more accommodating for your trip."

Elspeth eyed him uncertainly while Preston maintained his facade of calm reserve.

"The key, then," she demanded, thrusting out her hand. " 'Tis not proper for a young maid to be entertainin' a man in her room. Ye can talk to her without holdin' on to the key."

Preston clutched his fist around the key in his pocket with no intention of handing it over. "For appearance's sake, Bridget has been traveling as my sister," he explained.

"That's just fine," she retorted forcefully, tossing her head so that wispy strands of hair fell from her topknot. "But ye haven't any need of the key," she persisted.

Preston nodded in acquiescence. "You're quite right." He reached into his pocket and withdrew the key to his own chamber, dropping it into Elspeth's outstretched hand.

"Please remember that I wish to speak with Bridget before your departure," he reminded her.

A glimmer of triumph shone in Elspeth's icy blue eyes. "I'll remember."

After Elspeth had left with the key, Preston remained in the parlor, mulling over the information that the housekeeper had unknowingly provided. He could scarcely believe that Bridget was the long-lost cousin that Olivia Forster had written him about. He had not personally spoken with Olivia since receiving her letter, but he suspected that the investigator who had unearthed Bridget's whereabouts could not have been too specific regarding the details of the girl's unconventional upbringing. If he had, Preston mused, Olivia would never have arranged a court debut for the irascible, untrained hellion!

Of course, now that he knew her to be Olivia's cousin, the remaining mysteries surrounding Bridget's background might be resolved once they reached Sorrelby Hall. Increasingly involved in the maze of riddles that enveloped the Irish lass, Preston was more than eager for some clear answers.

Apprised of Bridget's orphaned state and, realizing that her only protector was the two-faced Elspeth Brady, he knew that Olivia would never forgive him, nor could he forgive himself, should he abandon Bridget to the care of such a person. He only hoped that after meeting Bridget, Olivia would forgive him for delivering such a bundle of mischief to her doorstep.

Inwardly groaning at the surprise in store for his friend, Preston proceeded to the front desk to speak with the innkeeper.

Distinctly uncomfortable with the knowledge that Elspeth and James now had access to his chamber, Preston thought it prudent to secure another room. Although it had been a reckless move to hand over the wrong key, at the time he had wanted only to pacify the woman so as not to alert her to his plans. And his plans included escorting

Bridget to Sorrelby Hall if it meant moving heaven and earth to do so.

"May I help you, Lord Campton?"

The proprietor's question interrupted Preston's pondering.

"Yes, I would like another room."

"Oh." The man's eyes widened in distress. "Is something wrong with your room, milord? 'Tis the finest in the inn."

Preston shook his head, reflecting on the dubious reputation he was garnering in lodging establishments throughout the kingdom. Another landlord questioning his sanity.

"Nothing at all," Preston returned. "I just have need of another room."

"Of course, my lord. Of course."

Ignoring the man's curious regard, Preston pocketed the key and strode upstairs. Assuring himself that neither Elspeth nor James was spying upon him, he cautiously let himself into Bridget's chamber. To his astonishment, he found her sleeping soundly in her bed. Preston laughed beneath his breath, thinking that the insatiably hungry woman must have been truly exhausted to succumb to slumber before taking her evening meal.

For a brief moment he stood above her, gazing down at her beauty. Faint violet shadows arched beneath the fan of her dark lashes, and he brooded as to what worries had been disturbing her sleep of late. Beneath his regard, however, she slept peacefully while Preston's thoughts churned with uncertainty.

Although it irked him to admit it, Elspeth's lies had pricked Preston's doubts. Still vulnerable from Bridget's earlier deception, he found the housekeeper's haunting words echoing mercilessly in his head.

He recalled Bridget telling him how the townspeople of Dunbriggan had nicknamed her the village leprechaun. Ruefully Preston wondered if Bridget was equally gifted with the trickery and subterfuge normally attributed to her fanciful namesake. Had she fooled him yet again? Was she not the innocent young woman he had been led to believe?

After all, she did swear as if she'd been raised on a boat full of sailors. Or, Preston darkly conjectured, as if she kept company with the likes of that sinister-looking James.

And she had lied to him again, this time about her father. Between the falsehoods perpetrated by both Bridget and Elspeth, how was he to determine where the lies let off and the truth began?

Shaking his head in disgust, Preston gazed down at Bridget's unblemished profile, dismayed by the suspicions still plaguing him. He could not be so wrong about her, could he?

"Have ye got it open?" Elspeth hissed, her gaze skittering nervously up and down the hallway.

James, bent over the door's lock, glared up at her. "If ye'd shut yer trap fer a minute, I'd 'ave it done," he growled back in a whisper.

Elspeth obligingly closed her mouth, though she began gnawing anxiously on her lower lip. If it weren't for that interfering Campton, she thought, she and Bridget could be well on their way to Sorrelby Hall by now. Last night, when she had discovered that Preston had given her the wrong key, she had flown into a rage that had sent James running for cover. But Preston's trickery had alerted Elspeth to his distrust, and during the night, she had devised a plan to ensure that when she, James, and Bridget took their leave this morning, Preston Campton would give them no further trouble.

A soft click announced James's success.

"Hurry, James," she quietly urged, pushing the big man into the room. "I hear people movin' around downstairs." Silently she pulled the door shut and took up her post in the hallway.

She did not have to wait too long, for within twenty minutes, she spied Preston walking toward her. Raking his nattily attired frame with hostile eyes, she masked her scorn, keeping her disdain of "them useless London dandies" to herself. She saw him frown as he recognized her.

"Oh, Mr. Campton," she greeted in hushed tones. " 'Tis glad I am that ye're here. Ye accidentally gave me the wrong key, sir." She held up the key he had passed to her last night. "I tried to check on Bridget this mornin' and the key didn't work."

The amateur actress lowered her brows in feigned concern, scarcely able to disguise her malicious smirk. "I'm worried about the lass, Mr. Campton. She didn't leave her room last night, and I'm prayin' she didn't give us the slip again."

Unwittingly, Elspeth had touched upon one of Preston's own concerns. He had hoped that Bridget would trust him enough to handle the situation, but it was always possible that her fears had sent her hurtling into another stranger's luggage. Although she had been asleep last night when he had checked on her, the evening had still been young. He had been surprised that she had retired for the night without her dinner, and Elspeth's suspicions fed into his own.

"It's still very early, Miss Brady. Perhaps, she still sleeps."

"Still, sir, I would rest easier knowing the lass hasn't flown off again," she persisted. "D'ye have the *right* key with ye, sir?"

Feeling as if he'd been backed into a corner, Preston fished Bridget's room key from his pocket. Elspeth snatched it from his palm and quickly inserted it into the lock. While Preston wondered at the woman's hurry, Elspeth threw the door open wide so that Preston had a clear view of the room's occupants.

"Bridget, for shame!" Elspeth shrieked as Preston roughly pushed past her into the room.

His turquoise eyes narrowed in fury as Bridget hurriedly sat up in bed, her hair tousled, her cerulean eyes wide and confused. Lying next to her, his naked body barely cloaked by a single sheet, was the infamous lover, James.

CHAPTER
9

Preston's fury slammed into Bridget with the force of a cannonball. She could feel the impact of his wrath like a physical blow to her midsection, and she gasped in reaction. The blood draining from her face, Bridget pushed herself back against the pillows in a futile effort to escape Preston's punishing gaze. In so doing, her hand brushed against something hot, coarse, and hairy.

A premonition of disaster instantly flashed through Bridget's consciousness, causing goose bumps to race across her flesh. Like an animal sensing danger, she froze, momentarily paralyzed. Infinitely slowly, as if in a dream, she pivoted her head around to stare into the emotionless black eyes of James Kenney. For a brief moment Bridget thought that she must be in the throes of a horrendous nightmare. James's rancid breath convinced her otherwise.

Her shriek of dismay appeared to galvanize Preston as he crossed the length of the room in three enormous strides. Bridget cowed to one side of the bed, frightened as she had never been before by the naked rage contorting Preston's aristocratic features. She watched in horror as he grabbed a fistful of James's abundant chest hair and nearly lifted the man straight from the bed.

For some unearthly reason James's yowl of pain reminded

Bridget of an amorous tomcat she had once owned, and a most inappropriate, unbidden giggle bubbled in her throat. She tried to suppress it, but as Preston yanked the howling highwayman from the bed, Bridget was unexpectedly presented with a view of James's hairy backside. The ridiculous tufts of whiskers sprouting from the man's posterior sent the agitated young woman over the edge. Convulsed with laughter, bordering on hysterics, Bridget suddenly doubled over on the bed clutching her sides. She chuckled and guffawed until tears streamed down her face.

Although she could feel Preston's eyes boring into her, Bridget could not control the paroxysm of giggles. 'Twas only the entrance of the uniformed men that finally tempered her insane mirth.

Through a blood red haze of fury, Preston glared at the lovely young woman protectively clutching the sheet to her chin. Her dark brown hair spilled onto the white lace nightrail she had borrowed from the ship's wardrobe, and Preston experienced an almost overwhelming desire to grab hold of those creamy shoulders and . . . and what?

Despite the acrid taste of betrayal choking him, Preston longed only to assuage its bitterness with the sweet promise of Bridget's lips. Jealousy was a foreign sensation to him, and it took Preston a few moments to recognize the emotion for what it was. His mind struggled with its acceptance while his heart congealed under its spell.

Bridget's startled cry arrested Preston from his paralyzing discovery. An undeniable burst of protectiveness, combined with white-hot anger, set him into motion. Never in all his years fighting on the Peninsula had Preston been so overpowered by bloodlust. He was going to tear James Kenney limb from limb.

Hefting the enormous man up from the bed, Preston read the fear in the other man's face and rejoiced in it while the empty sound of Bridget's hysterical laughter echoed loudly in the room. Preston's worried gaze flew to Bridget's bent head. If this cretin had even dared to lay a finger on her . . .

Suddenly a gnarled hand gently, yet firmly, restrained Preston's shoulder. Startled, he swiveled his head about, a snarl upon his lips, while still not relinquishing his hold on the mat of James's chest hair.

Knowing gray eyes met Preston's. In their silvery depths Preston read both sympathy and a warning as the hand fell away from his shoulder.

"We'll take him from here, lad," the man gruffly announced. The speaker was an older man, attired in the traditional dress of the Irish Guard.

Brows lowered in confusion, Preston's gaze swept the room. Standing inside the open doorway were six more officers of the guard.

The senior officer who had addressed Preston marched over to a pile of clothing lying beside the bed and tossed it toward the whimpering James. Reluctantly Preston loosened his hold, and James sank back onto the bed, one hand clutching his clothing, the other rubbing his sore chest.

"Get dressed, man," the officer barked. "You're under arrest, James Kenney, for the assault on Lord Kilgarry's coach two evenings past and the theft of his purse and his passenger's jewels."

Preston and Bridget exchanged shocked glances, and Bridget saw Preston rapidly scan the crowded room for Elspeth. Bridget had seen the housekeeper sneak out the door only a few seconds earlier, and when Preston's gaze returned to her, she shrugged slightly.

Grumbling and cursing, James crawled out of the bed while Bridget conscientiously averted her eyes.

"Ye dunna know what yer doin'," he protested in his gravelly voice.

"Keep your mouth shut, man, or I'll let this lad have another go at ye," the senior officer cautioned him. Looking over to his small troop of men, he roughly instructed, "Seize the accomplice."

Bewildered, Bridget watched as two of the officers sepa-

rated from the group and began walking toward her! Panic
rose like bile in her throat as she recognized their intent.
They were going to arrest her!

"Preston!" she cried, her frightened eyes turning to him
beseechingly.

For the briefest of seconds Bridget's petrified gaze caught
the fleeting glimmer of doubt in Preston's face before she
quickly whirled her head away to hide the scalding rise of
tears. My God, how could he? How could he believe that
of her?

Staring blankly at the cold white wall, Bridget refused
to look at the two soldiers standing patiently near the bed.
Her mind screamed out against the suspicion she had seen
in Preston's expression even as she bit back the words
proclaiming her innocence. The devil take him, but she'd
be damned before she'd stoop to pleading!

A wave of icy terror abruptly washed over her, followed
by a dizzying flush of heat. The prospect of prison abruptly
crystallized into a frightening reality. Breathing deeply,
Bridget steadied herself with one hand as she slowly arose
from the bed.

"Now, just a moment. You cannot—"

Somewhere, the distant recesses of Bridget's mind regis-
tered Preston's objection, but she forced herself to block out
his words. Moving woodenly, she accepted an overcoat that
one of the soldiers held out to her. The rough woolen garment fell past her ankles onto the floor, in odd juxtaposition
to the lacy, ivory nightrail. Bridget paid neither the coat nor
negligee any notice as she watched the remaining soldiers
lead the blanket-clad James out of the room. Expecting to
be likewise led away, she vaguely heard the commander
mumble an order to her guards.

To Bridget's surprise, it was not she, but Preston whom
the senior officer ushered toward the door. Crossing the
threshold, Preston turned about to look at her, and Bridget
quickly averted her eyes. She heard the portal shut and
glanced up to see that she had been left alone with the
two Irish sentinels.

*   *   *

"You have my word, Mr. O'Connell, that Miss Flannery
is not the woman you seek. Miss Flannery has been a guest
aboard my ship since we sailed from Bristol five days ago.
Since we only pulled into port yesterday morning, it would
have been impossible for her to accompany Mr. Kenney on
the evening of the ambush. Any member of my crew will
bear testimony to that effect."

Preston generously poured the gray-haired officer another
dram of whiskey as the two gentleman shared a bottle in the
privacy of Preston's room.

"That may be, milord, but Lord Kilgarry maintains that
his assailant was accompanied by a woman—a woman with
whom the highwayman appeared to be on familiar terms."

The emphasis placed on the word *familiar* caused the
hackles to rise on Preston's nape as he was certain that Mr.
O'Connell referred to finding Bridget in bed with James
Kenney. 'Twas a recollection that Preston would just as
soon have stricken from his memory.

"I may be of assistance there," Preston smoothly offered.
"Your highwayman enjoyed the company of one Elspeth
Brady. Thin, fair-haired, not exactly in the prime of youth."

"By all the saints!" Mr. O'Connell exclaimed, his rheumy
eyes widening in realization. "Why, of course! The woman
who had been in the room when we entered. My sights were
so keenly set on our blackguard that I failed to note her
disappearance!"

The officer shook his head, obviously dismayed by his
oversight.

"Never fear, Mr. O'Connell. I'm sure that you and your
men will be able to catch up with Miss Brady. She hails from
Dunbriggan," Preston explained, "as does Miss Flannery. I
believe that at one point she had been employed by the
Flannery family."

"Dunbriggan, eh?" The Irishman frowned and tossed
back his whiskey. "She won't get away so easily again,
I promise you, Lord Campton."

Preston smiled congenially. "Of that I am certain, Mr.

O'Connell. However, I would also like your assurances that Kenney will provide us no further inconvenience." Preston's smile assumed a lethal edge. "Should I encounter your highwayman again, sir, I warrant he will not live to swing."

Mr. O'Connell nodded slowly. "I take your meaning, my lord. Not to worry. James Kenney will be disturbin' you no more."

"Excellent." Preston refilled his guest's empty glass. "Now, about the matter of Miss Flannery . . ."

The officer shot him a jaundiced eye. "Just what is your relationship to Miss Flannery, Lord Campton?"

Preston hesitated. "She is cousin to a friend. She escaped Elspeth Brady's clutches, and I, fortunately, was available to assist her." He cleared his throat. "Er, I have been claiming her as my sister so as to protect Miss Flannery's reputation."

Levering a white brow, Mr. O'Connell concurred, "Naturally, naturally."

After a moment's contemplation the officer vigorously rubbed at his jowls. "A gentleman such as yourself, Lord Campton . . . should you tell me the lass is not guilty, I'm not in a position to be arguing with you. If you agree to accept responsibility for Miss Flannery, I will gladly release her into your custody."

Accept responsibility for Bridget? Phrased in that manner, it sounded to be a daunting prospect! Nevertheless, Preston emitted a weak smile. "Naturally, I accept responsibility, Mr. O'Connell. As I said, Miss Flannery's cousin is a good friend of mine, and I promise you that I shall see her safely delivered to her home."

Slapping the table with his palm, Mr. O'Connell arose. "Fine, my lord. Then she's all yours. I'll have my men bring her in, and you can explain the lot of it to her."

Preston intended to object to that proposition, but the cagey officer was already out the door.

Setting aside the half-empty bottle, Preston braced himself for his interview with Bridget; he anticipated that the feisty miss would not be in the most congenial of moods. Nothing like being arrested in your own bed to sour one's outlook on the day, Preston mused.

And although he still felt numb from discovering her abed with the highwayman, Preston simply could not believe that Bridget might have actually been *intime* with the disgusting Irishman. Yet . . . so much about Bridget remained a mystery to him. Niggling doubts continued to chafe at Preston's image of her as an innocent, indeed even vulnerable, young woman. Who was the real Bridget Flannery?

The door swung open and the subject of his contemplation entered, flanked by the pair of Irish officers. Saluting Preston, they spun about and quickly vanished, literally slamming the portal behind them.

Hoping to inject a note of levity into the awkward situation, Preston teased, "I hope that you weren't too rough on—"

With a scream that could have raised the dead, Bridget flung herself at Preston's chest, her tiny fists flying left and right as she cursed him with every vile term she had ever heard and then some new ones she invented on the spot.

"How dare you, you filthy rotten hunk of fishbait!" she wailed. "How dare you even *think* of me and that stinking hulk of a thief! Don't dare deny it, you cad! I saw it in your eyes!"

Fortunately for Preston, he outweighed Bridget by at least five stone, as her unexpected attack almost sent him sailing to the floor.

"Easy. Easy now," he tried to mollify her while attempting to catch her flurrying fists. She continued to fly at him, and when her right hand connected with his nose, he hastily barked, "For God's sake, woman, calm down!"

His shout slowed her enough for him to grab hold her wrists, and he pinioned her against his chest.

Shackled by Preston's strong arms, as securely as the irons she had just narrowly escaped, Bridget stared up at him mutinously.

Peering up into those glinting blue-green eyes, Bridget

despised Preston with an intensity that rocked her to her
toes. She hated the fact that he had been able to hurt her
so much.

After Preston had departed with the Irish officer, Bridget
had felt an almost overwhelming, uncharacteristic desire to
weep. His lack of trust had been a crushing blow to her,
one that had pained her very heart, but the presence of
the guards had prevented her from succumbing to tears.
With no other outlet for her misery, Bridget's anguish
found solace in anger. By the time that Mr. O'Connell
had returned, Bridget was one seething mass of emotion.

"Bridget, we have to talk," Preston stated.

"Talk?!" she nearly spat at him. "What can you possibly
say? I saw it in your eyes! You doubted me!"

Preston held tightly to her wrists as she struggled to
wrench away.

"Bridget, consider my view of this," Preston argued,
his expression hard. "You have not been exactly straightforward with me. You have lied to me from the very
beginning. You lied to me about your age. You lied to me
about your father. Then I find you in bed with a man—"
He frowned at her to stifle her protest. "Forgive me if I
was temporarily taken aback, but you have been the most
maddeningly puzzling wench from the moment I laid eyes
on you!"

Bridget scowled up at Preston while secretly conceding
some truth to his argument. In her efforts to return to
Ireland, she had unwittingly given him much fodder for
suspicion. But what choice had she? If she had given him
the whole of the truth, he would never have agreed to
take her home. Abruptly one of his arguments struck her
thoughts.

"I did not lie to you about my father!" she suddenly
retorted.

Preston lowered his tawny brows. "You told me that he
should soon be returning to Dunbriggan."

"He will!" Bridget cried desperately, feeling the shameful
sting of tears well in her eyes.

Through her tear-blurred vision, she saw a gleam of compassion touch Preston's face before he answered her, "If you believe he will return, then I'm sure that he will, Bridget. But until then, I cannot return you to Dunbriggan."

"You must!" Bridget protested. "You promised me!"

Preston released her wrists and gently reminded her, "I promised to return you to Ireland and I have done so. However, now that the authorities are hunting down Elspeth, you will be without a companion. Just as well, I might add, since the woman is a confirmed thief. Anyway, you see that I cannot leave you alone in Dunbriggan." He took a deep breath. "As it happens, I am well acquainted with your cousin, Olivia—"

"How did you learn of her?" Bridget gasped.

"Olivia Forster is married to my closest friend," Preston explained. "Colin and I have known each other for many years, and I have been acquainted with Olivia since their marriage.

"Elspeth let it slip that Sorrelby Hall was your destination, and by chance, I had recently received a letter from Olivia, informing me of her cousin's impending visit. Since I cannot possibly, in good conscience, abandon you here, I have no choice but to see you safely to Sorrelby Hall."

Bridget spun away from him, the oversized coat sweeping along the floor.

"I won't go!"

"Yes, you will, Bridget," Preston sternly advised, a threat explicit in his deep voice. "You are sadly mistaken about Olivia. I do not know how you came by the notion, but I assure you that she would never force you into marriage. She is not such a cold-hearted person as you seem to think."

Bridget stared at her bare feet, mutiny settling in her breast.

"You didn't read her letter," she remonstrated.

"You must have misinterpreted her," he shot back.

Squaring her chin, Bridget turned about and disdainfully informed Preston, "I didn't and I am *not* going!"

"Yes, you are!" He bit out each syllable with command-ing force.

"Make me!" Bridget childishly taunted, nearly sticking out her tongue to complete the infantile image.

As soon as the words left her mouth, Bridget knew that she had made a mistake. The flush of anger rising in Preston's cheeks told her that she had pushed too far. She saw his eyes quickly scan the room, and then, before she could take flight, he scooped her up in his arms.

"Wait! No—" she protested. In two strides he crossed the room, bent over, and suddenly, recognizing his intent, Bridget began to wail in earnest.

"No-o-o!"

But the lid falling closed on the trunk muted her cries as, once again, Bridget found herself neatly tucked into Preston Campton's expensive traveling case.

CHAPTER
10

Preston could not restrain a satisfied smirk as he lowered the lid over the gaping Bridget. Lord, but he'd spent the entire last week fantasizing about doing just this, he laughingly mused while fastening the latch with a flourish.

Bridget's muffled oaths seeped through the trunk's cracks, but, happily for Preston, her curses were too garbled for his overburdened ears to decipher. She noisily thumped on the lid, and Preston mischievously returned the knock.

"Who's there?" he cheerfully inquired, enjoying himself enormously.

A few more furious thuds sounded, followed by, what Preston assumed to be, another series of epithets.

Chuckling loudly, Preston advised, "Be a good girl, Bridget. I'll be back after breakfast."

He slammed the door shut and laughed the entire distance to the dining room downstairs.

While consuming an unusually healthy breakfast—Bridget's eating habits were beginning to rub off on him—Preston contemplated his dilemma with the beautiful, unpredictable Irishwoman.

Although it irked him to admit it, Preston acknowledged that Bridget had managed to worm her way under his thick English hide—the way a thorn works its way into one's flesh. His reaction this morning was evidence enough. The memories caused Preston's stomach to clench, and frowning, he felt the abrupt rise of anger as if witnessing the scene all over again. If the soldiers had not arrived when they did, Preston realized, he would have killed James Kenney with his bare hands.

Unconsciously Preston crushed a currant-laced scone to smithereens.

He had been jealous. Not merely jealous, but practically eaten alive by a primal need to repossess that which was his. And Bridget was his.

Scowling into his plate, Preston wondered at what point she had ceased to be the troublesome chit who had waylaid him at gunpoint and had become the mysterious woman who had his insides tied in knots. His desire for her bordered on painful. Luckily, whenever he felt on the verge of losing control of his passion, Bridget conveniently threw a tantrum, like the one just now, that sidetracked his burgeoning desire.

'Twas a handy trick the minx employed, but Preston could not help but speculate on her reaction should he some day lose that control. Although he had believed her an innocent, the episode this morning had sown seeds of doubt in Preston's fertile imagination. Would she welcome his kisses? Would she be a stranger to passion or had the highwayman already indoctrinated her into the wonders of desire?

Finding his appetite suddenly diminished, Preston arose from the table to seek out the inn's proprietor. Upon locating the innkeeper, Preston requested that a tray be prepared as he suspected that Bridget would be ravenous when finally released from the trunk. While awaiting the tray, he quickly penned a message to Olivia Forster.

Dear Olivia—
    Through an inexplicable quirk of fate, and a rather extraordinary tale that I will save for our arrival, I have set myself as escort to your cousin, Bridget.

Do not worry, she is well. I pray we meet no further delays, and I shall bring her to you as quickly as I am able.

Your friend and servant,
Preston

With the addition of a few coins, Preston consigned the letter to the landlord, asking that he send a messenger forthwith to Sorrelby Hall. Although Preston hoped to make quick time back to England, the vagaries of the Irish Channel's winds could impede their return voyage. Fearing that Olivia might be growing concerned regarding Bridget's tardiness, he thought it best to send a message straightaway.

The breakfast tray arrived, and Preston mounted the inn's staircase with his peace offering. Bridget would undeniably be miffed when he released her, yet he was hopeful that a good meal might turn away her anger and improve her spirits. He could not help smiling as he imagined the froth she had probably worked herself into whiling away this past hour in her tight quarters.

Tamping down his well-earned amusement, Preston pushed open the door and froze. His trunk was nowhere to be seen.

After exhausting her uncouth vocabulary, Bridget settled down among Preston's wardrobe and began plotting her revenge. 'Twas simply unthinkable that he had dared to lock her up! Her petite stature was to blame for this ignominious treatment, for as much as she might desire to retaliate in kind, Bridget held out no hopes of finding a trunk large enough to accommodate someone of Preston's size.

If she had been paying attention, she would have noticed that she was treading on thin ice with the taciturn baron, but she had been too overwrought with her own emotions to heed the signs of his rising ire. Next time, she vowed, she would be more astute!

But how could she avenge herself? If she pitched another fit, he would most likely pitch *her* back into the trunk. She would have to think of another way to convince him that she was not some wayward child who could be subdued by such stringent methods. Bridget sighed, realizing that she had just hit on the reason for her excessively foul humor. Preston was still treating her like a child!

She had hoped, after their sojourn on the *Circe,* that her attempts to emulate a lady had swayed Preston's opinion of her. Heavens, but she had honestly tried to leash her temper and thought she had succeeded—today being the exception, she mentally amended. Nevertheless, although Preston had behaved with courtesy these past few days, Bridget could hardly claim that he had taken an interest in the womanly version of Bridget. He had been polite, quiet, and altogether inoffensive.

If only she could appeal to him as a woman. Recalling the incident of that morning, Bridget's heart flared with hope. He could not be completely indifferent to her, she reasoned. He had appeared truly upset at finding James Kenney in her bed. But then again, Bridget argued with herself, had not some of that anger been directed toward her? Had he not, at least momentarily, questioned her innocence? Bridget tormented herself with arguments back and forth as her empty stomach growled its discomfort.

Suddenly she felt the trunk hoisted into the air. *Hell's bells,* she swore beneath her breath. Was he going to transport her to the ship this way? Not even to release her that she might walk on her own two feet? Bridget bit down hard on her lip, forcibly bridling her temper. She was not going to shame herself by crying out, begging for her freedom. No, she vowed, she would make Preston Campton pay for his high-handed treatment of her. And pay dearly he would.

What the blazes! Preston cursed, placing the tray on a table while furiously scanning the empty chamber. Was his little leprechaun actually gifted with magical powers? How had she spirited herself away?

Smacking himself upside the head, Preston jostled some common sense back into his fanciful thoughts. Don't be an idiot, man, he curtly scolded himself. The trunk had been stolen!

Preston tore out of the room and hurtled down the stairs, his bootheels clicking sharply along the polished floor. The innkeeper was consulting with a servant in the front room when Preston grabbed hold of his beefy arm, virtually accosting the startled innkeeper.

"I believe my trunk has been stolen from my room," he stated abruptly, declining to elaborate that his "sister" had been occupying the trunk at the time of the theft.

The hostler gaped at him in shock, his mouth opening and closing like a beached fish, stunned, no doubt, by both the information and its rather blunt delivery.

"Summon the servants immediately for questioning," Preston ordered, his piercing gaze managing to still the innkeeper's seesawing jaw.

Clearly aghast that his most prominent guest's luggage had been pilfered right under his noble nose, the hostler scurried to round up the staff.

Under Preston's direct questioning, one of the maids reported having seen a man leave with a trunk only twenty minutes earlier. When prompted, she recalled that the trunk had been emblazoned with a monogram, although she could not recall the letters. None of the servants remembered having seen Preston's dark-haired "sister" since their arrival yesterday.

After sending a message to the *Circe,* advising the captain to make ready for departure, Preston followed the trail to the inn's stables. He learned that a cart had been stationed outside the stables before being reclaimed by a man hefting an enormous engraved case. The stableboy's description of the man matched that of the maid's, solidifying Preston's conclusion that he had been the victim of a theft.

Facing down the quivering innkeeper, who had followed him to the stableyard, Preston struggled to control the anger throbbing in his voice. He realized that it was an anger born of fear—his fear for Bridget.

"I need a horse," he informed the proprietor. "A fast one."

The man anxiously bobbed his head in agreement, his voice cracking. "Aye, my lord. Anythin' at all you want. Take your pick of the stables."

"I want you to alert the authorities. Make certain," he lowered his brows menacingly, "that they understand the import of this search and give them the description of the man we seek. I am going to follow the cart's trail."

After the innkeeper had nervously assured him that the police would be notified immediately, Preston hastily mounted a promising-looking gelding and flew out of the stables like a bat out of hell.

Fortunately the recent drizzle plainly revealed the cart's tracks in the moist earth, and Preston effortlessly followed the trail. A slight mist had begun to fall, but Preston paid it no heed, leaning over the horse's neck, pushing his mount even faster. His heart thundered in his chest, rivaling the pounding of the horse's hooves, as man and beast flew down the streets of Dublin.

Preston's every thought centered on Bridget. He sent a silent prayer heavenward, hoping that the thief's greed had not compelled him to stop yet to examine his stolen treasures. Preston shuddered, not from the chill wind, but from envisioning what Bridget's fate might be at the hands of the scurrilous bandit.

If he had been in a different mood, Preston might have laughed, contemplating the mind-boggling string of events that had taken place since he had awoken that morning. James Kenney in Bridget's bed; the run-in with the Irish authorities; the argument with Bridget leading him to toss her into the trunk; and now this! Good God, what else could possibly happen to cap this disastrous day!

After leaving the boundaries of the city, Preston slowed his mount, wary of announcing his arrival to the thief. To his relief, the mist died down, and he ceased worrying that the rain might obliterate the signs of the cart's passage.

The country lane was quiet, and Preston slackened the animal's pace almost to a walk, thinking that his frenzied ride had covered enough ground to make up for the pilferer's headstart.

Advancing slowly, he concentrated all his senses to the pursuit of his prey. The rain had freshened the grasses so that their sweet green perfume wafted from the roadside to tease Preston with memories. Their fresh, floral scent reminded him of Bridget. How fitting, he thought, that she would smell like Ireland, and then he wryly smiled at his own poetic bent.

Suddenly the horse pricked forward its ears, only a second before Preston heard the faint jingling of a harness floating downwind toward him. Urging the mount forward, he turned a bend in the road, just glimpsing the tail end of the cart disappearing into the forest as the driver left the roadway.

Preston proceeded cautiously, cursing himself for a fool for leaving his pistol in the trunk. Since he did not know whether the thief was armed, he knew he would have to move very carefully so that Bridget would not be injured.

After looping the horse's reins over a branch, Preston slipped off the animal's back and noiselessly crept toward the spot where the cart had disappeared. The heavily wooded forest offered perfect camouflage for Preston's dark green superfine coat as he stealthily dodged from one tree to the next.

He had just moved into position when he saw the man yank the trunk down from the cart. Preston winced as the luggage, and therefore Bridget, landed with a thud on the forest floor. Glancing around the small clearing for a means to approach the thief from the back, Preston's heart suddenly lurched into his throat. With one forceful tug the thief had forced open the trunk and had thrown back the lid.

*   *   *

If Bridget was angry before, she was a raving lunatic after the excruciating jolt when the trunk was abruptly dropped. Despite her resolution not to fly into any more tantrums, the long, unexpected trip in the bumpy cart had whetted her fury to a fever pitch.

Initially she had resigned herself to the short trek from the inn to the wharf. Although miffed at Preston's need to humiliate her by hoisting her on board the *Circe* like a piece of cargo, she felt that she could endure the few minutes of traveling to the dock. However, as time passed, Bridget had begun to fume, wondering at what game Preston played.

Anticipating only a ten-minute ride, a full hour later Bridget was fit to be tied and more than ready to give Lord Campton a piece of her mind. While she was at it, she wouldn't mind taking a piece out of his backside if she could get her hands on a horsewhip!

So, when the trunk's lid was at last raised, 'twas a screaming, spitting virago, clothed only in a nightrail and a man's overcoat, that sprung from the trunk's recesses.

"Ye're going to die for this, ye no-account bastard!" she roared, her Irish accent thick as she leaped to her feet, her fists flailing in every direction.

Despite her inability to clearly define the form in front of her—her eyes had not yet adjusted from the trunk's darkness—Bridget did not slacken her attack.

"I'll see yer manhood nailed to the yardarm, ye—" Her tirade crashed to a halt as her vision finally adjusted to the bright sunlight.

The burly, bearded man staring back at her looked as if he had suddenly taken leave of his senses. His mouth hung open, revealing a dozen or so blackened teeth, while his eyes bugged out in his pockmarked face.

"What the—" Bridget sputtered, her gaze taking in her wooded surroundings. She looked back at the dumbfounded fellow, this time noting the poor quality of his clothing and the knife strapped to his thigh. "Perfect!" she announced to the hushed glade. "I've been stolen!"

Too furious to feel fear, Bridget bent over and began rummaging through the trunk. "Here it is."

She straightened, Preston's pistol in her hand. If possible, the man's eyes grew even wider.

"Be off with you," she ordered, wildly waving the familiar handgun. "I'm not in the mood for such shenanigans, and I'm of half a mind to put a bullet right through you!"

When the man did not move, the anger-bold Bridget stepped out of the trunk, brandishing the gun practically in the thief's face. However, as her foot landed on the damp grassy carpet, she slipped, and in her struggles to remain upright, her finger pulled back on the pistol.

The bullet's report echoed throughout the clearing as Bridget fell flat on her back, the gun still clutched in her fist. The impact of the fall had knocked the wind from her, and from her lowlying vantage point, she saw the man's tattered boots scamper past her toward the cart. In less than a trice the thief and cart were hurtling back to the roadway, and Bridget closed her eyes with relief.

Dazed, at first, she thought she was only imagining the rumbling chuckle. But then a well-known voice rang out, its silky tones heavily shaded with amusement.

"The way my luck has been running, I suppose it is too much to hope for that you have been knocked unconscious?"

Bridget raised her lids to discover a familiar twisted grin crowned by a pair of laughing aqua eyes.

"You were here the entire time?" she questioned evenly, still prostrate on the wet ground.

He smiled down at her. "I had planned to intercede but"— Preston shrugged eloquently—"you managed so nicely on your own."

Suddenly Bridget's foot lashed out, catching Preston behind his knee, and with a startled "oomph" he fell directly on top of her. Luckily for Bridget, Preston caught himself on one elbow before completely crushing her into the damp earth, but he still lay covering her from head to foot.

"Why, you little—" He stopped, staring down into the bluest eyes he had ever seen. Without thought his mouth slanted down and captured her soft lips.

CHAPTER
11

Too startled to object to this unforeseen intimacy, Bridget closed her eyes and surrendered to the marvelous sensations of her first kiss.

Preston's lips slid slowly across the satin surface of her mouth, insistently molding the shape of her lips to his own. The smooth play of his lips upon hers increased in pressure as his kiss grew more demanding. Instinctively Bridget responded.

Bringing her hands off the damp ground, she lay them on Preston's shoulders, reveling in the iron-hard muscles tensing beneath her fingertips. Faith, but he felt good, nearly as good as he looked, and Bridget unconsciously dug her fingers more deeply into his flesh.

Preston's seductive groan encouraged her, inflaming her senses. Tentatively she mimicked his soft sucking against his mouth. She thrilled to hear his faint gasp of pleasure at her boldness. The shifting persuasion of his lips urged her to open her mouth to him, and with her heart thudding painfully in her breast, she knew she must do as he silently asked of her. She parted her lips and welcomed his silky, hot invasion.

Suddenly Bridget felt as if she had let loose a torrent. Preston's tongue ravished her mouth, demanding and giving, until Bridget felt faint from the passion pounding through her body. Preston's hand slipped under the coarse woolen coat, unerringly finding her silk-covered breast. He ran the flat surface of his palm around its tip until the hard bud of her nipple pressed wantonly against his hand.

"Oh, God, I knew it would be like this," Preston hoarsely whispered as he trailed kisses to her ear.

Bridget did not understand, but she sensed the power of his words as they caressed her, heating her flesh. Preston's hand languidly massaged and molded her, and Bridget felt as if she were spinning out of control.

"Yes," she whispered. "Please, Preston, yes!"

Though too naive to know what she pleaded for, the need was there nevertheless. Panting deeply, Bridget breathed in the warm rich scent of the verdant forest, feeling that she, too, was coming alive beneath the nourishing rain of Preston's kisses.

"Uh-hmm."

The tactful cough served like a bucket of cold water upon the pair.

Preston jerked away from Bridget, whipping his head about. At the edge of the clearing three uniformed officers on horseback surveyed the passionate scene, their expressions ranging from mortified to amused.

"Lord Campton, I presume?" the leader of the trio addressed the scowling baron.

Preston could but nod as he did not trust his passion-thick voice. Although he would have preferred to stand, Bridget had buried her head in his shoulder, and he chose to remain on the ground to partially shield her from the men's curious regard.

"We received your message regarding the stolen trunk." The officer pointedly glanced in the direction of the open case. "I gather that you have already located your luggage and its bounty." At the word *bounty,* the man's insolent gaze swept Bridget, whose borrowed coat had fallen open, exposing the silken negligee and her creamy white skin.

Preston impatiently pulled her coat closed with one hand while impaling the impertinent officer with a piercing stare.

"Yes. I followed his trail, and the thief absconded at the threat of gunpoint." He declined to clarify who had wielded the weapon.

"Did you recover all of your property, milord?"

Again, the man's eyes raked Bridget's form, and Preston subdued an urge to leap at the officer's throat. 'Twas apparent that the man desired an explanation as to Bridget's role in the matter, but Preston was hardly of a mind to provide edification.

Perturbed by the guardsman's insolence, he nonetheless wished to rescue Bridget from this humiliating scene. Gritting his teeth, Preston essayed a diplomacy he was far from feeling.

"If your men would be so good as to see that my trunk is transported back to my ship, I will be appropriately grateful."

The officer did not mistake the promise of compensation and nodded his head in agreement. "Will the lady need assistance?" he inquired, the hoped for gold lending a note of respect to his previously patronizing tone.

"No. She shall return with me."

Again, the man briefly saluted Preston and motioned for his men to retreat into the woods to allow the couple a moment of privacy.

Preston waited until the officers had melted into the forest and then pushed himself up. He offered a hand to Bridget, who, after the briefest of hesitations, laid her palm in his. Uncharacteristically tongue-tied, Preston brushed the twigs and grass from Bridget's hair while she appeared spellbound by her bare feet.

"I guess I should apologize," he awkwardly suggested, then mentally cursed himself for acting like a gauche calfling.

Bridget's head shot up, her eyes glowing with some unidentifiable emotion. "Whatever for?"

"For . . . taking advantage." His voice sounded unnaturally rough as his hand fell away from her hair, dropping lifelessly to his side.

"I do not recall offering any objection, Preston."

Their eyes clashed, and Preston marveled at the direct-ness and honesty he saw there. Her unashamed declaration sparked a resurgence of the passion that had swept him only a few moments earlier.

'Twas he who finally tore his gaze away, severing their wordless exchange.

"My horse is tethered a short distance from here," he gruffly announced, unnerved by his rioting emotions. Anger, shame, and desire all warred within him as he mutely struck out in the direction of his mount. Hoping that Bridget would have the good sense to follow, he was gratified to hear the faint crackle of her footsteps behind him.

Silence reigned during their lengthy ride back to Dublin. Preston had placed Bridget in front of him on the saddle, and the proximity disturbed both riders' peace of mind. In light of the intimacies recently shared, neither Bridget nor Preston dared draw a deep breath for fear he might inch nearer to the warm body already too closely pressed against his own.

Preston rode directly to the wharfside dock of the *Circe*. After vaulting from the gelding's back, he reached up to assist Bridget, steeling himself against the desire to crush her against him once again. She fell into his arms as light as thistledown, reminding Preston that despite her Irish spunk, physically Bridget was still quite fragile. Gently he set her down, stepping back a few paces.

"You go aboard," he brusquely instructed her. "The cap-tain's expecting you."

"Where are you going?" Bridget asked, wringing her hands in the folds of the coat that fell past her fingers.

"To the inn. I have a few matters to clear up." Preston shot her a meaningful look. "When I return, we will discuss where we go from here."

Without elaborating on his cryptic statement, Preston leaped onto the horse's back and headed back toward town. Bridget watched him go until his tall form vanished in the distance. Unreasonably despondent, she boarded the *Circe*.

"Ach, dear lassie, are you all right?" the captain hailed her, hurrying across the gleaming deck, beaming from one elephantine ear to the next. His endearing Scottish brogue helped to ease Bridget's agitated spirits.

"Aye, Captain Mac," she returned, gracing him with a faint smile.

The carrot-topped captain frowned. "His Lordship hinted at some trouble in his note." His kind blue eyes skimmed her unusual attire. "Ye look as if ye could use a rest, lass. Go on down and I'll have a meal and bath sent to yer cabin."

Bridget should have been famished, not having eaten during the past twenty-four hours, but the sumptuous meal failed to excite her appetite. Overwrought by the day's events, she ignored the meal and instead sought solace in the steaming waters of the bath.

Closing her eyes, she leaned her head back, allowing the soothing warmth to coax her into relaxation. Having thrown off the nightrail and overcoat, she also threw away the mind-numbing shock that had gripped her since she had awoken to find James Kenney in her bed. The arrest and the abduction had so traumatized her that Bridget had been forced to bury her fears beneath her outrage, and it was only now that she was able to confront those anxieties.

Sighing heavily, she thought of Elspeth. Intuitively Bridget had always sensed the housekeeper's unfaithfulness, but to discover that Elspeth had been in league with a highwayman . . . Bridget shook her head sadly. Money had been the motivating force behind all Elspeth's actions, including her decision to remain with Bridget these past four years. The woman must have anticipated some financial benefit in bringing her to England, Bridget mused. Undoubtedly, lusting after Olivia Forster's wealth, Elspeth had hoped to finagle a portion for herself.

If that surprise were not enough, Bridget then had nearly been hauled off to an Irish prison. She grimaced with the remembered pain of Preston's doubting her. *Oh, Preston,* she moaned to herself, sinking deeper into the sheltering waters. From the moment she had laid eyes on his sculptured magnificence, he had captured her body and soul. He infuriated her, but, Lord, how the man affected her!

She was willing to forgive him his suspicions, to forgive him for locking her in the trunk, even to forgive him for standing by while she launched bullets at the knife-wielding thief! But she would have never forgiven him had he not initiated her into the rapture of passion. Having expected a sound thrashing, Bridget could not have been more surprised than when Preston had kissed her on the moss-covered ground. She had not dared even hope that he recognized her as a woman, but the truth crystallized in the pulsating currents that had hummed between them. Yes, she acknowledged with a smile, Preston knew that she was a woman.

However, as Preston had so eloquently phrased, where would they go from here? Most likely, he anticipated further battles with her in his desire to bring her back to England, but Bridget had discarded her arguments the moment his lips had touched hers. If she had entertained doubts before regarding her feelings for the enigmatic lord, his kisses had melted them completely away. She could not possibly leave him. She had no choice but to accompany him to Sorrelby if only to stay close to him.

After all, this man, this Preston Campton, had rescued her! As surely as any knight gallant, he had saved her—saved her from the loveless existence she had known these long four years since her father's disappearance.

Alone and frightened, Bridget had clung to her hopes of Da's return as a lifeline. What else had she to wish for? The villagers had scorned her, Elspeth secretly despised her. Bridget had naught else but hope and the forlorn memory of her parents' adoration.

But now she had love. Bridget nearly laughed out loud with the realization. She loved Preston with every ounce of her being. Although his handsomeness had intrigued her at first, she had come to realize this past week that he embodied everything she had unknowingly sought in a mate. Strong, levelheaded, decisive, witty, charming—when he chose to be. She had not known it, but her fate had been sealed.

Splashing merrily, Bridget tentatively rolled the words on her tongue. *I love Preston.* By Jove, that sounded right!

Like any young woman experiencing her first love, Bridget giggled happily at the immensity of her discovery. She playfully ran the bathing sponge up and down her arm, surrendering to her romantic bathtime fantasies.

Suddenly determining that her appetite had returned, she stepped from the bath, glowing both inside and out. After toweling dry, she chose a striking ruby sarcenet from the wardrobe, not bothering about the length. The skirts pooled about her feet, but Bridget made a beeline for the meal set out on the table.

With rediscovered relish she tore into a chicken leg, savoring the tasty morsel. Humming merrily, her mouth full, she finished off the leg and reached for a chunk of cheese—then abruptly froze mid-chew. *Wait a minute, Miss Flannery,* a little voice silently cautioned. *You might be in love with the dashing baron, but how does he feel about you?*

Preston felt furious! What in the bloody hell had he been thinking?

He downed another whiskey, then replenished his glass. He hadn't been thinking at all; therein lay the problem. He had been throbbing, vibrating, needing—everything but thinking. The woman was under his protection, for God's sake! She was one of his dearest friend's cousins! She was an innocent, a maiden untouched. Well, almost untouched, he amended.

If Preston had heretofore questioned the extent of Bridget's experience with men, those trembling, virginal lips had nullified any doubts. Damn, but she had tasted sweet! Exactly as he had imagined.

Disdaining the glass, Preston reached for the bottle and tipped it to his mouth. Errant drops of liquid amber slid down his chin and along his neck to stain his white cravat. Lowering the bottle, he welcomed the whiskey's harsh sting as it settled on his empty stomach. Better the burn of the alcohol than the burn of his unslaked desire.

The smoky, shadowed tavern fitted Preston's mood exactly. Mismatched tables were scattered across a floor that, Preston judged, had not seen a mop in a good many months. The scent of cheap spirits comingled with the pungent aroma of the sailors, obviously just into port, populating the pub. They were a rough, boisterous crew, but they paid the silent stranger no notice as they challenged each other to drinking contests.

Ensconced in the darkest corner, Preston bathed himself in whiskey and self-loathing. The worst of it, he seethed, was that Bridget had trusted him. She had placed herself in his care, not once disputing that he would conduct himself as a gentleman should. And he had wronged her! Taken her faith and thrown it back into her face. That lovely, bewitching face.

Preston groaned as he let his forehead drop to the rough wood table. Damn, he was a cad! What manner of beast allowed his passions to run unchecked to the detriment of a young woman's reputation? Although Bridget had intimated that his advances had not been abhorrent to her, the lass's naivety prevented her from understanding how unjust his actions had been.

With his recent understanding of Bridget's upbringing, Preston grasped the extent of her ignorance, the disadvantage in which she had been placed by the lack of parental influence. No mother had warned her to be wary of lascivious rakes or unscrupulous gentleman. No father had seen to her protection against desperate men or manipulating women. Bridget had had only herself on whom to rely.

Thank God that soon Olivia would be able to take the young woman under her wing! Glaring at the room at large,

Preston vowed that his goal would be to deliver Bridget safe and sound to the doorsteps of Sorrelby Hall with no further indiscretions to confess to his friend, Olivia. If he could not accomplish that, dammit, he was not fit to carry the Campton name!

CHAPTER
12

Bridget had just settled into a restless sleep when a persistent scratching at her door awoke her. Her heart leaped with both trepidation and excitement as she wondered at Preston's purpose in coming to her so late at night. "Faith," she whispered beneath her breath, her pulse suddenly accelerating. What was she to do? If he wanted to finish what they had begun this afternoon, should she—or could she—resist him?

Deciding that she could not allow Preston to alert the rest of the ship to his nocturnal visit, she quickly scrambled out of the bed.

"Pres—"

"No, it's not Preston, you foolish chit," Elspeth hissed as Bridget slid back the bolt and opened the door. Pushing past the startled woman, Elspeth marched into the moonlit cabin. "Or were ye expectin' him?" she sneered, her pale eyes scornfully raking Bridget.

"Elspeth! How dare you come here?" Bridget exclaimed in a loud whisper. "I would have thought your narrow escape this morning would have sent you fleeing Dublin."

"What do ye mean?"

"I mean that I was nearly arrested in your place!" Bridget shot back. "The Irish Guard is looking for a woman who assisted that highwayman, and they nearly carted me off to prison, believing that I was you!"

"Let them look," Elspeth mocked. "We'll be sailin' at dawn before they even know where to start lookin'."

"We?" Bridget echoed in astonishment.

"Of course, 'we,' " Elspeth irritably reiterated.

Horrified, Bridget stared at the woman. 'Twas evident that Elspeth had been at the bottle again. "You must be daft if you think that I am going anywhere with you! You've been deceiving me all along. You hid the letter from Olivia Forster while planning to sell me into marriage. And this morning!" she cried. "Planting that hideous man in my bed!"

"Bridget, ye're lookin' at this the wrong way," Elspeth wheedled, laying her hand on Bridget's shoulder. "I've only been thinking of ye, lass. I couldna let ye waste yer life away in Dunbriggan, and that interferin' Campton fella was just in the way."

Bridget shrugged Elspeth's hand off of her. "Preston is not interfering," she protested. "He is trying to help me."

Elspeth's sympathetic demeanor vanished as she pulled her thin lips back into a snarl.

"Hah! Ye'd be the daft one to believe that, girl. He's only interested in helpin' himself to yer innocence, if ye ask me."

"That's not true!"

"Why else would he be wastin' his time on ye, then?" Elspeth derisively queried. "It's not like he's in love with ye!"

Bridget winced, grateful that her face was in the shadows.

"I did not say that he was in love with me. He only means to help me."

"O' course," the housekeeper jeered. "Yer own da cannot be bothered with ye, yet ye believe some hoity-toity London gent is takin' care of ye just to be friendly-like. Faith, Bridget, don't be blind!"

Bridget held her breath, determined not to allow Elspeth's cruel barbs to wound her. She knew that the housekeeper wanted to manipulate her by throwing her father's abandonment in her face. Deep down, however, Elspeth's spiteful words conjured up all the pain Bridget had hidden away these many years.

"Come on, girl. Time's wastin'. Gather yer things and let's go."

"Elspeth, I am not going with you." Bridget's voice was firm.

"*What?!* Ye're goin' to run off with this Campton fella to be some . . . some kind of harlot?" Elspeth cried. "Yer dear mum must be turnin' over in her grave!"

"Don't talk like that," Bridget ordered, her resolve steady, but her voice now slightly shaking. "Preston is merely escorting me to Sorrelby Hall."

"But that's where I'm takin' ye, lass!" Elspeth argued.

Bridget shook her head. "No, you are not. I cannot trust you, Elspeth. I never have and I never will. Preston will take me to my cousin."

"Ye're such a child, Bridget," Elspeth spat, her tone now strident with frustration. "Forever lookin' fer someone to love ye when nobody does. This man will make a fool of ye, mark my words."

Bridget bit down hard on her lip to still its quivering. "You'd better leave. The authorities are looking for you."

"I'm leavin'," Elspeth scoffed, "but I swear to ye, ye'll rue the day ye thought any man could care fer ye, ye silly girl."

On that dire prediction Elspeth exited the cabin, slamming the door behind her.

Bridget stared at the closed portal, wishing she could be rid of the malicious images that Elspeth had generated, but the housekeeper's prophecies were woven too tightly to Bridget's own fears. The woman had assailed Bridget's greatest vulnerability and fanned to life her self-doubts. Lurking evilly in the farthest corner of Bridget's mind lay the question: *Was she worthy of anyone's love?*

Preston did not return to the *Circe* that night. The following morning Bridget paced the deck back and forth like a caged animal.

"Now, now, lassie," Captain Mac advised, "ye're beginnin' to wear a hole in me ship! We kinna be havin' that now kin we?"

Bridget halted her incessant pacing merely to mollify the man, but she immediately wished that she had not. Torn between the doubts that Elspeth's visit had generated and the hopes that Preston's embrace had fueled, Bridget could not sit still. She knew that Preston would eventually have to return to the ship, but her fear of abandonment, that Elspeth had reawakened last night, made her skittish to the extreme.

"Don't you think, Mac, that you should send someone to look for him?" she asked.

"Lord Campton is a capable lad, Bridget. Ye need have no worries."

"But he might have run into that thief," she argued, "and done something foolishly heroic like challenge him to a duel."

"Not a man alive who could best His Lordship, be it with pistol or saber," Mac assured her, beaming, obviously proud of his master's prowess. "Besides," he added, his eyes squinting into the distance, "here he comes now."

Bridget spun about, looking into the direction of the captain's gaze. Sure enough, a tall, regal figure, mounted on an enormous chestnut steed, trotted into view. The morning sunshine glinted off Preston's light blond hair, and as he drew closer, Bridget felt something tighten in her chest.

The man and beast made a striking pair: Both were large, heavily muscled creatures, distinctly comfortable with their strength. Bridget grinned widely, thinking it little wonder that she had fallen in love with this magnificent man.

She quickly smothered her smile as Preston approached the ship, not certain what type of greeting was appropriate in the aftermath of their interlude yesterday. Should she pretend that nothing had transpired? But she doubted that was possible—already feeling her pulse quicken its beat.

Preston dismounted, removed a package that had been strapped behind the saddle, and then handed the reins to a young wharfhand standing nearby. The boy accepted horse and coin with an affable nod and headed back toward town.

Lacing her fingers together to quiet their nervous fidgeting, Bridget almost held her breath as Preston came aboard with the package. Her apprizing gaze immediately discerned the bloodshot eyes and the limp cravat. His mouth seemed drawn and his vigorous color a bit off, she noted, frowning slightly.

He raised his red-rimmed eyes to her, and her heart plummeted within her breast. She did not know what she had expected to find within his regard, but certainly not the emotionless courtesy with which he surveyed her at this moment. She forced a stiff smile of greeting to her lips.

"Bridget," he briefly saluted her, dipping his head in imitation of a bow.

She noted with perplexity the grimace he tried to conceal as he righted himself.

"Preston," she evenly returned.

From the corner of her eye she saw Captain Mac study this stilted exchange. The strained silence expanded until Mac questioned, "Make sail, milord?"

"Aye, Mac. As soon as you see fit."

Although the words had been addressed to the captain, Preston's impassive gaze had not left the small woman standing at the captain's side. An enormous grin of understanding suddenly split Mac's ruddy face in two as he turned to Bridget, offered her an exaggerated wink, and whistling, strode off to give orders to heave anchor.

Bridget blinked once or twice in bewilderment at Mac's curious one-eyed signal. What was that about? she wondered. Had they shared a secret communication that she had overlooked?

A sharp whistle sounded at the far side of the *Circe,* indicating that the ship was preparing to leave port. Preston raised two fingers to his temple in a pained gesture, and Bridget, worried, rushed to his side.

"Preston, are you ill?"

"No," he groaned into his chest, avoiding her eyes. "I quarreled with a bottle of whiskey last night, and the damn bottle won."

"Oh."

Bridget had not known Preston to overindulge before, but after having lived with Elspeth these past years, she knew how to treat this particular ailment.

"Well, you're in luck, sir," she advised, slipping her arm through his. "I've just requested an early tea be sent to my cabin, and there's nothing like a fine cup of black tea to set you straight again."

Preston slanted her a rheumy look. "Tea?"

"Just the thing," she briskly affirmed. "However, if the tea doesn't work, I know of an egg concoction that will put you back on your feet in no time."

Preston shuddered while consenting to be led away. "Tea, it is."

In her cabin, Bridget attacked the teapot and its accoutrements with gusto, apparently unaware of England's age-old ceremony as to the correct manner to partake of tea. Saucers rattled, milk spilled, and sugar catapulted from a wayward spoon as Bridget saw to the business of filling two small teacups.

While Preston gingerly nibbled at a piece of toast, ignoring the milk and sugar flying about the cabin, Bridget studied him from beneath her lashes.

Although Preston's implacable manner had amused and irritated her in the past, she had, by way of her own impetuosity, been successful in breaking through his maddening control. However, the cool detachment that he currently presented doubly frustrated her as Bridget felt certain that his sudden reserve resulted from yesterday's shared passion. Even her laughable attempts to deposit a few drops of tea into their cups failed to garner even an amused smirk.

Not knowing how to broach such a delicate topic as their romantic interlude, Bridget thought to divert Preston by changing the subject.

"Elspeth came to see me last night."

Preston peered over his cup. "I know."

"You know?"

"Officer O'Connell notified me this morning that she had been apprehended leaving the *Circe*."

Bridget shook her head in dismay. " 'Twas a senseless risk she took to come here. I assume she is to be imprisoned?"

Preston nodded. "Does that distress you?"

Shrugging, Bridget's lips twisted downward. "She made the mistake of resorting to a life of crime. She must pay her dues, I guess, although I cannot help but feel a bit sorry for her."

"That's most generous of you," Preston dryly returned, "considering her plans for you."

"True enough," Bridget agreed, staring blindly into her tea. "She hoped to barter me like a piece of property. She never really cared for me."

As soon as the words left her mouth, Bridget regretted them, recalling Elspeth's prophecy that no man would ever love her. Bridget shoved the pain-filled thought to a corner of her mind and seized another topic of discussion.

"What's in the package?" she abruptly questioned.

Preston looked over to the box he had laid aside.

"I picked up a dress for you. One which I hope is closer to your size than the two you've been forced to shorten."

Bridget's eyes widened in amazement.

"You bought me a gown?"

"It's nothing," he assured her, his voice unnaturally rough. "I just didn't want you to arrive at Sorrelby looking any less than you should."

"What makes you think I'm going to Sorrelby Hall?" Bridget testily retorted, angered at his assumption even though she had already decided to go.

Preston's eyes narrowed threateningly. "I'm *not* in the mood, Bridget," he warned. "You're going to your cousin Olivia's and that's final."

"Hmph." Bridget tossed the chocolate curls that she had painstakingly pinned up that morning. "As it happens, I had already decided to visit the Forsters before you issued your ultimatum," she flippantly rejoined. "And I'll have you know, Lord Campton, that your highhanded declarations do not have any effect on me whatsoever."

A hint of a smile played around Preston's lips before he hid behind his teacup. Bridget warmed to see that expression again, pleased that her sauciness had penetrated his aloof facade.

Setting the cup down, Preston smoothly returned, "Since we are in agreement—for once—why don't you see if the gown suits you?"

Bridget eagerly reached for the package, tearing it open with childlike enthusiasm.

"Oh, Preston," she gasped. "It must be the most beautiful dress in the world!"

Although only a day gown, the kelly green robe of merino crepe shimmered against its matching trim of emerald satin bows. 'Twas evident, even to Bridget's inexperienced eye, that the garment was of the highest quality and undoubtedly expensive.

"My favorite color!" she enthused. "How did you know?"

Pleasure glinted in Preston's aquamarine gaze. "What other color would a leprechaun favor?"

Bridget looked up into the face of the man she loved and unashamedly felt the abrupt rise of tears. It had been four years since she had last received a present, and this gift from Preston touched her more than she cared to admit. Impulsively she leaned forward to place a kiss of gratitude upon his cheek, but as her lips gently skimmed his jaw, he stiffly recoiled from her touch.

Disguising her hurt beneath a glittering smile, Bridget sat back, turning her tear-brimmed eyes to the lovely gown. The thought that Preston had personally chosen the dress for her eased some of the pain of his withdrawal, but a new fear settled within her breast. Why suddenly did he loathe her touch when before he had appeared to crave it? Had her wanton response yesterday disgusted him?

Fustian, Bridget swore to herself, her gaze still pinned to the glorious gown. If only she knew what a man expected of a lady! But therein lay the problem, an insidious voice whispered to her—she was no lady. She was nothing more than a roughly reared Irish hoyden who hadn't the first inkling how to please a gentleman like Preston Campton. The best she could do was to force him to laughter or to fury by her high-spirited antics, but to lead him to love . . . She knew that she was only kidding herself.

Preston stood, his expression shuttered.

"Unfortunately, I have accounts to review before we reach England, so I will be unable to entertain you this afternoon."

"I am not a child in need of divertissement," Bridget asserted, her hurt lending a shrillness to her tone. "I am perfectly capable of occupying myself, thank you."

His curt nod caused her to regret her shrewish retort, and Bridget softened her voice.

"What I mean is . . . thank you again, Preston, for the beautiful gift. I shall treasure it always."

Not meeting her eyes, Preston bowed in acknowledgment, then wordlessly turned toward the portal. His large, brown hand had wrapped around the door's latch when Bridget abruptly asked, "Is your pain eased?"

She noted Preston pause for a long moment before he softly murmured beneath his breath, "I doubt it shall ever be."

Straining to catch his low-pitched response, Bridget frowned, certain that she had misunderstood the enigmatic reply. Before she could ask him to repeat it, however, Preston had left, closing the door behind him.

CHAPTER
13

Quelling the desire to return to Bridget's cabin and alleviate his torment, Preston stalked to his own cabin, a stormy glower darkening his brow. He threw open the door to his chamber and then slammed it shut with equal force. The noisy crashing of the portal penetrated the fog muddling Preston's thoughts, and he lowered his chin to his chest. No use teasing himself into a lather, he silently berated. The prudent thing to do would be to refocus his attention elsewhere. Determinedly he strode over to his desk, sat down, and withdrew the Welsh horse-breeding papers from a drawer.

Staring blindly at the pile of parchment, Preston allowed his mind to drift. He thought back to his last encounter with Lord Frances Pitham—the chance meeting that had spurred him to embark on this course of investigation.

"I say, Preston, you've really outdone yourself this time! He's a stunner!"

Preston politely inclined his blond head in acknowledgment of his companion's praise as the two gentlemen rode through London's Hyde Park. Fallen leaves crackled underfoot although summer had not yet yielded her reign to autumn and the air still lay warm and heavy.

Leaning forward, Preston patted the neck of his newly acquired stallion, Mercury, the subject of Lord Wyefort's compliments. The dark chestnut horse whinnied loudly in response to his rider's caress, tossing his magnificent head.

"The fellows at White's will be green with envy once again, you sly dog," Geoffrey Wyefort continued.

"Well," drawled Preston as he flashed a sardonic smile, "their discomfiture alone should be worth the price of Mercury, wouldn't you agree?"

Geoffrey half smiled, apparently uncertain as to whether Preston joked with him or spoke seriously. "I say," he asked, suddenly squinting into the sun at an advancing rider. "Is that Pitham?"

Preston looked in the direction Geoffrey indicated and immediately recognized Frances Pitham's garish riding attire. He was coming upon them quickly, pushing his mount at too rapid a pace for the park, stirring up a cloud of dust in his wake.

"Pitham does seem to favor that shade of chartreuse, doesn't he?" Preston commented as he slowed Mercury to a trot and Geoffrey followed suit.

Frances Pitham did not slacken his approach, but charged up to within a few feet of them, reining in his horse at the last possible moment, causing both Preston's and Geoffrey's mounts to shy. Preston deftly reigned in Mercury while Geoffrey struggled with his own startled animal.

Frances Pitham smiled, his yellowed teeth reflecting not only the color of his jaundiced complexion, but also the hue of his curly, straw-colored hair. His jacket fit poorly, the buttons straining atop the round expanse of a well-fed belly. His overall appearance, coupled with the chartreuse riding jacket, reminded Preston of nothing more than an underripe lemon.

"Nice piece of horseflesh, Campton," Lord Pitham hailed in his nasally voice. "Where did you find him?"

"Pitham," Preston curtly acknowledged, bobbing his head in the smallest of greetings while choosing to ignore the man's inquiry.

"I say, Pitham," Geoffrey protested with a glare, finally calming his horse. "You needn't have overrun us, you know."

"Sorry if you can't control your animal, Wyefort." He dismissed the complaint, and its issuer, with an insolent shrug of his plump shoulder, turning his attention back to Preston and the impatient Mercury.

"Damn fine horse," Pitham ventured again. When no answer was forthcoming from the stone-faced Lord Campton, Pitham assayed another tact. "Your stables must nearly rival my own with your new addition there, Campton, and that's saying something. All of London knows I have the best eye for horseflesh, and my stables are proof of that."

Lord Pitham puffed up his chest, further straining the jacket's beleaguered buttons. "Beautiful animals, but you've got to know what to look for. Breeding is everything, you know, everything. Both in animals and men." He chuckled smugly at his own joke.

"Yes," Preston responded coolly, his hands relaxed on the reins. "I understand that you recently turned a handsome profit on the sale of a pair of matched sorrels."

Preston noted the man's slight hesitation before he responded.

"That I did, that I did," he answered, his tone unnaturally hearty. His eyes narrowed suspiciously as he looked up at the taller man. "Surprised you heard of it, Campton."

Preston merely responded with an enigmatic smile.

"But," Lord Pitham continued with forced joviality, toying with his pocket watch, "I don't mind sharing my expertise with others. When you've got a discerning eye like mine, you can afford to be magnanimous."

"Well, I wouldn't be too cocky if I were you, Pitham," retorted Lord Wyefort, angered by the man's arrogance. "Campton is planning a trip to Wales to purchase a new stud that will surely outshine your prizewinner."

"Wales?" croaked Pitham, a slight crack in his nasal voice.

Preston's keen eye noted the flicker of agitation in Frances Pitham's face, and before Geoffrey could elaborate, Preston shot his friend a warning sidelong look.

"When are you heading to Wales?" questioned Pitham in an offhanded manner, his gaze straying from Preston to Geoffrey and back again.

"Just talk, old man," Preston answered easily. "I've been bored in London lately and thought I'd leave town for a while. Might go up to Sorrelby Hall instead."

"Good idea," advised Lord Pitham. "Weather in Wales this time of year would be hellish. Absolute hell. Rains constantly, I hear." He shifted uncomfortably in the saddle. "Well, I've got to be off. Meeting Lady Magby at the other side of the park for a ride. Good to talk with you fellows."

With a jerk of the reins, he turned his steed about, leaning back with one parting shot. "Remember what I said about the weather in Wales, Campton. Pure hell," he called as he rode off in a cloud of dust.

While Preston recalled his fateful encounter with Lord Pitham, Bridget toiled at her toilette. Rapturously she donned her new gown, feeling marvelously elegant and sophisticated. Through practice, her dexterity at playing hairdresser had vastly improved, and it was with considerable satisfaction that she surveyed the results in her mirror.

Although undermined by her lack of confidence as a woman, Bridget's Irish tenacity compensated for the wont of self-esteem. Living in Dunbriggan had not taught her to be a lady, but it had taught her other valuable skills—such as fishing. Any successful angler would say that fishing was simply a question of casting out the proper lures. Bridget reckoned that landing a man could not be much different than landing a fish; she just needed to determine what type of bait would attract Preston.

Gazing into the mirror, she deliberated on her choice of lure. Perhaps she should try flirting. Although Bridget didn't have much expertise in the area, she had heard that the art of flirting comprised a large part of a London debutante's training.

She practiced batting her eyelashes a few dozen times in the mirror, then toyed with a coy backward glimpse over her shoulder. She could not help but chuckle at her own reflection. Lord, but she looked positively ridiculous! Striving as she was to appear sincere—was that even possible while flirting?—she was convinced that the lowliest of actresses would succeed where she was destined to fail. Preston would most likely laugh himself sick should she direct such a cow-eyed face toward the unsuspecting man!

Wrinkling her nose at her image, Bridget abandoned the flirting concept. What had worked for her yesterday? Contact, physical contact. When Preston had fallen on top of her, he had seemed to lose that last vestige of control, letting loose the mind-numbing passion that had held Bridget spellbound upon the dank Irish earth. Yes, she mused, that had done it. She would have to engineer the situation so that they were in close proximity again.

Of course, how to manage that was another dilemma entirely. She could hardly just throw herself at him, could she? *Could she?* she asked the face staring back at her in the mirror. Her reflection smiled at her saucily, apparently finding the notion not entirely implausible. Bridget wagged her finger at the audacious miss grinning in the glass, before fussing with the bows on her dress one last time.

Gulping past the nervousness clogging her throat, Bridget took a deep breath and headed for Preston's cabin.

"Come in."

Preston slid the papers into his desk and arose as Bridget entered. All thoughts of Pitham departed as his gaze fell on the blushing young woman.

Damn, Preston silently cursed. *If I'd been thinking straight, I would have bought her a coarse black sack to wear!*

He would not have believed it possible a week ago, when that scraggly ragamuffin had leaped from his trunk, but Preston felt more attraction for this one petite female than any other woman he had known in his twenty-eight years. How in God's name was he supposed to keep his hands off her after having sampled the delights of that creamy flesh?

Gritting his teeth, Preston gestured toward the table.

"Dinner has already been brought in. Shall we?"

He noted Bridget's crestfallen expression when he failed to comment on her appearance, but he ruthlessly checked the complimentary words as they threatened to burst forth. He had to keep distance between them if he were to deliver her to Sorrelby Hall with her virtue intact!

As the meal progressed, Preston spoke not once. He admired Bridget's determined efforts to uphold a one-sided conversation, but he feared should he open his mouth to respond, heated declarations of need would spill from his tongue. At last, apparently tiring of her fruitless monologue, Bridget posed a direct question.

"What is Cousin Olivia like?"

Preston expelled a deep breath. "Olivia Forster is one of the loveliest people I know, in more than one sense. Although her beauty is renowned, she is completely devoid of vanity. She is a thoughtful, considerate woman, a loving wife, and a devoted mother."

Bridget, who had been sipping at her wine, began gulping heavily. When finally she emptied her goblet, she dryly replied, "My, what a paragon."

Preston ignored her sarcasm. "You are fortunate to be related to such a person, Bridget. She will teach you well."

"Teach me?" Bridget echoed sharply. "What do you mean by that?" She helped herself to another glass of wine from the bottle.

"I only mean that due to your upbringing, you have been deprived of certain . . . education. She can help you with some of the issues that your mother might have shared with you."

Preston frowned as Bridget downed her third glass of wine in one brief guzzle.

"In other words, she can teach me to be a lady, isn't that what you mean?" Bridget slammed the crystal glass down on the tabletop.

"I am not implying that you are deficient in any way. It's just that Olivia is near your age. She—"

"You think I should model myself after this exemplary female, don't you, Preston?" Bridget interrupted. "Is she the type of woman you admire? Someone soft and cooing, biddable and weak? Is that what you want in a woman, my lord?"

Bloody hell, Preston silently swore, if she had the slightest inkling what he wanted at this moment, she'd run like the very devil! Feeling his temper rise to the boiling point, Preston pushed away from the table. He dared not lose control of any passions, for he knew which ones would rise to the forefront.

Deflecting her question, he rose to his feet. "If you'll excuse me. I have more work to review."

Moving to the far side of the room, he distanced himself as much as possible from the fiery-eyed Bridget while hoping that she would take the not-so-subtle hint and leave.

She complied by also rising.

"Certainly, my lord."

But instead of heading for the doorway, as Preston had expected her to do, Bridget stepped forward, cornering him against his desk.

"Good night, Preston. From a not very exemplary female."

Without warning, she reached up on tiptoe, wrapped an arm around his head, and planted a wine-laced kiss smack on his lips.

Initially Preston resisted her embrace, holding himself stiffly as Bridget's soft mouth caressed his own. But within a matter of seconds his resolve melted beneath the warmth of her lips. Groaning under his breath, he crushed her to him, returning her embrace with unbridled desire.

Locked together, they both stumbled as the floor suddenly pitched violently beneath their feet. Tearing his mouth away from hers, Preston flung out an arm to steady them while the floor heaved again in the opposite direction.

"I've heard of the earth moving . . ." Bridget hazarded, her expression somewhat dazed as she clung to Preston's lapels. "Is it the ship or did I drink too much wine?"

"Both," Preston answered sardonically, staring down into her wide-eyed countenance. "Go back to your cabin, Bridget. We might be in for a rough time of it."

Bridget looked as if she might protest, but another furious tilt of the ship, accompanied by a crack of thunder, appeared to convince her of the merit of Preston's suggestion.

Releasing her hold on his coat, she gazed for a long moment into Preston's inscrutable aqua eyes before bolting for the door.

CHAPTER 14

Bridget clung to her bunk as the ship rolled and pitched, riding the turbulent waves of the storm-lashed Irish Channel. The thunder seemed to grow louder with each blast, its deafening roar coinciding with the day-bright flashes of lightning that illuminated the dark cabin.

Although it seemed an eternity, perhaps only an hour or two had passed since Bridget had left Preston's cabin. She had not bothered to light a lamp or to change into her nightrail. The storm and Preston were too all-consuming to consider such mundane matters. Staring unseeing into the indigo shadows, Bridget nearly cried with frustration.

On returning to her cabin, Bridget had fluently cursed her misfortune. Why had the storm arrived upon them at such an inopportune moment? Emboldened by the wine, Bridget had dared that courageous kiss, the final outcome of which she could only now guess at. If not separated by the storm, what would have been the ultimate conclusion to her presumptuous embrace?

Whereas Preston had recoiled from her earlier in the day, Bridget had provoked a completely different response from him this evening. She had gambled, hoping not to alienate him by her forwardness, but, unfortunately, she would have to wait for another opportunity to see where such boldness might lead.

Bridget's musings came up short. Where did she want her experiment to lead? She loved Preston. And she wanted his love in return. She did not believe him indifferent to her, and, in fact, Bridget thought that perhaps Preston felt a degree of attraction to her. But was that enough of a basis on which for love to flourish?

Tortured by so many questions, Bridget had, at first, not noticed the mounting savagery of the storm outside. But as she skittered back and forth across her bed, clutching madly to the mattress to keep from being tossed to the other side of the room, she began to take note of the tempest besetting the ship. Louder and louder grew the thunder as the *Circe* pitched violently up and down like some crazed animal.

Suddenly an ear-shattering splintering, louder yet than the ferocious thunder, reverberated throughout the darkness. The *Circe* shuddered and groaned, her wooden slats whining like the howling wind, as the ship began listing to port. While Bridget huddled beneath a blanket, the cabin's portal was abruptly thrown open, and a flash of lightning cast Preston's taut expression into bright white relief. Bridget felt the blood drain from her own face as she read the controlled fear in his countenance.

Without a word he strode into the cabin, water pouring from his hair and clothing, instantly creating massive puddles upon the cabin floor. Without preface he scooped Bridget into his arms, blanket and all. She shivered as the icy dampness that enveloped Preston penetrated the woolen coverlet's warmth.

"Preston, what is it?" Bridget felt ashamed to hear her voice tremble.

Marching out the door into the pounding rain, he had to nearly shout his answer to be heard.

"We're abandoning ship. She's going down."

Horror shot through Bridget, and she dazedly stared up at Preston. She did not know a great deal about ships and ocean travel, but surely a simple storm could be ridden out by a sound vessel. Or had she underestimated the ferocity of the gales buffeting the sleek *Circe*?

"But how could that be?"

Bridget did not know whether her voice, carried away by the screeching wind, reached Preston's ears, but he answered her anyway.

"We've been sabotaged. Someone had weakened the mast, and the storm completed the job. She's not going to stay afloat."

Tightening her hold on Preston's neck, Bridget battled her terror. *Sabotage*.

Her stomach roiled and clenched as the sickening movement of the ship intensified the sudden spasm in her gut. Valiantly she collected herself, trying to shunt aside her fear.

Preston had been carefully moving along the corridor, holding fast to the ship's interior wall, bound for the stairway leading to the upper deck. As they passed his cabin, Bridget, suddenly and inexplicably, recalled Preston's mission.

"Preston, the documents!"

Sheltered momentarily from the falling rain, Preston leaned against the wall.

"The horse-breeding documents," she explained in response to his apparent confusion. "I think that they're important."

If they had not been standing directly outside his cabin door, Bridget felt certain that he would have refused to go after the papers. However, after a brief hesitation, Preston kicked open the portal and strode into his cabin. Gently he lay Bridget upon the bed, his hair dripping icy pellets as he leaned over her, and in a thrice had recovered the documents. He also withdrew from his desk a metal tube in which he placed the parchment.

Shivering upon the bed, Bridget marveled at his composure. His ship was sinking to the bottom of the Irish Sea, and yet, the expressionless mask of his features revealed nothing. The initial fear that Bridget had witnessed there had vanished, leaving only a spasming muscle in his ironhard jaw.

After having tucked the tube into his coat pocket, Preston turned about.

"I-I can walk," Bridget hesitantly offered. Preston appeared not to hear her as he slid his arms beneath her, easily hoisting her up against his broad chest. The ship groaned and heaved again, listing more steeply into the churning sea. Miraculously Preston maintained his footing, and with increased speed, he vaulted out the door and up the stairs to the deck.

The full force of the punishing rain assaulted them as they came onto the exposed deck. Any protection that the blanket had offered against the chill downpour disappeared, and Bridget huddled more closely against Preston.

Waves relentlessly crashed over the side of the ship, then receded back into the sea only to return again with renewed velocity. Each mountain of water that leaped over the railing hit the deck in a thunderous collision, and Bridget brought her hands to her ears to stifle the ocean's roar.

Agog, she watched the crew scurry to ready the skiffs. Despite the horrendous conditions, the men seemed to move quickly and efficiently even though the deck beneath them continued its descent into the frigid waters. The men's clothing, plastered to their bodies by the wind and rain, outlined their heaving muscles and wiry frames while they labored to align the smaller boats.

Once the skiffs had been laid out, Preston carried Bridget over and placed her into one of the waiting boats. Thunder and lightning crackled against the ebony sky, and Bridget cringed, cowering beneath the soaked blanket.

"Lower her over," Preston ordered.

"No!" Bridget screamed, raising her arms to clasp hold of Preston. Feeling like the veriest of cowards, she clutched him frantically, panic throbbing through her veins.

He leaned over and grabbed hold her upper arms, his eyes piercing her with their fevered light. "I will join you, never fear. I must see that my men get away safely."

Bridget gulped back the tears and released him, nodding her acquiescence. Preston stepped back from the boat, and the crew levered her over the side as Bridget clung fearfully to her seat.

Bobbing alongside the ship, Bridget felt relieved to note that the skiff was still tethered to the *Circe*. At least she would not be washed away to sea while Preston remained aboard the ship. Two more skiffs were sent over and splashed into the roiling waters beside her. She closed her eyes and sent a fervent prayer heavenward that they would all escape this terror unharmed.

Shimmying down the ropes, the crew took possession of the other skiffs. Thankfully, thought Bridget, the odds favored their survival since the six sailors, the captain, Phillips, Preston, and herself were easily accommodated by the three lifeboats.

Shielding her eyes from the rain, Bridget raised a hand to her brow, straining to see the deck. Another flash of lightning revealed the remaining occupants of the doomed ship, the easily identifiable, redheaded Captain Mac . . . and Preston.

Standing, legs widespread, against the dramatic backdrop of the stormy night sky, Preston appeared to Bridget to be the absolute essence of man. His lank hair whipping about his head, his fists firmly planted upon his hips, he seemed to challenge the very elements to best him. It was man against nature in a primitive battle for life.

As Bridget studied the heroic figure, Preston and the captain simultaneously reached for a rope, each man beginning the descent to the skiffs below. The wind had increased its ferocity, and the gusts swept the two figures haphazardly back and forth. Captain Mac was the first to settle into a boat. Pulling a knife from his coat, he quickly sliced through the mooring ropes to all but Bridget's skiff.

Preston had nearly reached the relative safety of the boat when a rushing roar of water signaled the *Circe*'s surrender to the ocean. Canting heavily, the ship abruptly lurched in the water, slamming Preston into the ship's side.

Bridget gasped, one hand covering her mouth, as Preston tenaciously cleaved to the hemp lifeline. He hung there, flattened against the ship's side, while Bridget's heart constricted her throat. Then she saw his fist grapple lower on the rope, and he slipped, dropping the remaining distance into the skiff.

He landed feet first into the boat, immediately crumpling over onto the seat. Bridget rushed forward, nearly losing her balance.

"Preston!" She grabbed his shoulders, trying to pull him up into a sitting position, but his weight proved too much for her. As he slumped forward again into a ball, Bridget placed her lips nearly against his ear and shouted, "Preston!"

His head lolled back, and his eyes flickered open.

"The knife, Bridget." She struggled to catch his murmured words. "You must cut us away, or we'll go down with her."

Startled, Bridget glanced back to the ship that already lay half-submerged beneath the bubbling sea. Dear God, yes! If she did not hurry, they would be pulled down by the ship! Frantically she strained to find the other skiffs through the darkness, but neither moonlight nor lightning assisted her.

Leaning over Preston's shoulder, Bridget fumbled in his heavy, wet coat until her hand wrapped around a metallic object, the tube of documents. Frustrated, she slid the container back into his pocket and continued her search, the gurglings of the sinking ship magnifying the urgency.

With a startled cry Bridget felt her finger unexpectedly slice against a honed edge, drawing blood. Ignoring the pain, she carefully extracted the knife from Preston's front so as not to accidentally stab the semiconscious man. She grasped the handle of the blade in a death grip and began to hack fiercely at the mooring ropes. After two or three slashes against the corded hemp, the rope gave away, and she and Preston floated free into the stormy black night.

CHAPTER
15

The storm passed as quickly as it had come. The clouds skittered away, permitting the moon to grace the solitary travelers with an occasional beam of ivory light. The sea abandoned her frantic heaving, settling into a lolling rhythm of waves.

Through the brief patches of luminescence, Bridget searched for the other two skiffs. At one point she thought she heard a voice calling in the distance, but it grew more faint until it vanished into the gloom.

Preston still sat hunched over, half-conscious, his head hanging limply below his knees. Bridget finally succeeded in pulling him down to lay flat across the seats by wrapping her arms around his back and levering her feet against the seat. She tucked the wet blanket beneath his head for a pillow, and then set about tugging and pulling at his lifeless limbs until they were arranged in a more natural, and she hoped, more comfortable, manner. Exhausted from the trauma and her efforts at moving Preston, she lay down next to his prone form. Despite the dampness of his clothes, his body radiated heat, and Bridget snuggled closely against him. Almost immediately she succumbed to the rocking of the boat, falling asleep with the comforting thud of Preston's heart beating against her ear.

The earliest rose-hued light awoke Bridget, and she was

amazed to see how calmly the sea rolled beneath them. Dawn anointed the horizon with a dazzling display of color, its golden-pink promise of a better day lifting her spirits.

She turned back to Preston, wishing that he could share the glory of the sunrise with her, when she noted the ugly, purple gash marring the center of his forehead. Her fingers delicately outlined the injury as a frown settled between her winged brows. He had obviously sustained a terrific blow last night when he had collided with the ship.

Bridget bit down hard on her lip, surveying the wound. She knew little of the healing arts, but she had heard of head injuries proving fatal. Shaking her head, she refused even to contemplate such a fate.

She brushed Preston's hair away from the gash, the pads of her thumbs softly massaging his temples. Beneath her fingertips, she could sense the steady pulsing of blood flowing through his veins, and she smiled to herself. Preston was too alive, too vital to be felled by a mere blow to the head. She recalled the vision that he had presented last night, his long, muscled legs straddling the deck of the sinking ship, the lightning glinting off his blond hair. He had seemed more than a man to her, a veritable force of nature. Her heart thrilled with the memory as she gazed down into his pale face. *No,* she whispered reassuringly to herself, *'twould take more than a scratch upon the forehead to bring down Preston Campton.*

Her eyes caressed each detail of his face, taking advantage of this unusual opportunity to savor his masculine beauty. In repose his features were more relaxed, lending him a more youthful appearance. Not that he looked older than twenty-eight, Bridget decided, but the sardonic twist to his smile and the arrogant gleam to his aspect when awake produced an illusion of cynicism, suggesting a man of more advanced years.

Staring down at the mouth that had shown her such pleasure, Bridget could not resist placing a butterfly-light caress upon his parted lips. Their rough texture surprised her, and, pulling away from the kiss, Bridget noticed that his lips were dry and chapped. For the first time she recognized the gravity of their situation. She had no fresh water to offer him.

In one corner of the boat a small packet of provisions had been stored, but Bridget doubted that fresh water would be among them. Nevertheless, she cautiously stepped around Preston, mindful not to dump herself into the sea, and unwrapped the bundle. Dried beef, hard biscuits, and a bottle of ale comprised their emergency stores.

The sun had continued its ascent into the sky, and Bridget welcomed the heat as morning advanced. The damp wool gown steamed under the warming rays, emitting a faintly unpleasant odor reminiscent of wet sheep. Preston did not awaken throughout the morning, but Bridget was pleased to see that his breathing remained even and his color had improved. She removed the blanket from beneath his head, laying it out flat to dry in the sun, cradling his head in her lap as he continued to sleep.

Bridget wished she knew in which direction they were floating, wondering how long it might be before they came upon land. For that reason she had delayed partaking of their stores, despite her mounting appetite, until Preston awakened. He would probably have a better idea as to the number of days they might be expected to drift along.

Judging from the position of the sun, Bridget estimated that they were heading north. Grimacing, she regretted that she had not continued her study of geography after her father had disappeared, since she could not guess whether north would yield land or not.

The day progressed and Bridget entertained herself with reminiscences of her younger days when she, her mother, and her father had been together, a happy family. The sun toasted her face as its intensity grew in the afternoon hours, and she huddled over Preston, hoping to protect him from the escalating heat of the sun's rays.

Memories of her tenth birthday party danced through her head, when suddenly Preston stirred in her lap, emitting a soft groan.

"Preston," Bridget whispered, her heart soaring with relief, "are you awake?"

He did not open his eyes, but his lips moved slightly and Bridget bent forward to catch his rasping words.

"How could anyone sleep with their ear pressed against the roar of your stomach?"

She blinked. The man had been unconscious all day, and *this* was the first thing he had to say to her?

"Hmph," she grumbled. "I guess you're not going to die just yet, then."

Preston's eyes opened to the barest of slits. "Not just yet," he answered.

He tried to push himself up into a sitting position, but immediately fell back onto Bridget's lap with a pained groan.

"Whatever happened to my head?"

"Don't you remember colliding into the ship? You were climbing down the rope—"

"I remember, I remember," Preston interrupted her, scowling. He brought his hand up to his head to probe the injury, wincing as his fingers found the gash. "Ow! A regular rammer, eh? Is it splendid?"

Bridget smirked. "Well, I don't believe it shall scar, if that's what you're worried about."

Preston's scowl deepened. "I am not concerned about a little blemish," he vehemently protested. "I'm sure I've suffered worse at Gentleman Jack's."

Eyeing him speculatively from her upside-down position, Bridget could not resist a mild jibe. "Perhaps. Though it is unfortunate that it's smack in the center of your forehead. Should it scar—after all, what do I know?—'twould be a pity."

Preston flexed an amused brow. "My looks would be destroyed, is that it?"

"Well," Bridget drawled, "I don't know about destroyed—"

"And you would no longer find me attractive?" he pressed, a curious gleam lighting his eyes.

Bridget blushed and the glimmer in Preston's gaze sharpened.

"And since I shall surely lose my hearing from the din your stomach is making, I take it a deaf, scarred old baron would hold little appeal for you, hmm, Bridget?"

The man was a rogue. He toyed with her, and yet she knew his game was a dangerous one. If she did not watch her tongue, she might reveal more than she cared to at this point.

Flashing him an arch smile, Bridget lightly retorted, "I daresay you must have some other attributes to render you acceptable."

"What do you suppose those might be?"

His teasing smile wreaked havoc on Bridget's senses, and she struggled to maintain the playful banter.

"A pleasant temperament?" she proposed, feigning contemplation. Shaking her head sorrowfully, she answered her own question. "No, I think not. Wit? Women do enjoy a clever man. Hmm . . ." Pausing, she tilted her head to one side, a regretful moue curling her mouth. "Perhaps, a sensitive nature—"

"I have been complimented before on my talent at kissing," Preston interrupted with a wicked grin.

Bridget gasped. "Oh, you are a scoundrel!"

Impetuously she pushed his head off her lap, and it thudded against the wooden seat.

"Youch!" Preston rubbed the back of his head. "That was a bit rough!"

"You deserved it," Bridget shot back as she flounced to the other side of the bench.

Preston both smiled and winced as he sat up, turning to face the pink-cheeked Bridget.

"Is that the sun's effects, or have I put you to the blush?"

"The sun," Bridget primly retorted.

"Come now, let us be honest."

"I said 'the sun,' " she forcefully reiterated, glaring down her pert nose.

"That is a relief." Preston's lips twitched. "I would hate

to think I might have embarrassed you by discussing amorous exploits."

"Embarrassed?!" Bridget looked aghast. "Why should I be embarrassed? Dash it, I shouldn't care if you've kissed every female in England!"

"Ah, but it's not the English kisses I was referring to," Preston mischievously taunted.

"Oh, really!" Bridget spluttered as she felt the burning rush of color to her cheeks.

Preston chuckled while Bridget turned to study the horizon with renewed concentration. His gaze followed hers, and he dropped one elbow to his knee.

"We're in quite a coil, aren't we?"

At first Bridget thought that he referred to their mysteriously complex relationship, but when she pivoted around, she saw that his eyes were fixed on the endless blue vista surrounding them.

"It appears so," she said, sighing. "Where do you think we're headed?"

"I am not entirely sure. The storm took us off course, and we've been drifting at least, oh"—he glanced to the sun's position—"eighteen or so hours. . . . I'd wager that's Scotland there to the east."

"What?" Bridget excitedly cried, sitting forward to peer into the east. "Land! Preston, it's land!"

"Indeed."

Bridget's face fell with the realization that although they might be able to see it, reaching it was another matter entirely.

"Damn," she muttered. "Now what shall we do?"

"I'd suggest we eat," Preston casually returned. "I'm famished."

Bridget worried her lip with her teeth. "What if we consume all our provisions?"

"I shouldn't worry, Bridget," Preston confidently assured. "I'd think it unlikely we'd pass through the North Channel without being rescued, or, more likely, the tides will pull us into one of the many bays."

"So, we shan't breathe our last floating about on the Scottish Sea?"

Preston grinned endearingly into her worried expression. " 'Tis extremely doubtful, my dear."

Preston's prediction proved correct, for, as the sun teetered on the brink of the horizon, the skiff washed to within a few hundred yards of a rocky beach.

"You are certain that you can swim?" Preston questioned for perhaps the sixth time as the sunburned pair gaped at the watery distance separating the shore and their craft.

"Of course," Bridget repeated with exasperation. "I told you that I was raised in a fishing village. Everyone swims."

"But it is farther than you might imagine, Bridget. It will be no mean feat, fighting the surf into the beach."

Bridget sighed, pushing a lock of hair away from her damp face. The afternoon had proved terribly warm, especially for Bridget in her woolen gown.

"I might look delicate, Preston, but I warrant I'll reach the beachhead before even you," she brashly challenged.

Although anxious about Bridget's ability to span the stretch of sea, Preston smiled despite himself. His diminutive Bridget had more spunk than most of the soldiers that had served under him during the war. The saucebox probably didn't even know the meaning of the word *defeat*.

"All right, minx. I'll take that wager," Preston agreed with a nod. "I think, however, that you will need to divest yourself of"—he coughed uncomfortably, contemplating the ramifications of his suggestion—"some of your clothing. It might prove too weighty once you are in the water."

Bridget glanced down with dismay at her lovely emerald gown. "I cannot possibly leave it behind," she protested. "It's the only gift I—" She clamped shut her jaw.

"No, I refuse to leave it," she stubbornly declared.

Preston rolled his eyes heavenward. On occasion that admirable spunk of hers proved irksome to the extreme.

"I will carry the gown for you," he patiently offered.

"However, we have not all day to discuss this, Bridget. The tide will soon turn."

Preston's warning caused Bridget to nervously glance from beach to sea, and then, with sudden determination, she began unfastening the gown.

Preston hastily averted his gaze while sternly admonishing himself to be a gentleman. Although tempted beyond endurance to view what his palm had once so joyously caressed, he fastened his gaze to the shore and did not remove it until Bridget thrust a wad of fabric into his hands.

"The race is on, my lord." And without further ado, Bridget stood and dived cleanly into the blue-green waters.

CHAPTER 16

"Eeeks!"

Bridget's squeal as she resurfaced from the icy depths was met by a wholeheartedly unsympathetic chuckle from Preston.

"I shouldn't laugh too hard if I were you," Bridget warned, scowling while she fanned her arms back and forth, treading water. "Unless you wish to be washed out to sea, you'll have to join me shortly." She spluttered as an errant wave caught her openmouthed, and Preston renewed his laughter.

"Never fear, little one," Preston returned. "I have never backed down from a dare and I fully intend to best you in this race."

Her eyes squinting into the setting sun, Bridget watched as Preston stood and began shrugging out of his jacket. For a brief moment she experienced a twinge of regret, wondering if her brash challenge might have been foolhardy in light of Preston's recent injury. If he had been weakened by his head wound, overexertion in the form of their race might prove too much for him. His size and weight would make it impossible for Bridget to tow him to shore should he falter.

However, her worries dissipated as Preston stretched his arms overhead, the fine linen of his shirt pulling tautly across his sculptured chest. Surely, she thought, no man could be a finer specimen of health than this one. Head wound notwithstanding, Preston exemplified the essence of masculine strength and power. Her fears eased, and instead, Bridget concentrated on her competition.

'Twould be most improbable, she mused, to best Preston in this contest. The advantage his size afforded him would far outdistance her swimming skills. Bridget smiled wickedly to herself and straightaway struck out for the shore.

"Hey, now," Preston shouted. "No fair!"

But Bridget ignored him and put her head down, establishing a smooth, even stroke as she steadily plowed through the gentle waves. A splash announced Preston's pursuit, and Bridget counted in her head, wondering how many seconds would lapse before he overtook her. One, two, three . . . Much sooner than she had thought.

"I hadn't taken you for a cheat," Preston accused as he came even with her.

Bridget swallowed a gulp of air, retorting, "Don't waste your breath on excuses, my lord. If you dallied, 'tis your own fault."

She could not read his expression as the waves softly splashed around her, although she heard Preston cough wetly on a response.

After a few more minutes of steady stroking, Bridget paused to gauge their progress. Preston had not sped ahead of her as she had anticipated, but rather had matched her pace. He, too, paused, treading water.

"Do you tire?" he asked.

"Huh," Bridget grunted, spewing water like a fountain. "You would wish so, but a Flannery is made of sterner stuff than you might think."

"We have gone nearly halfway," he encouraged.

Bridget eyed the shore, so tantalizingly close and yet still a good ten minutes' swim away. The sky had lost the brightness of day as the pale violet twilight descended on the rocky beach.

"Let's be off, then," she answered. "I have no desire to spend another night asea."

Determinedly she cleaved through the waves, Preston adhering to her side. Although Bridget was confident in her swimming abilities, she felt reassured to have Preston near as the minutes ticked by, the sky darkening and the waters growing more chill.

At last her foot struck rock, and she scrambled to her feet, wading in the final few yards to the welcoming shore. Her chest heaved, and she flashed an elated smile as Preston joined her upon the pebbled beach.

"Whew," she breathed. "I guess we'd have to call it a draw. I don't think—"

Bridget's voice congealed in her throat as she met the searing heat of Preston's turquoise eyes. She drew her breath in sharply, mesmerized by the sensuality radiating from those blue-green orbs.

His gaze raked her, each touch of his eyes burning Bridget's flesh where they contacted her. She followed his consuming gaze, suddenly realizing that her white cotton chemise clung to her so closely that it outlined every curve and crevice of her damp body. She gasped to see herself so clearly revealed, her deep breaths thrusting her feminine curves more firmly against the thin fabric.

The shadowed coolness of dusk had teased her nipples into tautness, their cherry peaks easily discernible, and Bridget blushed furiously in the face of her near nakedness.

Aghast, her eyes flew back to Preston. He had turned his head away, his jaw clenched tightly as he surveyed the far horizon. Bridget saw that familiar muscle in his cheek clench in spasms and noted the tumultuous pulsing of the vein running down his thick neck.

Without looking at her again, he untied the small bundle of clothing he had tied to his waist. He tossed his soaked jacket toward her where it fell near her feet.

"Put this on," he ordered, his voice curiously gruff.

Bridget wordlessly complied, slipping her arms into the enormous coat. Although the dripping wet jacket further chilled her, she made no protest.

Preston turned toward her again, and Bridget noted the steely mask he had settled over his features. His hair was slicked back from his forehead, highlighting the angular planes of his face. He briefly scanned her appearance, his expression tight.

The coat fell past Bridget's knees, and with one hand she self-consciously clutched the lapels together at the neck to prevent the garment from gaping open. Unaccountably she trembled, her knees knocking together.

"Dark will be upon us soon. We should hasten to find some form of shelter."

Bridget nodded, unable to locate her voice. She was still too stunned by the naked desire she had seen in Preston's visage. Her entire body quivered with the memory of the passion she had witnessed, its fire leaving an imprint upon her skin. Faith, Bridget whispered to herself, if his mere look could so scorch her, would she not melt beneath the inferno of his unrestrained passion?

Although she had experienced a small measure of his ardor the other day in the woods, the intensity that she had seen in him only minutes ago astounded her. She had never imagined that she could so inflame a man. With the realization, a sharp joy flooded Bridget's heart. Preston desired her! Fervently. Surely, she naively thought, love could not follow far behind. Such depth of feeling must certainly suggest a degree of affection.

Trudging behind Preston as they wound their way up an overgrown trail, Bridget stared longingly at his broad back. Could such a dream come true for Dunbriggan's gamine? Would she ever again know the warmth of reciprocated love? So many loveless years had passed that Bridget almost dared not hope that she would be rewarded with someone like Preston Campton. Except for his one flaw, that being born an Englishman—make that two flaws, she quickly amended with a secret smile, recalling Preston's arrogance—he embodied every woman's fantasy.

Bridget sighed heavily, and Preston abruptly spun about, a frown etched across his scarred brow.

"Do you need to rest? I did not mean to push you so hard, but night is nearly upon us." His voice was husky, yet measured. Eyes narrowing, he surveyed the purpling sky.

"No, I am fine. Really."

Preston slanted a dubious glance at her bare feet.

"You are not uncomfortable unshod?"

Bridget smiled, peering down at his own bare toes.

"Not in the slightest. At home I hardly ever bother with shoes, to tell you the truth."

"I, unfortunately, am accustomed to my Hessians, which are currently floating aimlessly about the Irish Sea."

Bridget grinned ruefully. "Perhaps an octopus can put them to good use."

Humor flickered around Preston's mouth. "I doubt Hoby would be amused to hear of it."

"Hoby?"

"My London bootmaker," Preston dryly explained.

As Bridget's heart rate slowed, she realized that this discussion of footwear had been merely contrived by Preston as an opportunity for her to catch her breath. He must have known that her pride would never have permitted her to ask for a respite, and she smiled at his thoughtfulness.

"Shall we push on?" she suggested.

They marched across the stark countryside, the piercing wind picking up in strength as they came onto a bluff above the beach. Long grasses billowed and swayed about them, very few trees breaking the barren panorama. They had just climbed onto a small hillock when Preston suddenly came to a halt.

"Thank God," Bridget heard him mutter.

Drawing abreast, she understood his prayer of thanks. In the small vale below, a stone cottage stood, awaiting two weary travelers.

"It appears abandoned."

"Is that good or bad?" Bridget questioned from the doorway.

Preston strode quickly about the single-room dwelling, looking for signs of recent occupation.

"Both, I would say," he answered, rummaging through a chest to the side of the fireplace. "Bad since we have no food nor change of clothing. Good because we do not have to worry about our welcome." He stood up, gesturing to the hearth. "At least a few pieces of firewood remain. We shall have a fire even if we have nothing to cook."

Bridget bit her lip as she approached Preston. "Not another missed meal," she groaned. "I cannot understand why I am forever hungry when I am with you."

Pivoting his head about over his shoulder, Preston impaled Bridget with an enigmatic stare. Her innocent regard convinced him that she had not intended the double meaning her words had implied. He turned back to his task of lighting the fire, attempting to quench the sudden lust that her inadvertent statement had wrought. If she only knew, he privately agonized, how hungry a man he truly was!

He hungered for her to the point of starving. The sight of her rising from the sea had nearly set him to salivating! The perfection of her diminutive form, the glow of animation to her piquant features . . . Damn, but it had been a close thing! Only his iron will had kept him from throwing her onto the beach and devouring her inch by inch.

"I am going to take a look around before it grows too dark," Bridget stated at his back. "I am quite a proficient scavenger. There must be something to eat around here."

Preston nodded, continuing his labors at kindling the fire. He had laid Bridget's gown over a chair to dry, placing it near the roaring blaze in the fireplace, and had stripped off his shirt to do the same, when Bridget entered. She appeared to stumble at the threshold, her eyes alighting on Preston's bare chest, but hastily recovered.

Casting her eyes downward, she hesitantly announced, "Um . . . I have dug up a few potatoes and onions. And found a handful of mushrooms." Preston saw her peek at him from beneath her lowered lashes. "There's a well only a little ways away. I thought if you could bring in some fresh water, we could wash up, and I could throw together a soup."

Preston wanted to laugh at Bridget's uncharacteristic shyness, but he refrained. Instead, he apologized.

"Forgive my lack of modesty, but I am sure, like you, the damp clothing grows uncomfortable."

A puckish grin twinkled at the corners of Bridget's lips as she raised her eyes to his. "Your bare chest is not nearly as shocking as other views you have afforded me in the past, my lord."

Preston shook his head at Bridget's audacity. Had he only a moment earlier thought her bashful?

"Point taken, minx," he retorted, his playful tone feigning rebuke at her boldness. "I'll see to that water."

Scant light remained, and as the moon had not yet arisen, Preston relied on instinct to navigate the path to the well. At moments like these, he appreciated the rigorous training he had suffered serving on the Peninsula. Although, to Preston's thinking, little good had come of the wars, he, personally, had benefitted. Before his military stint, Preston had not wholly appreciated all with which he had been blessed: his health, his station in life, his myriad abundance of riches, both material and intangible.

When he had returned to London after his service, the scope of his advantages had hit him full on. And it was during this period that the *ennui* of Society life settled upon him. Before, he had taken for granted the butterfly-like existence that the *ton* enjoyed, flitting about aimlessly from one social function to the next. With the horrors of war fresh in his mind as contrast, Preston had inevitably grown cynical and bored by the shallowness of Society.

Padding through the frigid darkness, Preston felt far from bored. In fact, he cursed the fates that had brought Bridget and him to this unfortunate pass. 'Twas simply inconceivable the series of disastrous incidents that had plagued the pair these past two weeks. Hefting the bucket from the well, Preston wondered for the first time if more than ill luck lay behind their situation.

Pushing open the wooden-plank door, Preston frowned to find Bridget huddled before the fire, her teeth chattering. Setting the bucket down, he rushed to her side.

"What are you still doing in those wet clothes?" he questioned, concerned by the bluish tinge to her pale lips.

"I-I have nothing else to wear," she feebly protested. "The gown is still damp."

Roughly pulling her up by her shoulders, he glared at her. "Don't get missish on me now, for God's sake, Bridget. We've long ago surpassed the bounds of propriety, as you only recently reminded me yourself!"

He released her shoulders and stalked over to the crudely crafted wooden bed, where he retrieved a dusty blanket.

"It's not especially clean, but you'll have to suffer it until your gown dries." He shook out the blanket and then tossed it to her, gruffly instructing, "Get out of those wet garments. Now."

Pivoting about, Preston offered her a space of privacy while he fought down his irritation. What was the little ninny trying to do? Catch her death of cold? If matters weren't grave enough, the last thing he needed was a feverish female on his hands! His concern for Bridget, combined with his frustrated physical needs, whetted Preston's annoyance, and when he finally turned about, a threatening scowl lay across his brow.

Bridget had wrapped the gray woolen blanket around her toga-style, leaving a great expanse of creamy skin revealed on one shoulder. Preston's glower deepened, and he winced as the facial contortions pulled at his wound.

"Does your head bother you?" Bridget asked, stepping forward to examine the injury.

Preston automatically stepped back, evading her touch.

"No," he curtly lied. "I am but hungry."

Bridget's expression closed, and Preston knew that he had hurt her with his brusqueness, but he also knew that no matter how much he hurt her, he had to maintain distance between them. He had erred earlier today in the dinghy, by teasing and flirting with her, but he had not been thinking straight when he had awakened from the blow to his head.

"Then I'll start dinner," Bridget evenly replied, vainly trying to keep the hurt from her voice. Without looking at Preston, she turned to the trestle table in the middle of the room and began chopping the vegetables with Preston's knife.

The stew Bridget improvised, though not haute cuisine, tasted simply delicious to the hungry pair. Preston and Bridget easily finished off the pot, their hunger keeping conversation to a minimum. Although heavy with unspoken thoughts, the silence suited Preston, for his emotions simmered too close to the surface for him to feign casual conversation.

Bridget rinsed out the bowls and tossed the dirty water out the front door, shivering as the frosty night air swirled into the cabin.

"We're lucky," she commented as she closed the door behind her, "to have found this cottage. A fire, cooking utensils, a roof over our heads—heavens, we might have been forced to bed down in the fields."

Preston narrowed his eyes contemplatively, leaning back in the rickety chair. "Odd you should use the word *lucky*. Earlier, I was thinking how very unlucky the incidents of the past fortnight had been."

Bridget turned to him, frowning. "Whatever do you mean?"

"I mean," Preston elaborated, a mischievous gleam to his eyes, "that for a self-proclaimed leprechaun, Miss Flannery, you have brought me naught but ill fortune."

CHAPTER
17

Bridget gasped in outrage, thrusting her fists to her hips in a clearly indignant gesture.

"How dare you!" she squeaked. "You would blame me for your misfortune? I—"

"I was jesting," Preston interrupted with a conciliatory smile. "But you must admit the irony of the situation. A leprechaun is supposed to lead one to a pot of gold, not to disaster."

Throwing up her hands in disgust, Bridget had to make a hasty grab for the blanket that came loose with the motion. Tucking the folds of the blanket back into place, she glowered at Preston, who sat watching her rearrange her make-shift gown.

"Fat lot you know of leprechauns, Lord Campton," she angrily retorted. "First, after catching a leprechaun, you must be clever enough to force him into revealing his hidden treasure. Leprechauns do not happily turn over their gold to their captor. In fact, they do all in their power to rid themselves of their jailer, resorting to any manner of magical tricks and disguises to secure their freedom and their treasure."

"Well," Preston lazily drawled, "you certainly have lived up to that aspect of your moniker."

"Hah!" Bridget's eyebrows threatened to disappear into

her hairline. "And what, pray tell, do you mean by that?"

"Exactly as I said," Preston smoothly replied, subduing a smirk at Bridget's aggravation. She was marvelously entertaining when in a pique. "You cannot deny that you have resorted to disguises and, verily, your desire to secure your freedom was the basis for our meeting in the first place."

"That still does not mean that I have brought you bad luck," she argued, flopping inelegantly into the other wooden chair.

"I must disagree."

Of course, Preston conceded to himself, he did not really believe Bridget responsible for the hapless events, but he was so enjoying the game, he could not resist teasing her a bit.

"The sinking of the *Circe*, the theft of my trunk, the confrontation with the Irish guard, the wheel breaking on my carriage." Preston catalogued each event, ticking them off on his long, tanned fingers. "What other explanation could there be?"

"Now, just a moment," Bridget objected, wagging her finger to emphasize her point. "I had not even met you at the time of the carriage accident."

"We might not have officially met," Preston countered, "*but* you were already stowed away in the carriage. Is that not so?"

Bridget clamped shut her jaw on a remonstration, her brows wrinkled in thought. Abruptly she remembered, "But you told me that the ship's mast had been sabotaged. Do not say that I am to be condemned for that?!"

Preston's lighthearted expression evaporated. "No, Bridget, I was but joking with you. The sabotage, however, is no joking matter and, according to Captain Mac, very real."

"But why would someone wish to sabotage the ship?"

Frowning, Preston echoed her question in his mind. Up to now he had been too preoccupied with their mere survival to consider the events that had placed them in this predicament. However, Bridget's query forced him to reevaluate the mystery.

Bridget tapped her fingers rhythmically on the table while Preston, distracted from his thoughts, admired the dimple in her cheek. The dimple popped in and out as Bridget chewed thoughtfully on her lower lip, mesmerizing Preston.

"You know, Preston," she haltingly began, flashing him an uncertain look from beneath her lashes. "I did have a strong sense of intuition at the time of the shipwreck."

"Yes?" he prompted her, curious.

"Do you remember that I insisted you retrieve the horse-breeding documents before we abandoned the *Circe*?"

"Of course I remember. I have them right here."

"Well, you did mention that they might prove incriminating, did you not?"

Preston frowned across the table at her, suddenly grasping her train of thought. "Are you suggesting that someone sabotaged my ship merely to see the papers destroyed?"

Bridget tilted her head, delicately shrugging the one bare shoulder. "You did not mention whom you were investigating, however, if it is someone of importance and they suspected your involvement . . ."

Something clicked in Preston's consciousness as Bridget's hypothesis became clear. Although somewhat far-fetched, her argument was not without merit.

"Frances Pitham is a nobleman, a member of the House of Lords," he slowly explained. "He travels in some of the best circles. It would mean both financial and social ruin should my suspicions prove correct."

"Could he have known of your expedition to Wales?"

Preston nodded his head. "He did. London is a very small community, and I made no secret of the trip. Naturally, I did not discuss my objective. However, Pitham might have suspected since he and I had words regarding my friend's purchase from his stables."

"Why, though, if he's a wealthy lord, would he take such a risk engaging in fraud?" Bridget queried.

Preston tossed her a shrewd glance, impressed by her acuity. " 'Twas not common knowledge, but last year I had learned from a banking associate that Pitham had fallen upon hard times. He seemed to recover, perhaps due to these fraudulent horse transactions."

"Why, that could explain everything!" Bridget breathed excitedly. "Had you not wondered about the theft of the trunk? On reflection, it seems rather a gamble for a common thief to lug away an entire trunk, don't you think? He must have known that he had little time to make a search for the papers, and so he absconded with all your luggage.

"Yes," she breathlessly continued, her eyes gleaming with the discovery. "Perhaps that is why I was able to scare him away so easily. He figured that he would have another opportunity to go after the documents, and he did not want to give away his purpose."

Nodding his head in agreement, Preston pursued her theory.

"Pitham had probably instructed his henchman to retrieve the documents or, at the very least, ensure that they were destroyed. When the hired brigand realized we planned to sail back to England, he took such drastic measures in case we reached London before him."

"That's not very likely now," Bridget woefully commented, her eyes scanning their humble accommodations.

"No, but it might work to our benefit. Pitham's minions could not possibly have trailed us, and our return to England should be worry-free. What is important is that we have the documents, thanks to you, Bridget."

Without conscious volition, Preston reached across the table and clasped Bridget's hand in his. The spark that flew between their fingertips caused Preston to immediately pull his hand away, but not before he noted Bridget flush in obvious awareness of the physical pull between them.

Unmistakably disconcerted, Bridget's words stumbled into the awkward stillness. "I . . . um, I guess that would mean that I have brought you luck after all."

Preston studied her for a long moment, the fading fire casting a golden glow to her hopeful countenance. She seemed to desperately need his affirmation, exposing a vulnerability that deeply touched Preston.

Softly, he whispered, "I would say that right now, Bridget, I am the luckiest man alive."

After another meal of boiled potatoes, Bridget and Preston struck out the following morning to explore. Stifling a yawn behind her palm, Bridget half ran half walked to keep up with Preston as his long legs strode along the path away from the cottage.

Frankly, she wondered where Preston had found such energy, for she knew that he had slept little, if at all, the previous night. Of course, she knew this because she herself had barely caught more than a dozen winks as the agonizingly long night had advanced.

Preston had made a pallet of his jacket in front of the hearth, insisting that Bridget make use of the rustic bed. Although she had felt guilty for allowing Preston to sleep upon the hard floor, she could hardly have invited him into her bed, and 'twould have been foolish for both of them to take to the ground and leave the bed unoccupied.

In the long run it had not mattered one way or the other, for both she and Preston had lain awake listening to the other's breathing as the moon rose slowly into the sky. More than once she had been tempted to speak into the oppressive silence, but something had held her back, and so the two of them had passed the hours by politely feigning sleep.

"I feared just this."

Bridget blinked at Preston's statement, nearly colliding into his back as he abruptly drew up at the top of a small hill.

"What's that?" she asked in confusion.

"An island," he flatly announced, his eyes squinting into the morning sun. "We have marooned ourselves on an island."

Bridget's own blue eyes widened in astonishment as she stepped forward to confirm Preston's observation.

"Are you certain?" she questioned, although the vista clearly supported Preston's claim.

"But look," she declared, pointing into the horizon. "Land lays just across that strait."

"Indeed, but as skilled a swimmer as you might be, I doubt either of us are strong enough to span that distance."

"What shall we do?" Bridget anxiously inquired, silently wondering how many more potatoes lay buried in the abandoned garden.

"We keep searching. Scotland is dotted with hundreds of islands, some scarcely populated. Judging by the cottage's condition, it has not been more than a few months since it was last inhabited and, if we are fortunate, we might find a small enclave on the other side of that ridge."

Bridget's gaze followed the indicated direction. The basin on the other side of the ridge was the only area not visible from their vantage point.

" 'Tis a very small island. If that site were occupied, would we not have seen or smelled the smoke from their fires by now?"

Preston shot her an assessing look. "Most likely," he conceded. "However, it still bears investigating."

They trudged along for another hour or so, encircling the island. As they waded through fields of waist-high grass—at least waist-high on Bridget—the once-lovely emerald gown attracted an impressive collection of seeds and prickles.

"My dress is ruined," she lamented, vainly attempting to remove the hundreds of stickers clinging to her skirts while hurrying to keep up with Preston.

Plainly intent on reaching the unexplored valley, Preston did not turn around or slow his stride. "Don't fret, love, I shall get you another," he distractedly reassured her.

Bridget froze in her tracks, dazed by the endearment that had just fallen from Preston's lips. *Love.* He had called her his *love.* A wave of giddy pleasure swamped her, sending her crashing into an emotional whirlpool. She wanted to both laugh and cry. She felt like singing to the skies. She felt positively dizzy.

Bridget meant to rush to him, for Preston had outdistanced her a good measure already, when a shifting of the shrubbery below halted her steps. They had just descended into the basin, and the peculiar ebb and flow of the brown and beige grasses struck Bridget as odd. Was the vegetation actually advancing upon them?

Suddenly she realized that the low-lying bushes were not bushes at all but a herd of sheep moving toward the unsuspecting duo. Bridget had no fear of sheep, as it were, but the hundreds of woolen bodies coming toward them sparked a glimmer of anxiety.

Preston had stopped just ahead of her, apparently becoming aware of the impending stampede.

"Um, Preston," Bridget nervously ventured. "I do not know a great deal about livestock, but I fear we are in danger of being trampled."

The pounding of the advancing hooves lent credence to her prediction, and suddenly, Bridget and Preston were racing along, pursued by a large contingent of bleating sheep.

Only a scant moment before Bridget's warning, Preston, too, had realized that he and Bridget were not the only creatures standing in the vale. Initially he had not been concerned for sheep were well-known for their placidness. However, these Scottish sheep seemed to be of a more aggressive temperament.

Within a few seconds it became clear that he and Bridget had best make haste unless they wished to be overrun by a pack of marauding ewes and rams. Breaking into a run, Preston was amazed to see Bridget fly past him as if on wings. With Mercurial speed, she sped across the field, her feet flying nimbly, despite the confining gown.

Preston labored to catch her, but he immediately realized he had no hope of matching her amazing speed. He cast a furtive glance over his shoulder, dismayed to see that the damned sheep still pursued them. In fact, they seemed to be closing in on him, and at this distance he thought he detected the unmistakable gleam of bloodlust in the lead-ers' eyes. He had yet to hear of man-eating sheep, but the gruesome notion spurred Preston on, and he redoubled his efforts to catch up with Bridget.

Although he was in prime physical condition, fatigue was setting in when Preston mounted a hill, spying their cottage just ahead. Once again, he glanced backward and sighed with relief to note that the attacking livestock had abandoned their pursuit. He slowed down and walked the remaining yards to the cottage.

Perspiration beaded his brow as he strolled through the open portal, panting. He glanced across the room to where Bridget lay flat on the bed, her arms widespread, her dirty feet hanging over the side. At his entrance she levered herself up, leaning back on her elbows.

"I never thought I'd live to see the day that Preston Campton fled in terror from a lamb!" she announced with obvious amusement, her dark brown hair spilling about her in wild disarray. "You should have seen yourself! 'Twas a wondrous sight, I assure you."

Preston answered with a smile. "You weren't exactly cozying up to the woolen beasts yourself, madam. In fact, you flew by me as if pursued by the very hounds of hell."

Laughing, Bridget threw back her head, exposing her pale throat. "They were a ferocious group," she conceded.

"Indeed. I feared for my very life," Preston mocked. Sauntering over to the bed, he teased, "I suppose that this is yet another brush with death for which I should deem myself fortunate for having survived?"

Bridget giggled, falling back upon the straw mattress. "Oh, no, you don't. You're not to blame me. This lepre-chaun had naught to do with those killer sheep!"

Preston gazed down at her flushed, beaming face, think-ing that she appeared especially carefree all of a sudden. He considered the subtle change in her, wondering if the invigorating race had elevated her spirits. She had told him before that she enjoyed running for the sheer joy of the activity.

"Has our race through the fields brought that sparkle to your eye?" he questioned, curious as to her lightheartedness.

Something flickered behind Bridget's eyes before she blithely answered, "What you see there, my lord, is nothing but sheer hunger. I fear it's potato-hunting time again."

Preston contemplated her for a moment before issuing a mental shrug. Whatever had altered, he would soon decipher it. Bridget had become too important for him not to be fascinated by every mysterious aspect of her.

"So what do we do now," she asked, "aside from dig up more potatoes?"

"Well," Preston drawled, "although I believe those sheep belong to someone, it's impossible to say when their owner might happen by to rescue us. Therefore, tomorrow, we start building a raft."

"A raft? From what?"

"Wood may be scarce, but I believe I may have hit upon just the thing." He pointedly stared at Bridget's bed.

"You're going to take apart my bed?" she halfheartedly protested. "What if the raft proves unsuccessful? Then I'm stuck on the floor with you."

Preston shrugged innocently, attempting to hide the burst of pleasure the idea had produced.

CHAPTER
18

"You, sir, are no fisherman."

Preston spun about, glowering at his impertinent critic. Perched above him on a rocky outcrop, Bridget regarded him with scornful superiority. After nearly an hour of unproductive baiting and casting, Bridget all the meanwhile nattering about fishing dos and don'ts, Preston was clearly not in the best of humors.

"The fish aren't biting," he retorted.

"Fish are always hungry," she corrected. "You've been—"

"Enough!" Preston gruffly interrupted. "If you know so damn much about fishing, why, instead of harping at me this past hour, haven't you had a go of it yourself?"

Bridget pursed her lips. "You didn't ask me," she primly replied.

Rolling his eyes and sighing heavily, Preston passed the crudely fashioned pole to Bridget, who accepted it with a simpering "thank you."

Scampering nimbly over the rocks, she took a position a few feet away from Preston and, with a condescending arch of her eyebrow, flung the hapless worm into the sea.

From the corner of her eye she watched Preston as he gazed with lowered brows at the line bobbing in the water.

He looked so positively adorable, his masculine pride clearly threatened, that Bridget wanted to throw her arms about him and smother him with kisses. However, her thoughts this afternoon had left her in emotional turmoil.

During lunch (boiled potatoes, again), Bridget had waited for Preston to expound on his use of the term *love*. She had not known what to expect, but after the endearment he had earlier employed, she had assumed it to be only a matter of time until he declared his feelings for her.

Judiciously she had checked her caustic tongue and controlled her temper, not wishing to sour the atmosphere. Their playful banter after the sheep attack had left both of them in a jovial mood, and Bridget had done her utmost to maintain the pleasant tone.

However, when naught but idle chatter passed between them, she had begun to despair. Had she only imagined that he had called her his love? Had the wind played tricks upon her ears? No, Bridget was certain that she had heard him employ that all-important word. But, how could he call her his love and then pretend he had not?

Ultimately she had begun to believe that Preston had not even realized that he had used the endearment. She recalled that he had seemed rather distracted at the time, focused as he was on exploring the valley. The word *love* must have slipped from his tongue without him recognizing the chaotic effect such a term might have on Bridget's heart.

Woefully Bridget wondered if he habitually referred to all female acquaintances in such an intimate manner. Perhaps he had meant nothing by it. Perhaps Bridget had placed too much value on the casual reference.

She worried her lip as the wind rose around them. A salty spray misted the pair as they sat beneath the warming afternoon sun.

Bridget slanted a glance at Preston, smiling wistfully at the handsome picture he made. The sun's rays glinted off his light hair, the blond waves falling naturally about his head. His tawny brows were drawn together, contemplating the fishing line.

Bridget's heart twisted in her chest and her self-doubts insinuated themselves into her tormented thoughts. Why did she continue to delude herself? She had thought she had seen desire in Preston's gaze yesterday, but he most likely would have regarded any woman with such interest if she were in a similarly unclad condition. Why should she, of all women, think herself so lucky as to win Preston's love?

Abruptly, an unbidden memory flashed to Bridget's mind.

"Preston. Do you remember on the ship when you were telling me about your trip to Wales?"

"Hmm-mm," he murmured. "When I thought you to be twelve and not eighteen."

Embarrassed, Bridget lowered her lashes. "Yes, well anyway," she muttered. "Do you recall how I had thought it odd for you to make such a lengthy trip for your friend? And how you had said you had been eager to get away from London?"

Bridget felt the heat of Preston's stare, but kept her gaze on the sea.

"Yes, what of it?" he tersely asked.

She swallowed nervously, gathering her courage.

"Was there a woman involved?"

The silence held for what seemed a lifetime to Bridget.

"Why do you ask?"

"I am only curious." Her voice sounded pathetically thin.

Preston moved and Bridget shot him a furtive look, but saw that he merely folded his arms across his chest.

"Yes, there was a woman."

Gnawing on the inside of her cheek, Bridget prayed that her expression revealed none of her despair.

"Our relationship was ending," Preston emotionlessly continued, "and I thought it prudent to leave town for a while."

"Oh." Bridget's emotions somersaulted in her breast.

"Does that appease your curiosity?"

Bridget nodded woodenly, although what she really wanted to know is if Preston had loved the woman. Who had ended their affair? And most important, did he love her still?

While struggling to pose such questions, the fishing line suddenly jerked in Bridget's hands.

Preston shouted, "You've got one!" as he leaped to his feet.

Blinking, Bridget concentrated on pulling in her catch. The doomed fish put up a heroic fight, but Bridget's perseverance prevailed. As an enormous bass finally came to rest at her feet, Preston whooped with delight.

Clapping her upon the back, he praised, "You may do all the fishing from here on out, Bridget. I bow to your expertise."

With a weak smile Bridget commented, "I couldn't have managed without the hook you improvised."

Grinning widely, obviously pleased by his contribution, Preston scooped up the prize and headed back toward the cottage.

Preston had already cleaned the fish and dug up more potatoes by the time Bridget returned from the beach. After a lengthy discussion as to the fish's preparation, it was decided that stew would maximize their bountiful yield, and Preston took up the pail to retrieve more water.

Striding down the pathway to the well, he slowed his pace as the memory of their recent conversation resurfaced. He had been surprised when Bridget had asked about his mistress. Preston had hardly even thought of the singularly self-centered Chelsea since meeting the Irish spitfire. And on the rare occasions when Chelsea had come to mind, it generally had been in the context of an unfavorable comparison of his ex-lover to the intriguing Bridget.

Preston frowned, thinking that the two women were as alike as night and day. Chelsea had been very aware of her beauty and had used it to manipulate men, bending them to her will. Within a short time he had grown to resent her ploys, especially the way she had employed sex as a weapon, withholding her affections should her desires be unmet.

Bridget, on the other hand, appeared completely unconscious of the spell her loveliness wove. Devoid of arti-
fice, her charms slowly wrapped their way around a man;
not bowling one over as Chelsea's flamboyant seduction
had done.

And whereas the widow Chesterhaven, absorbed in
her own self-adoration, had never doubted her allure,
Bridget's vulnerability touched a chord of protectiveness
within Preston. Behind that spunky armor of hers, he saw
how Bridget concealed her fears and self-doubts. More and
more, he felt a need to dispel those doubts and soothe those
fears by taking her into his arms and proving to her that her
appeal was both genuine and powerful.

But to take such a step, he ruefully admitted, would
be a mistake. Despoiling a virgin, especially the cousin
of his dearest friend, would be shamefully dishonorable.
Bridget deserved better than that. She deserved an honest
man, one who could cherish her spirit and nurture her fun-
loving nature. She deserved marriage, family, a home . . .
and love.

Preston nearly dropped the pail back into the well as that
last word snuck unwelcome into his mind. He immediately
shrunk away from such thoughts. Although he respected the
exalted emotion, and even envied his friends, the Forsters,
who had managed to find it, Preston had seen too much
perfidy and misery in relationships to believe that similar
happiness was within everyone's grasp. The cynicism that
had forced him to leave London was not so easily discarded,
and, perversely, he took refuge in such pessimism.

Besides, he argued with his protesting heart, a man would
have to be braver even than he was to fall in love with such
a wayward creature as Bridget Flannery. Forever battling
her hot temper and impetuosity would drive the most virtuous and tolerant of men to a state of dementia. And he
was neither virtuous nor tolerant. Though perhaps a trifle
demented, an inner voice taunted.

Lugging the bucket back to the cottage, he sought to
quell his sudden emotional pandemonia. The cynical side

of Preston maintained that his many weeks of celibacy had so frustrated him that he saw tenderness where only lust reigned. His desire for Bridget had grown so consuming that perhaps he deluded himself by justifying his passion behind a veil of sentiment. "Yes, that's it," he mumbled aloud, "I need a woman."

And then and there, he vowed to avail himself of the first willing female he could lay his hands on, Bridget excepted.

With grim determination, he pushed open the door to the stone cottage.

"Oh, there you are!" Bridget exclaimed. "I was beginning to wonder if you had fallen into the well."

"No such luck," Preston wryly returned, privately thinking that a cold dunking might do him some good right about now. Particularly since Bridget presented a rather fetching picture of domesticity outlined against the firelight. Her dark chocolate tresses, piled haphazardly atop her head, were tied into place with a scrap of fabric, allowing thick, brown ringlets to fall about her rosy face.

She glanced up at him from where she sat slicing potatoes. "There you go again, talking about luck." Her smile teased him. "You simply must stop blaming me for your tribulations. I know you refuse to believe it, but I assure you that I have brought you nothing but the best of luck."

Deciding that the bantering might provide diversion from his single-minded lust, Preston parried her jibe.

"I'll believe it when I see it," he laconically drawled. "A ship at the bottom of the Irish Sea has hardly convinced me that you are a good-luck talisman."

Bridget slanted him a look from beneath her lashes. "Well, Lord Campton, I am beginning to believe that *you* are the one bringing misfortune down upon my head."

On a half-swallowed chuckle Preston admonished, "Do not speak such blasphemy, woman!"

Bridget began to laugh, then cried out, "Ow!" Pouting, she sucked on her thumb where the knife had slipped. "Look what you've made me do," she mockingly accused.

"Now, if that's not proof, I do not know what is!"

Impulsively Preston stepped over to the table and pulled Bridget's hand toward him to examine the injury. Two brilliant drops of crimson shone against her skin and, unthinking, Preston raised her hand to his lips to lick clean the wound. Cradling her palm in his hand, he brought her thumb to his mouth, then abruptly froze as his eyes collided with Bridget's. He dropped her palm as if it had burned him.

Lowering his gaze, he ordered, "Let me have the knife. I'll take over."

Wordlessly Bridget handed him the blade, and Preston continued paring the potatoes as if nothing had passed between them. In silence they prepared their meal, the quiet only intensifying the torrid undercurrents vibrating in the room. They ate their stew and cleaned their bowls, both of them exceedingly conscious of the mounting tension.

The mundane chores complete, Preston stood awkwardly in the middle of the room. Having restacked their meager firewood three times, his idle hands had begun to twitch with a need to sink them into Bridget's soft flesh.

He had tried not to make eye contact during these past hours, and suddenly, as Bridget's eyes squarely met his, Preston knew that he was at the breaking point.

"It has been a long day." The low-pitched words rushed out of him on a single breath. "I think I'll retire."

Bridget forced a wan smile. "I think I'll take a walk before doing the same."

Preston nodded, jerkily removed his jacket, and laid it upon the hearth. Silently Bridget quickly slipped out the door.

Heaving deep breaths of the sea air, Bridget strode down to the beach, the full moon acting as a beacon to guide her. God in Heaven, but she barely knew herself tonight! A longing, so desperate and so deep, consumed every fiber of her being to the point where she could not remain in the same room with Preston.

Loving was not a simple affair. Bridget grimaced into the darkness, wishing for the thousandth time that she had a mother or father to explain this complex emotion to her. She had not known that love could be so painful, ripping the very heart from one's chest.

Bridget clutched a hand to her bosom, the frantic pounding there reassuring her that the lovesick organ remained where it should. The ache within it, however, could not be dispelled.

Again, she had tried to keep the mood light this evening but to no avail. She was too distraught, her emotions too convoluted, to convincingly sustain the breezy pretense. Better to put some space between her and her unsuspecting tormentor.

As she reached a sandy portion of the shore, Bridget felt the salty wind beckon to her. Impetuously she tied her skirts up to mid-thigh and gazed down the moonswept beach, thrilling in anticipated exhilaration. With a glad cry, she took off, her feet flying. She sped along forever, dashing through the grass when the trail disappeared, deftly skimming over the rocks. Her hair came loose, sailing about her.

When she had exhausted herself and could not run another step, she staggered to a stop. Leaning forward, she placed her hands on her bare knees, struggling for breath. Faith, but she could not remember ever running so fast or so hard.

Grinning with the release of tension, she righted herself. The grin instantly faded, however, as her eyes alit on Preston standing but a few yards away, his back to the moonlight, his face in shadows.

Shakily Bridget wiped her sleeve across her damp brow. How long, she wondered, had he been watching her? Had he witnessed her desperate flight along the beach? Did he know from what she was running?

Her voice died in her throat as her arm fell limply to her side. Preston's figure, delineated against the stark white rays of the moon, reminded her of the night the storm had crippled the *Circe*. That vision of him, contrasted against the ghostly lightning, returned to her in full force. This evening, as she had done once before, Bridget recognized on the most basic, visceral level the primal male essence that constituted this man.

She shivered, either in awareness of his masculinity or in reaction to the night air cooling her damp skin. Her eyes widened in wonder as the dark silhouette advanced upon her.

From the shadows Preston stepped into the colorless light. The breath whooshed from Bridget's body as she recognized the naked desire in his gaze. There was no mistaking the look she had seen their first day here on the beach. Pure unadulterated hunger.

Her surprise held her spellbound as Preston moved to within a few inches of her. She saw his hands reach out and grab hold of her shoulders, his fingers like a vise. For a split second Bridget thought that surely the full moon was responsible for the madness gripping them tonight. But then Preston's mouth took possession of hers, and Bridget ceased to think at all.

Mercilessly he plundered her mouth, not bothering to temper his ardor. His tongue and teeth ravished her, nipping and licking and sucking while Bridget instinctively matched his passion. Crushed against him, her head was thrown back, her toes barely skimming the sand as Preston effortlessly held her erect.

Helpless in his bruising embrace, she could but respond. As she satisfied his unspoken demands, his kisses gentled, and Bridget felt herself being lowered to the ground.

Preston blanketed her body with his own, his large hands cradling her head, holding it immobile for his caresses. He knew that he was a man possessed. From the moment he had arrived at the bluff and seen the unearthly angel floating across the sands, he had ceased to be Lord Preston Campton. He had surrendered to the elemental being within.

The sight of Bridget's long, firm legs flashing white against the blackness and the pure joy on her face, transforming her beauty into something surreal, had stripped away his civilized veneer. At this moment he was simply a man who needed his woman.

"I have never seen anything more beautiful," he hoarsely murmured while gently nibbling on her earlobe. "I want you so desperately, Bridget, more than I have ever wanted another woman."

"Yes, Preston, yes," Bridget breathed, transported by the night's magic. "I love you so very much."

Preston froze, his passion instantly quenched. *Love*. An icy curtain of dismay enveloped him. Damn it to hell, he was a fool! Of course, she wanted love, his mind screamed at him. She was young, pure, innocent. What right did he have to take from her without giving her what she needed and deserved? None at all, he harshly berated himself, none at all!

Rolling away from Bridget, Preston sensed the hurt emanating from her as if it were palpable. He could not stop to explain, however, he simply had to get away before he seized that innocence which was so sweetly offered him.

Bounding to his feet, Preston turned and vanished into the darkness.

CHAPTER 19

Much later that night Bridget heard Preston creep into the cottage and quietly drop onto his pallet on the hearth. She sent a silent prayer of gratitude heavenward that he had not returned before she had completed her bout of crying. She knew that she would have died of mortification should he have discovered her sobbing as if her heart had been broken. Of course, that was exactly the case.

In the midst of their embrace, when she had felt Preston stiffen above her, she had wanted to scream at her folly. She would have given her very life in that instant to call back the fateful words. But the damage had already been done.

Thankfully, Preston had melted into the shadows before the scalding rush of tears had overtaken her. The tears had been especially painful, for they had been buried so long that it seemed their heat had accumulated over the years until Bridget was certain that they burned lavalike trails onto her cheeks.

Six years had passed since Bridget had last wept, that time at her mother's funeral. Since then she had endured her father's disappearance, her loneliness, the villagers' ridicule, all without shedding a tear. Love, however, had brought her to her knees. She had dared to hope, had dared to believe herself worthy of love, and for this, she had been shot down as surely as Icarus had been felled from the sky.

Lying motionless upon the cot, Bridget fought her humiliation. She might have made a fool of herself, but she would rather die than admit it. Tomorrow, she would have to carry on as if nothing were amiss, as if that asinine declaration of love had never slipped from her tongue.

All her life Bridget had been a fighter and a survivor. Realistically she knew that she would survive this humbling episode just as she had survived others. If she lost her heart,'twas the price she'd have to pay for flying too close to the sun.

"Hello there!"

The deep voice boomed through the cottage as an insistent rapping fell upon the door.

Preston jerked awake. A voice!

The gray filtered light indicated that the day had not yet fully dawned. He was surprised that he had slept at all, for he had passed most of the night cursing himself and his monumental stupidity.

Leaping to his feet, excited, yet wary, Preston grabbed the knife from the table as he crossed the room. He threw a glance toward Bridget and saw that she was burrowed beneath the blanket, invisible except for the small lump she made on the bed.

He opened the door a crack, instantly sizing up their unexpected visitor.

An elderly gentleman, attired in peasant dress, stood at the doorway leaning upon a staff. His bushy white hair and beard draped his friendly face, curiosity tingeing his brown eyes.

"The wife had said she'd seen smoke from the island, but I didna believe her," he greeted straightforwardly.

"Our thanks to your wife," Preston answered with a smile, his fears put to rest by the stranger's innocuous appearance. "We hardly dared hope to be rescued so soon. Come in."

The man entered slowly, employing his staff as a walking aid. He held out his gnarled hand to Preston. "Cowden is the name. Brian Cowden."

Preston shook the man's hand, ushering him toward the table where he put the knife aside.

"Preston Campton. And my sister, Bridget." Preston tossed his head to indicate the bundle shuffling on the bed. "Our ship went down."

"Ach," the man clucked sympathetically. "How long have ye been 'ere?"

"Two nights."

"Well, it's a good thing I found ye when I did. Not much firewood to be had," Cowden explained, "and I canna imagine ye'd find much in the way of victuals."

"Fortunately, Bridget is amazingly resourceful. We've made do with potatoes and fish."

The old gentleman nodded. "I keep my sheep on the island, but me and Mrs. Cowden live just across the water there. The sheep do well, grazing free, and I row over and check on 'em every once in a while. At shearing, me and me boys stay over here in the cottage."

"We, uh, met your flock." Preston's lips twitched with the memory.

Cowden's attention abruptly fixed on the bed, and Preston pivoted about as Bridget's dark head emerged from the blanket.

"Hello."

"Good mornin' to ye, Miss Campton," Cowden greeted.

"It appears we've been rescued, *Sis*," Preston pointedly interjected when Bridget frowned in confusion at the unfamiliar salutation.

"Oh." Her blue eyes expanded. "How wonderful!"

Cowden's shrewd brown gaze returned to Preston, a knowing gleam behind the old man's eyes.

"If ye're ready to go, the missus will be expecting ye for breakfast, I imagine. She was so convinced that someone had gone adrift here, she'd already begun puttin' fresh linens on the beds."

He shook his head in apparent wonder at his wife's clairvoyance. "I'll wait for ye two outside. Me skiff is just down at the end of the trail."

"Thank you, Mr. Cowden."

After the door had shut, Preston turned around to look at Bridget. She was making a great show of smoothing out her wrinkled skirts.

"Bridget—"

"Such luck, hmm?" she cheerfully interrupted. "To be rescued after but one day. He seems like a dear man. And to think his wife has a hot breakfast awaiting us. I only hope it's not potatoes."

"Bridget, I think we should—"

"Don't dither, Preston. I, for one, will be glad to get off this godforsaken island. A bath and a decent meal. Why, I'll almost feel human again." She deliberately turned her back to him and began plaiting her hair.

Her forced smile had not fooled Preston. He saw the hurt shadowing her eyes, but he decided now was not the time to push the matter. Cowden was waiting, and Preston figured they would have ample opportunity later to clear the air.

Gathering up his jacket and the knife, he waited until Bridget had tied off her braid, and, together, they walked away from their island refuge without a backward glance.

Approaching the Cowden home, Bridget felt the prick of tears threaten and instantly squelched them before they dared spill over her eyes. *Faith,* she chastised herself, *after all these years, am I suddenly becoming a watering pot?* After that storm of tears last night, Bridget assumed she wouldn't be due for another for at least another six years.

But the cheery cottage standing in the glade had abruptly reminded her of her own home before she had lost her mother and father. The handmade tatted lace curtains at the windows, the smoke curling invitingly from the chimney, the bright flowers dotting the walkway; Bridget felt as if she were coming home.

The door swung open before they had even mounted the porch stairs and a female version of Mr. Cowden appeared on the threshold. A puff of white hair lay beneath a pink-ribboned cap, this adorning a rosy, round, slightly wrinkled face. Wiping her hands across her apron, Mrs. Cowden beamed at the approaching group.

"I told ye so, Brian Cowden," she triumphantly announced. "I knew in me bones someone needed our help out there."

She bustled forward as her husband made the introductions.

"This is me missus and this here is Lord Preston Campton and his sister, Bridget."

Mrs. Cowden's bright blue eyes flew from Preston to Bridget and back again. "Sister? What are ye tryin' to pull, Brian Cowden? Why, this—"

She cut herself off short as Bridget felt the guilty rise of blood to her cheeks.

"Listen to me, goin' on," the Scotswoman muttered, clucking her tongue. "This poor lamb needs a hot bath, somethin' clean to wear, and a hearty Scots breakfast," she cooed, wrapping her arm around Bridget's shoulders. "Come, lassie, let's get ye fixed up, shall we?"

Bridget allowed herself to be led away in the comforting arms of Pat Cowden.

The intoxicating aroma of freshly baked scones assaulted Bridget's senses as Mrs. Cowden ushered her into the spotlessly clean house. Every square inch shone with a deep luster, the wood furnishings polished to a gleam. Hand-woven rugs warmed the cobblestone floor, and a fire burned in the hearth.

"You have a pretty home, Mrs. Cowden," Bridget remarked as the woman showed her into a side bedroom. A copper tub already sat before a roaring fire, the clean scent of lavender permeating the room.

"Thank you, love. Mr. Cowden and his brother built it when they was just young men. Lyle, his brother, went to seek his fortune in the Americas, but me and Brian stayed on and filled the house with four strappin' lads."

Bridget heard the note of pride in the elder woman's voice as she spoke of her sons.

"Four boys," she dutifully commented. "How nice for you and your husband."

Mrs. Cowden picked up a bucket of water warming near the fire. Her face was wreathed in smiles as she dumped the water into the tub.

"The joy of my life, those lads. Each one as dear as ye could ever imagine." Looking about at the room, her dreamy expression assumed a wistful glow. "They're all married now, raising their own families. Sometimes, the house seems a wee bit empty without them."

She appeared to shake off her melancholy, her tone brightening. "But whenever I start thinkin' the cottage is too big for me and Brian, they bring over the little ones, and I swear to ye, the house shrinks to half its size."

Instinctively Bridget warmed to the sweet, Scottish grandmother, smiling at the picture of their family gatherings in this inviting home. Sighing, she wondered if she might ever know such a sense of family and belonging. Many years ago, she had experienced those feelings, but they seemed very far away.

Swishing her fingers through the water to test the temperature, Mrs. Cowden pronounced it "Just right. Ye go ahead, dear, and enjoy yerself. Yer breakfast will be waitin' for ye when ye come out. On the bed I've left a dress that belongs to my widowed niece. She stays with us sometimes. As a matter of fact, she might be comin' today for a visit."

"She won't mind?" Bridget asked, unweaving her braid as she prepared for her bath.

"Faith, no. She's a dear child."

Mrs. Cowden waved her fingers as she let herself out the door.

Although the bath was heavenly, Bridget rushed through washing her hair and scrubbing herself clean. The last thing she wanted was time for reflection since, unquestionably, her thoughts would drift to last night's fiasco. Preston's rejection still pained her too much. So, hurrying through her toilette, Bridget concentrated on the toasty scent of the baking scones and not the memories of Preston's musky, warm scent.

The Cowdens and Preston still remained at the table by the time Bridget entered the kitchen. The long pine table, piled high with scones, preserves, oatmeal, and smoked salmon, set Bridget's stomach to growling, and she eagerly accepted the seat next to Mrs. Cowden.

Unfortunately, the seating arrangement placed her directly across from Preston. His smiling composure did little to alleviate Bridget's silent heartache. *How could he sit there,* she fumed to herself, *as if last night had not happened?* His easy banter with their host and hostess exhibited none of the emotional chaos that Bridget was experiencing.

From the corner of her eye she peeked at him from time to time, hoping to find a hint of the devastation racking her own soul. But Preston appeared completely at ease. And why shouldn't he? His heart had not been torn asunder last night. His declaration of love not ruthlessly thrown back in his face.

Counseling herself to be strong, Bridget summoned her damaged pride and focused on her breakfast. She promised herself all manner of dire retribution should she weaken and her eyes stray to him again.

"By all the saints," Mr. Cowden boomed as Bridget polished off her third scone. "I wouldna believe such a wee thing had such a good Scottish appetite. Are ye sure ye ain't a Scotswoman, lass?"

"Stop now, Brian. Nothing wrong with a healthy lass eatin' her fill," Mrs. Cowden sternly advised.

Bridget flashed a smile at the white-haired gentleman. "Irish through and through, sir," she answered without thinking.

Suddenly she felt Preston pierce her with a warning glance.

"That is," she stammered, seeking an explanation that would not be a blatant lie. "I spent my youth in Ireland while Preston was reared in England."

"Yes," Preston smoothly interjected. "Bridget's mother was Irish. Personally, I find the lilt she has acquired to be most endearing, don't you agree?"

Bridget appreciated the effortless smile Preston flashed the Cowdens' as he handily extricated her from her blunder.

"Where were ye headed when yer ship went down?" Mr. Cowden inquired.

"A cousin outside of London has invited Bridget to stay with them for her coming out, and I am escorting her to them," Preston answered.

"London," Mrs. Cowden repeated in awe. "Ach, what I wouldn't give to see the sights. Ye must be thrilled, lass."

"I am." Bridget stretched her lips in the facsimile of a smile.

A knock at the door rescued her from further falsehoods, and Mrs. Cowden arose to answer it while Bridget reapplied herself to her breakfast.

"Leah! So happy to see ye, love." Mrs. Cowden's jubilant welcome could be heard clearly at the kitchen table. "We have guests, dear. Come in and meet them."

At Mrs. Cowden's side entered a small, raven-haired woman whose black eyes and wide mouth contributed to a pretty face.

"Leah, let me introduce Lord Preston Campton and his sister, Bridget. Their ship went down, poor dears, and they washed up here in Largs. Preston, Bridget, this is our niece, Mrs. Leah Harriston. She hails from Cumberland. Widowed last year, poor love." Mrs. Cowden patted the woman's arm consolingly.

Mrs. Harriston, however, did not appear in need of consolation, Bridget noted, as the widow's eyes fell appreciatively upon the stunning blond man arising from the table.

"Preston Campton. A pleasure." Politely, he bowed over Leah's hand.

Scowling, Bridget resisted the urge to wrench Mrs. Harriston's fingers from Preston's. The widow's ebony eyes openly appraised the comely stranger, her interest patently obvious.

"My sister, Bridget," Preston introduced, waving his hand to where Bridget sat, stuffing another scone into her mouth.

Temporarily incapacitated, Bridget could but nod a stiff greeting.

"Your sister?" The woman's interest sharpened.

"Different mothers," Preston succinctly replied.

"I see." Her gaze flickered briefly over Bridget before she fluttered her lashes at Preston. "How long do you plan to visit, my lord?"

"Preston, please."

Bridget suddenly choked on a crumb that lodged in her throat. Mr. Cowden hopped up from his seat and obligingly patted her back until the coughing subsided.

Hell's bells, she cursed, eyeing the handsome pair from beneath her lashes. How lethally charming Preston could be! That sardonic twist to his lips already had the Scottish widow panting after him like a cat after cream.

Painfully, Bridget wondered if Preston would turn away the flirtatious Mrs. Harriston as indifferently as he had her last night. The widow would probably be too astute to spew words of undying devotion while in the throes of passion.

"As for our departure," Preston responded to her inquiry, "I'll be riding into town this afternoon to rent a post-chaise."

"So soon?" Mrs. Cowden asked with obvious dismay.

"Unfortunately, yes," he answered. "No doubt, the Forsters must be concerned by our delay and I have my crew to think of as well. I need to check for news of Mac and the men."

A pang of alarm sliced through Bridget as she thought of the fiery-haired captain. Her worried gaze traveled to Mrs. Harriston who had thrust out her lower lip in a disappointed pout.

"What a pity that you cannot prolong your visit," the widow protested, slanting Preston a smoldering look.

All concern for Mac vanished as Bridget felt the hackles rise at the nape of her neck. The fire in Leah Harriston's eyes might as well have been heating Bridget's seat for she suddenly shot to her feet, indignant at the woman's brazenness.

"Isn't it, though?" she caustically intoned. "Well, brother, I imagine you should be on your way to town then." Waving her hands, she tried to shoo him out the door. "The Forsters are probably counting the minutes until our arrival."

Preston tossed her a quizzical look before Mrs. Cowden interceded.

"Oh, now, wait a minute, love. I'll just start the water heating for your bath. Ye can at least wash up afore ye go dashing off."

"A bath would be most welcome, madam," Preston agreed. "Point me to the well and I will see to the water."

Preston and Mrs. Cowden exited through the kitchen's back door leaving Bridget, Mr. Cowden, and the feline Leah Harriston. The woman's black eyes skirted over Bridget, clearly assessing her, and Bridget's spine stiffened in automatic defense.

Too tired to fend off any of the widow's inevitable curiosity about Preston, Bridget quickly excused herself, citing the need for a nap.

To her surprise, she fell asleep as soon as she laid her head upon her pillow. She had not realized the extent of her exhaustion until she awoke in the late afternoon, having slept nearly the entire day.

Padding barefoot through the quiet house, Bridget followed the sound of muted humming to the kitchen. Mrs. Cowden, elbow-deep in a bowl of dough, popped her head up at Bridget's entrance.

"Feelin' better?"

"Yes, thank you." She smiled sheepishly.

"I left a pair of slippers out for ye, lass. I hadna realized that ye had no shoes even." She shook her head. "Ye musta been frightened out of your wits, poor lamb, your ship sinkin' and then floatin' helplessly about the ocean."

Donning the slippers, Bridget considered the woman's words. "Odd as it may seem, I really was not that frightened. Intuitively, I guess I knew that Preston would take care of us." She shrugged. "And he did."

Bridget listened to the lyrical chirping of the birds outside. "Where is everyone?"

"Leah has gone to say hello to me boys, and Brian and your brother rode into town to see about renting a coach."

Bridget dropped her lashes at Mrs. Cowden's pointed emphasis on the word *brother*. Ruefully she silently admitted that their deception, although her idea, had become utterly preposterous.

Coming over to sit at the table, Bridget watched the older woman knead the dough for a few minutes.

"I suppose you know that Preston is not my brother," she finally stated.

"Figured as much." She continued her pounding of the dough.

Bridget licked her lips nervously. "I know it's completely improper for an unmarried woman to be traveling with an unwed man, but circumstances were such that I had no other choice."

Mrs. Cowden glanced up from her work with a reassuring smile. "I'm not one to judge people, lass. Ye dunna have to explain to me."

"Yes, well. I did not want you to think that anything improper was going on between us."

Mrs. Cowden wiped her hands on her apron. "What happens between a man and a woman is their business alone, I figure."

Bridget studied that round, open countenance, wondering if she dared speak with the warm-hearted Scotswoman about her troubles.

"Mrs. Cowden?"

"Aye?"

"About what happens between a man and a woman . . ."

CHAPTER
20

Setting the bowl aside, Mrs. Cowden clasped her flour-white hands together on the table.

"What ails ye, lassie?"

"I, uh, was just wondering." She lowered her eyes. "My own mother died when I was twelve. I was wondering if I could ask you a few questions about . . ."

"About love?" the older woman kindly supplied.

Bridget took a deep, ragged breath. "Yes."

"Now, now, lass," Mrs. Cowden advised, patting Bridget's hand with her own. " 'Tis nothin' to be embarrassed about. Ye think ye're in love with Lord Campton, is that it?"

Bridget nodded helplessly.

"And what of him? How does he feel about ye?"

Shrugging, Bridget sent her a confused look. "I honestly could not say. Sometimes, I think that he finds me, um, attractive." She squirmed uncomfortably, adding in a whisper, "He's kissed me."

Darting a glance at Mrs. Cowden's smiling expression, Bridget was relieved to see that she had not scandalized the woman with her confession.

"And he hasn't discussed his feelings fer ye?"

Vigorously Bridget shook her dark head.

"Explain to me how it is that ye came to travel with him,

lass," Mrs. Cowden asked with a knowing smile.

Bridget related their meeting and subsequent adventures as concisely as possible, blushing as she related the two occasions on which Preston had kissed her.

Mrs. Cowden carefully listened to the tale.

"Sounds to me as if Lord Campton's got himself in a tangle, if ye ask me," she announced at the end of the narration. "He has a duty to return ye to yer cousin, but maybe he has plans of his own fer ye."

"Plans?"

"Let's say that he did have tender feelings fer ye . . . 'twouldn't be gentlemanly to do anythin' about it afore he delivered ye to yer cousin. I figure the only way yer goin' to find out how he feels is to put it to him direct-like."

"But what if he doesn't care for me? I'll make a complete fool of myself!" Bridget protested.

Mrs. Cowden shrugged philosophically. "Ye wouldna be the first, lass."

Bridget chewed on her lip, studying Mrs. Cowden's sympathetic face. Surely, this woman knew what she was talking about, Bridget determined. She simply had to cut right to the heart of the matter with Preston. And do it soon. Bridget seriously doubted that she could survive another day beneath this torment of indecision and uncertainty.

"Thank you so much, Mrs. Cowden. You've helped me come to a decision."

Rising from the table, Bridget walked over and planted a grateful peck on the older woman's cheek before setting out in search of Preston.

Preston pulled into the Cowdens' barn after a long day of haggling and string-pulling. His efforts had been worthwhile, however, as he'd been able to procure a loan against his London accounts, permitting him not only to hire a coach for their trip, but also to purchase clothing and toiletries for both himself and Bridget. The coach and riders were scheduled to arrive tomorrow morning shortly after daybreak.

Although he'd had no information as to the fate of his crew, he'd sent a messenger to London this very night to search for word of Captain Mac and his men. He trusted they were well.

Mr. Cowden, who had accompanied him into town, and had proved most helpful, had stopped by at a neighbor's house for a short visit. Exhausted from lack of sleep, as well as the difficult day, Preston had decided to head directly back to the Cowden home.

Since he was a small boy, Preston had harbored a great love of riding, and so he found the aroma of hay and horses strangely comforting as he led his borrowed mount into her stall.

After unsaddling the mare and removing the packet of purchases, he took up a brush to give the animal a quick grooming. Preston had ridden her hard on the last stretch home, needing to release the tension that had been escalating in him steadily since last night.

Bridget's unexpected declaration of love had thrown Preston into shock. Never would he have anticipated such a turn of events. Ridiculously he had not once stopped to consider Bridget's feelings while his own desire for her had increased on a daily basis. Attracted to her, he had seen the answering attraction in her eyes and had selfishly acted upon it. Thinking only of himself, he had forgotten her inexperience and conducted himself abominably.

Looking back on these past weeks, Preston realized that he had not been himself since first he had met the blue-eyed hellion. The obsession he had developed for the lovely imp had shaken his usual equanimity. He had surrendered to more emotional outbursts of jealousy and anger during this last fortnight than he could ever recall doing before. Nothing in his past, not even the war, had provoked him to such extremes. And, if he were brutally honest, the realization scared the hell out of him.

The combing complete, Preston checked the mare's hooves for stones, then straightened, rubbing his neck with one large hand. *God, what a mess—*

"Preston, what a pleasant surprise."

The soft voice startled him from his musings, and he whirled about to find Leah Harriston leaning against a wall. *Surprise, indeed.*

"Mrs. Harriston." His voice was cautiously polite.

"Oh, please, call me Leah. I thought we had dispensed with the formalities."

She pushed away from the wall, swaying her hips seductively as she approached him. Her perfume clashed strangely with the stable's sweet grass smell, and Preston momentarily yearned for the scent of hay.

He studied her with detachment as she crossed the barn toward him. An attractive woman, her small stature reminded him of Bridget. There, however, the similarities ended, for the woman's sensual awareness, as contrasted to Bridget's innocent allure, was readily apparent in the invitation explicit in her glittering, midnight eyes. 'Twas evident that she was no novice to the ways of the flesh; no virgin that Preston need fear compromising. A lonely widow, she merely sought a night's entertainment in the arms of a stranger.

Leah walked up to him, brazenly placing her hands on his chest.

"I had thought we might take this opportunity to get to know each other better," she addressed him in sultry tones. "If you are leaving tomorrow, we don't have much time in which to get acquainted."

A month earlier Preston would not have hesitated to avail himself of the woman's blatant offering, but as he only had just realized, he was not the same man who had left London. Irritated by his reluctance to take up the widow's invitation, Preston abruptly remembered his pledge to slake his lust on the first willing female he could find. Mrs. Harriston certainly appeared willing.

Conquering a spurt of irrational guilt, Preston deliberately lowered his head, slanting his lips over hers.

Granted, he had to admire her enthusiasm. Her tongue parried his as they met in a wet, openmouthed kiss. And yet,

the embrace left him cold. Something was missing. In the
back of Preston's mind he recalled the sweet virgin honey
of Bridget's mouth, but immediately and forcefully stifled
the comparison.

Closing his eyes, he tried to muster up a degree of passion
for the Scotswoman. After all, he had been overcome with
desire these past days to the point where he could barely
function. It could not be so very difficult to rekindle the
ardor that had been bubbling at the surface of his consciousness. But as his mouth possessed hers, he found his
traitorous thoughts again straying. *If I picture her eyes blue,
not black, and her skin softer . . .*

"What's wrong, darling?" she cooed, flicking her tongue
around his ear.

No, I cannot do this, he admitted to himself. *Even pretending she is Bridget is not enough.*

Preston grabbed hold of Leah's arms, his heart suddenly
pounding with the knowledge that no woman would ever
be enough. No woman could ever replace Bridget. For the
rest of his life, she would be the only woman for him.

This earth-shattering realization came at a most inauspi-
cious time, however, since Leah hung panting in his arms.
How could he possibly explain that, while embracing her,
he had just discovered that he was in love with another
woman?

"I am sorry, Leah."

"Sorry?" She pulled back from him, clearly confused.

"I . . . I should not be doing this."

Her frustrated pout spoke volumes. "What—"

The sudden crackle of footsteps upon the hay alerted
them both to an intruder. A warning signaled in Preston's
head, but alas, too late.

As Bridget rounded the corner of a stall, Preston easily
interpreted the series of emotions, so clear on her expressive
face, that followed her initial shock: pain, anger, and then,
withdrawal. Before he had a chance to speak, or even to
release his hold on Leah, Bridget spun about and ran from
the barn.

Preston's hands dropped away from Leah, falling heavily to his sides.

"Now I am the one who is sorry." Leah's chagrined expression conveyed her embarrassment. "I had not believed that story about her being your sister, but I did not realize that there was something between you. I shouldn't have—"

Preston interrupted her. "Do not blame yourself. In another time I would have been flattered by your interest. This is entirely my fault. If I had not been so obtuse in regard to my own feelings, this situation would not have grown so tangled."

He sighed heavily, massaging his forehead with the heel of his hand.

"You love her, then?"

Hearing the words spoken aloud brought a painful spasm in the vicinity of Preston's heart.

"I do."

My God, what in heaven's name was he confessing to? Of all women, he had fallen in love with that incorrigible, uncontrollable, outrageous . . . passionate, spirited, irresistible Irish lass.

"And she loves you?" Leah's question sounded more like a statement.

Preston smiled wryly. "She's too innocent to even know what love is. I would guess that I'm the first man to show her any kindness, to allow her to see herself as a woman." He shook his head dispassionately. "She might be grateful, even somewhat infatuated, but she hasn't seen enough of the world to understand the depth of the emotion."

Folding her arms across her chest, Leah countered, "She is not a child, Preston."

"If you only knew," he sarcastically retorted.

The enigmatic statement clearly puzzled the young widow.

"Besides," Preston explained, "I have a duty to transport her to her cousin. 'Twould be dishonorable of me to take advantage of her naivety, exploiting her first girlish *tendre*." Preston's voice unconsciously roughened, "She's going to

London for her debut. She'll meet many men there."

"You still ought to explain what she witnessed here," Leah urged. "She appeared most overset."

Smiling softly, Preston laid a hand upon her shoulder. "You're a fine woman, Leah. Not many would have acted so graciously in these circumstances."

She shrugged lightly. "I loved once."

"Only once?"

With a meaningful look she wistfully answered, "I don't think that many of us are given more than one chance."

One chance, Preston repeated to himself. *Only one.*

Bridget threw herself face down upon the bed, sinking her fingernails into her palms to keep from crying. *Blast it,* she swore, *I am not going to shed one more damn tear over Preston Campton!* She was a ninny, a complete idiot!

The worst of it was that she couldn't even begin to sort out her sentiments. She loved Preston and she hated him. She felt furious and, at the same time, crushed. After vowing to carry on as if nothing had occurred last night, she had done naught but stew on the disastrous encounter all damn day!

Then, after her talk with Mrs. Cowden, she had mustered the nerve to confront him about last night, and to reveal the entirety of her feelings, only to discover him in a heated embrace with that woman!

Naively Bridget had taken hope from Mrs. Cowden. Perhaps, she had thought, Preston did care for her, but felt honor-bound not to declare himself until delivering her to Sorrelby. She had desperately believed what she had wanted to believe until the shock of finding Preston and Leah together had brought her crashing back to reality.

God, but he must have had a good laugh at her expense! The silly, Irish chit who thought herself in love with the godlike baron. Even Bridget had to admit that it was utterly insane.

She pounded her fists into the mattress. *Damn it to hell, it just wasn't fair!* For the briefest of moments last night, beneath the magic moonlight, Bridget had felt beautiful. Preston's whispered words had gone straight to her heart, and she had clung to them with the fervor of a dying woman. He had called her beautiful, and she had believed him. She had believed herself desirable, alluring, and . . . wanted. Finally someone wanted her. Elspeth hadn't, the villagers hadn't, apparently even her own father had not wanted her.

But for a tiny space of time Bridget had glimpsed paradise. Then, because of her own clumsiness, her rash words had driven him from her. She had ripped the potential for happiness from her grasp and sent Preston tumbling into the next pair of feminine arms he could find. She should have been satisfied that Preston merely desired her, but she had greedily yearned for more. She had wanted his love. If only she could be content with just his passion, she thought dismally, but she could not. She needed more.

A knock on the door arrested Bridget's melancholy meditation.

"Who is it?" she called.

"It's Mrs. Cowden, dear."

"Come in."

"What's wrong, lass?" Mrs. Cowden asked in concern as she hurried over to the bedside. She sat herself down next to Bridget.

One corner of Bridget's mouth twisted downward in a pain-filled smirk. "I took the risk and ended up the fool."

"Oh, no!" Mrs. Cowden cried. "Are ye sure, lass?"

"Quite."

Pulling Bridget gently into her arms, Mrs. Cowden murmured her sympathy. "Ach, I am so sorry, Bridget."

Bridget snuggled in the maternal embrace, finding solace in the spicy aroma of Mrs. Cowden's cooking apron. Faith, but how she had missed these shows of affection during the past years!

"If 'tis any comfort, lass, ye'll be at yer cousin's in five or six days," Mrs. Cowden stated, patting the young woman on the back.

Bridget's head came up in inquiry.

"Aye. Preston says that he's found a coach and that ye'd be leavin' at daybreak. He said that he wanted to get to Sorrelby Hall as fast as he could. Plans to change horses at nearly every stop." Mrs. Cowden shook her head. "I'm afraid 'twill be a rough trip fer ye, lass."

"Huh," Bridget derisively snorted. "He probably wants to be rid of me as quickly as possible."

Mrs. Cowden made no reply to that comment. Instead, she ventured, "He did get ye a few necessities while he was in Largs. Another gown. And I cleaned up the pretty green one you was wearing, so ye'll have two dresses to wear till ye get to yer cousin's."

She gestured with a nod of her head to the pile of clothing that she had brought in.

"Thank you, Mrs. Cowden," Bridget gratefully answered while silently vowing never to don that particular emerald gown again.

Brightly the Scotswoman announced, "Mr. Cowden has returned, so we'll be eatin' soon."

Bridget smiled, appreciating the woman's attempts to cheer her with the promise of food.

"If it's all right with you, I'd prefer a tray in my room. I doubt that I could face Preston just yet."

Frowning sadly, Mrs. Cowden reminded her, "Dinna forget, love, that ye'll be travelin' with him in the same coach for nearly a sennight. Ye're goin' to have to face him sooner or later."

"I know." Bridget sighed. " 'Tis only that I need tonight to set myself straight."

Mrs. Cowden ran a gentle hand across Bridget's hair. "All right, love. I'll tell him ye're too tired to come out for the meal. Ye have a rest, and I'll bring ye in yer dinner soon."

"Thank you again." Smiling, Bridget gave her a warm hug before Mrs. Cowden arose and left the chamber.

CHAPTER 21

His features rigidly controlled, Preston watched as Bridget entered the kitchen attired in the gown he had purchased for her yesterday. Apparently, Mrs. Cowden had seen to the alterations, for the daffodil-yellow dress clung enticingly to Bridget's petite form. Although not of the first quality, to Preston's eyes, the modest attire rivaled Worth's finest creation once placed upon the lovely young woman.

He studied Bridget's face over the rim of his coffee cup. Last night he had been perturbed to learn that she refused to join them for dinner since he had been hoping for an opportunity to speak with her regarding the encounter in the barn. Although he had resolved to keep his newfound sentiments to himself, he had heeded Leah's advice and had decided to clarify the scene that Bridget had witnessed.

Preston had given a great deal of thought to yesterday's startling revelation—specifically, that he was madly, wildly, insanely in love. The logical side of his brain told him that he should have seen it coming. The spectrum of emotions that Bridget had triggered in him should have provided ample warning of his heart's involvement. But the cynical component of his nature had obviously overridden the signals. And now he was truly caught, the love-bound prisoner of an azure-eyed leprechaun.

Although his primal male instincts demanded that he claim Bridget for his own, Preston had experienced sufficient guilt over his inappropriate behavior to temper such base yearnings. In the wee hours of the morning, when sleep yet again eluded him, he had privately sworn not to take further advantage of Bridget's naivety.

Naturally, he reasoned, Bridget believed herself enamored of him—he was the first man to have ever kissed her, the first to have introduced her to passion. And whereas he felt ashamed of his conduct, it seemed inevitable that the innocent young woman might be temporarily blinded by infatuation.

No, Preston had decided, the only decent recourse left to him was to transport her to Sorrelby posthaste that she might be introduced into Society. Once the London gentlemen laid eyes on her, she would be inundated with their attentions, and, most likely, her fixation on Preston would dissolve into a fond memory of their days together.

Nevertheless, Preston did not want her remembrance of him to be soured by what she thought she had seen transpire between him and Leah last evening. Confidently, he hoped that once Bridget had entered the *ton,* he might also throw his hat into the arena for her affections. There was no reason that he, too, could not pursue her. After he had given her sufficient time to experience the thrill of her debut, and to meet other men, he might still have a chance at winning her affections.

However, gazing over the rim of his cup at the coolly composed Bridget Flannery, the possibility of such appeared remote at best. Her gaze sweeping the room, she afforded him a chilled nod when his eyes met hers.

"Preston."

"Good morning, Bridget," he cautiously returned.

"There ye are, love," Mrs. Cowden greeted, placing a lid on a pot and rushing over to Bridget's side. "Only one day and ye're leavin' us already. I should have words with Preston here, but I doubt 'twould do any good."

"Regretfully, Mrs. Cowden, we must be on our way," Preston reiterated.

"Not afore the lass has her breakfast," the woman clucked, leading Bridget to the table where she piled high a plate and lay it before her.

"Now, ye go ahead, dear, and eat yer fill. The horses might be waitin' but I won't have ye leavin' us without a decent meal in ye."

Turning to Preston, the Scotswoman warned, "I know ye're in a hurry to get the lass home, but remember, she's not just a piece of luggage ye're transportin'."

Preston choked on his coffee, and Bridget suddenly blushed, dropping her attention to her plate. Unaware of the private joke shared by the couple, Mrs. Cowden continued her instructions.

"Be sure ye stop regularly fer her to stretch her legs. I've packed a basket fer ye to nibble on durin' the trip, but that doesn't mean you canna stop at midday fer yer meal."

"I assure you, Mrs. Cowden, that I will be solicitous to a fault."

"Hrmph," Bridget jeered through a mouthful of porridge.

Surprised by the mocking protest that had broken through Bridget's icy demeanor, Preston hid a smile. Try as she might to appear aloof and composed, Bridget's basic nature could not help asserting itself.

"You said something, Bridget?" he asked in amusement, arching a questioning brow.

"Nothing at all," she returned, the malicious gleam in her eyes contradicting her syrupy tone.

While Preston sipped at his coffee, Bridget ate her breakfast, pointedly ignoring him as she conversed with Mrs. Cowden.

"I'm sorry that I won't be able to say goodbye to your husband."

"Aye, but out here, we all rely on each other, and the Rafferty boy said for Mr. Cowden to come quick. If there's a problem, ye have to be able to call on yer neighbor. Mr.

Cowden was gone afore the sun even came up."

"And your niece?" Bridget politely inquired, studiously refusing to glance in Preston's direction.

"Leah decided to stay with me oldest boy," Mrs. Cowden answered with a slight frown. "Surprised me, it did, but she left afore dinner last evening. She did ask me to say goodbye to ye, though."

Nonplussed, Bridget hoped that it did not show in her expression. "How nice," she weakly responded, abruptly lost in thought.

Why had the widow bid such a hasty departure from the Cowden home? Had Leah and Preston consummated their passion in the barn after she had accidentally stumbled upon them? If so, it seemed peculiar to Bridget that the woman would leave so hastily. Or, she wondered, was that common practice after an illicit tryst?

"If you're done, Bridget, we should be off. We have many miles to travel before we reach Sorrelby."

Preston's words jarred her back to the present, and Bridget glanced down to her empty plate, realizing that she could not stall him any further. This lengthy trip to England would undoubtedly prove an arduous test for her, but she was committed to keeping Preston at arm's length. Determined to hold conversation to the minimum and to maintain her composure at all costs, she vowed to conduct herself with dignity, giving no clues as to her pain.

Arising from the table, she gave Mrs. Cowden a last hug before stalwartly striding from the room.

The traveling coach appeared out of place in the rural setting, the liveried riders starkly formal in contrast to the quaint Cowden cottage. The juxtaposition reminded Bridget of the life she left and the one she was about to enter when she reached Sorrelby Hall.

Two weeks ago such a prospect had terrified her, but Bridget had grown up this past fortnight. Once and for all, she had shed her childlike masquerade, admitting to herself that she was indeed a woman and capable of accepting the responsibilities of adulthood.

Squaring her shoulders, she marched through the coach door that the footman held open and resolutely settled herself on the banquette.

After only a brief moment Preston joined her, carrying the promised basket of goodies.

As the coach rolled into motion, Bridget leaned back against the squabs, closing her eyes.

"This is rather different than our last coach trip, is it not?"

The memory of the ride to Bristol, when she had first become aware of Preston as a man and herself as a woman, rushed forcefully into her mind. She turned it aside, however, not deigning to raise her lids to respond.

"Indeed," Bridget starchly returned, adding, "If you don't mind, I believe that I shall have a rest."

"Are you fatigued?"

"Frightfully fagged out," she lied, eyes still closed.

"By all means, then."

She heard the sarcastic edge to his voice and emitted a mental shrug. As far as she was concerned, 'twas simply too bad if Preston did not enjoy her quiet company. He would have to get used to it since she planned to hide behind this device for the balance of their journey.

She must have actually nodded off while feigning sleep for the jostling of the coach as it came to a stop awoke her from a dream. Bridget had been dreaming of that wondrous night upon the deserted island, reexperiencing the rapture she had known in Preston's arms. So, when she sleepily opened her eyes and found the subject of her fantasies sitting across from her, she unknowingly allowed a sensual catlike grin to spread across her lips.

"You were tired," Preston commented, glancing at his newly acquired pocket watch. "You've been asleep nearly five hours."

"You must be joking," she returned. "Five hours?"

Yawning delicately, Bridget suddenly recalled the reserve she wished to maintain with Preston, and reluctantly letting go of the pleasant dream, she stiffened.

Replacing his pocket watch, Preston appeared not to note her rigid demeanor. "Five hours to the dot. We've made good time. We'll take our meal at this inn, change horses, and be on our way again."

Bridget glanced out the window to the small, neatly kept inn. Despite her resolve, she could not help commenting, " 'Tis difficult to believe that we will be traveling like this for nearly a week."

Reaching for the jacket that he had earlier removed, Preston shrugged into the fawn-colored coat. "If we are fortunate with our horses, we might make Sorrelby in as little as four and a half days."

Turning her head, Bridget bit down on her lip. Good God, but Preston was in a rush to be rid of her! She wondered whether he would even bother to stay and visit with his friends, the Forsters. Or, in his eagerness to dispose of her, would he merely drive by the entrance to Sorrelby and shove her from the moving coach!

Masking her irritation as the door opened, she took the footman's hand and stepped down from the coach.

Although midday, Bridget shivered, reacting to the chill that hung in the October air. These past weeks she had forgotten that the seasons had changed, summer finally relenting to autumn. So much had altered in her own life that Bridget had overlooked the passage of the year's cycles.

"Shall I fetch your cloak?" Preston asked at her ear.

Bridget started, unnerved by the husky inquiry just behind her. The man was too perceptive by half. If she had accidentally ignored the shifting seasons, Preston had not. In his inimitably competent way, he had included a coat for her in his purchases yesterday. Bridget frowned, irked by his ever-present efficacy.

"No, thank you," she tightly replied.

Preston's mouth screwed up at one corner in obvious reaction to her severe answer. Wordlessly he grabbed hold of her elbow, steering her into the inn.

The front room was vacant, five small tables forlornly awaiting traveling diners. A fire in the hearth welcomed them, its smoky fragrance a refreshing change from the coach's closeness. The filtered light passing through the windows shone on the dust-free tabletops.

As Preston released Bridget's elbow, a plump woman suddenly bustled through a back doorway. Apparently, the landlady had not heard them enter, for she looked taken aback to find visitors standing in the entrance. She hastened to seat them, however, and promised them the most delicious meal to be had in all of Scotland as she scurried toward the kitchen.

"I daresay that Mrs. Cowden would take issue with the proprietress's claim on Scottish cuisine," Preston stated, seating himself across the table from Bridget.

Glancing around, Bridget ignored his comment, wishing that she and Preston were not alone in the small dining room. If she could not rely on other people for distraction,'twas going to be a very long trip indeed.

"Hmm," she mumbled noncommittally, her eyes fixed to the kitchen door, hoping that she could summon the proprietress through sheer force of will.

"Bridget—"

Preston's serious tone captured Bridget's attention, and automatically her gaze pivoted about to his.

"I have a matter to discuss with you," he broached, his expression solemn.

Bridget's dark brows veed together in consternation.

"Yesterday, when you came upon Mrs. Harriston and me—"

"I don't want to hear about it," Bridget interrupted, her frown clearing. Alarmed, she swiftly waved away his words with her small hand, loath to hear the details of his amorous encounter with the sultry widow.

"I think it's important that you understand—"

"I understand perfectly," she interjected, feeling the hot rise of color to her cheeks.

"I don't think that you do," Preston gravely persisted.

"Of course, I do," she countered, shooting frantic, pleading glances to the kitchen door. Where was that landlady?

"Bridget, I know that you were upset—"

"Why should I be upset?" Her reedy voice wafted nervously in the still room.

"Well," Preston slowly began, "the night before you had mentioned that you . . . had certain tender feelings for me."

Bridget fixed her wide eyes on Preston. "I . . . was carried away," she stuttered. "S-surely, you don't think . . ."

Preston's expression closed. "Of course not," he succinctly returned. "I only wanted to assure you that nothing transpired between me and Leah."

"Preston, really," Bridget anxiously breathed while her gaze flitted around the room. "You needn't make up tales on my account. Whatever passed between you and Mrs. Harriston, my missish declaration amounts to nothing. Please do not dissemble merely to protect my feelings."

Bridget's palms grew sweaty, and she wiped them on her skirt, fervently praying that the proprietress would soon return. She could feel her heart pounding in her breast, her anxiety increasing. She had never expected Preston to address the delicate issue head-on, and she was completely confounded by his need to lie to her about it. How unlike him it seemed!

"Bridget." His tone compelled her to meet his eyes. "I am not lying. Nothing happened between me and Leah Harriston."

Bridget lost herself in his gaze. As she fell deeper and deeper into those turquoise depths, a roaring swelled in her ears, sending her reeling. He spoke the truth. She blinked rapidly, striving for equilibrium.

"I can't see that it matters any to me." She had wanted the remark to sound flippant, but it had left her mouth as a whisper.

"Perhaps not," Preston softly answered, his aqua eyes plumbing hers. "It was important to me, however, that you not misinterpret the incident."

Bridget thought that her heart might burst through her chest. What was Preston trying to say?

"Why?" she rasped.

Preston suddenly grew fascinated with the toes of his boots. "I am aware of your opinion of London's fast bucks," he lightly replied, "and I did not want you to think that I indulge in such dalliances."

"You do not?"

Preston shifted on his chair. "Not anymore."

"Why not?" The words were drawn from her almost without volition.

An emotion skittered across Preston's features and disappeared before Bridget could put a name to it.

"I have changed."

"Changed? How have you changed?"

"I do not know," Preston gruffly returned, his gaze now darting between her and the apparently mesmerizing boots. "Anyhow, that is not the point."

"You do not know how you have changed?" Bridget insisted.

"Let us leave it, shall we?"

Preston's terseness did not faze her. Instinctively she knew that there was more underlying his confession than he had told her.

"No, Preston." Bridget shook her head. "I do not want to leave it. How have you changed?"

"For God's sake, Bridget, can't you just leave well enough alone!" Gone was the gentle gaze as he glared down his patrician nose at her.

"No, I cannot." She patiently folded her hands upon the table. "I sense that it is most important that you explain to me this change."

Preston closed his eyes and threw back his head as if battling for self-control. When he brought his head back down, his aspect was steely with purpose.

"My affairs are not your concern," he bit out. "Once and for all, let me make myself clear." He delivered each word with acerbic intensity. "I only wanted you to know that I had not *been* with the woman. All right?"

Bridget crossed her arms across her chest, her expression curious. "Why should you care what I think?"

Preston clenched his jaw, and Bridget fancifully imagined she could hear the grating of his teeth as he ground them together.

"I just do."

"Why?"

"Why?!"

"Yes, why?" she queried again, silently wondering if it was the play of the shadows or if steam were actually coming from Preston's ears.

"I did not want you to think badly of me," he spat, his voice rising in volume.

"Why?"

Preston's eyes bulged from his head as his tenuous hold on his patience evidently shattered. Slamming his fist upon the table, his bellow shook the entire room. "Because, dammit, I hoped to win your affections!"

'Twas Bridget's turn to appear bug-eyed. Sitting up in her chair, she echoed hollowly, "You hoped to win my affections?"

Preston squeezed shut his eyes, slamming that same fist into his forehead.

"Preston," Bridget whispered, "you care for me?"

Not opening his eyes, Preston dropped his elbow to the table, cradling his forehead in his palm. His shoulders sagged in defeat as he muttered in exasperation, "Bridget, you are the most maddeningly tenacious wench I have ever had the misfortune to meet."

"But you care for me?" Bridget insisted, a giddiness lacing her voice.

Preston bobbed his head dispiritedly.

"How much?"

Although his face was lowered to the table, Bridget saw Preston's shoulders shake, as if in mirth, while a glimmer of a smile passed across his visage.

"I love you, imp. Are you satisfied?"

Bridget felt as if the heavens had opened up and rained joy upon her head. She sat dazed, the unbelievable declaration echoing in her ears. Preston loved her. He loved her.

A piercing joy shot through her as she hammered the words over and over again into her mind.

Abruptly seizing his hand in hers, she stood up, roughly pulling him along with her.

"You, sir, are coming with me!"

The sun hovered on the horizon, its last crimson rays tinting the sky, as Preston slowly mounted the inn's creaky staircase. Arriving outside the door, he stood for a long moment, his breath unnaturally short, before slipping into the room. With a shaky hand, he turned the key in the lock then, straightening, pivoted about on his booted heel. His eyes instantly flew to the bed where Bridget lay, a shy smile playing about her lips.

He laughed quietly to himself, thinking that this afternoon had been the most extraordinary of his life. As Bridget's expectant blue gaze met his, Preston realized that the day held yet even greater promise.

CHAPTER
22

"How much longer?"

"Ten minutes less than the last time you asked," Preston patiently answered, gazing down at the pocket watch that he had not bothered to replace in his coat after Bridget's sixth inquiry.

"Come now, Preston," Bridget urged, "I have lost track of the time. Are we close to Sorrelby?"

"Another three hours or so," he calculated with an understanding grin. "Are you very nervous?"

"A trifle," Bridget breezily replied, smoothing the skirt of her gown. She then began patting at imaginary loose tendrils falling from her chignon. "Do I need to repair my coiffure?"

Preston obediently examined the neat knot atop her head. "You look lovely."

"Oh." Bridget stifled a sigh. Peering out the coach window at the landscape flying past them, she commented, "Do you think we should rest the horses?"

"No, I do not."

"But—"

"Bridget," Preston cut short her anxious protest, "you have nothing to worry about, I assure you. The Forsters are going to adore you."

Bridget gnawed nervously at her lower lip. "Are they

truly as wonderful as you say?"

"Truly. Colin and Olivia are first-rate people, a remarkable couple. Devilishly handsome, Colin has also been blessed with a keen intellect. He was instrumental in penetrating the French forces during his stint with Wellesley. And Olivia . . . Olivia is a diamond of the first water."

"Faith, you make them sound positively perfect."

"By no means," Preston contradicted her on a laugh. "Colin has sown enough wild oats in his days to make me look the saint. And Olivia has a stubborn streak—why, it rather reminds me of you, my dear." Preston ignored the tongue Bridget displayed in response. " 'Tis evident to everyone who knows them that they were meant for each other."

.Preston tilted his head slightly as if reminiscing. "I remember a time, not so very long ago, when I envied them their unique relationship. Unlike so many other couples of our time, they honestly care for each other. Often I would watch them together, regretting that I would never be able to share my life with someone in a similar way."

He bent over to whisper in Bridget's ear. "Until I met you, my lady leprechaun."

Bridget laughed softly. Ironically, the dubious title the Dunbrigganers had given her so many years ago had evolved into a term of endearment.

Wrapping her arms around Preston, Bridget squeezed tightly. As she did so, she felt the small bulge of the cylinder beneath Preston's coat. Thoughtfully she patted the lump. "Preston, what exactly do you intend to do with these papers?"

"Well," Preston answered, unconsciously scowling. "First I must return to London. I shall have to compare the Welsh documents against the supposedly fraudulent papers that Pitham provided Jamison and a few other purchasers. Once it is clear that he forged the animals' credentials, I shall take the evidence to the authorities and allow them to proceed."

A pensive frown crinkled Bridget's brow. "So you won't have to confront this Pitham fellow directly?"

"I hope not to. I would prefer to keep my presence in London quiet so as not to alert him. He might flee should he realize how close I am to exposing him."

Satisfied that Preston would not be at peril, Bridget relaxed. "Since I already know everything about my cousin and her husband, why do you not tell me about your London friends," she prompted. "Jamison, for example."

Preston began to describe his friends and acquaintances, and, as usual, the insatiably curious Bridget bombarded him with questions about everything and everyone.

While deftly trying to evade her blunt inquiries regarding his past mistresses, a sudden hoarse shout erupted from the coachman's perch.

The horses whinnied in alarm as the carriage was drawn up sharply, and Bridget clung to Preston's arm to keep from falling to the floor.

"Stand and deliver!"

The command rang out loudly, immediately followed by the menacing report of a pistol. A pain-filled howl established that the pistol's bullet had achieved its mark, and Bridget bit down hard on her lip to keep from crying out. Was that their coachman who had shrieked in anguish?

Moving with lightning speed, Preston pushed Bridget down to the carriage floor, his body covering hers. "Keep low," he whispered in her ear.

Bridget raised her head to question him, but Preston's hand shoved her back down. "I mean it, Bridget, stay down," he hissed between his teeth.

The musty smell of dust and damp nearly suffocated her as Preston's palm pushed her nose directly into the coach's floor. She muffled a cough by shoving her fist into her mouth, although the need to cough, coupled with Preston's weight upon her, nearly drove all breath from her body.

Terrified, Bridget wanted to scream out loud as she felt Preston lever himself off of her, and then she heard the creak of the coach door swinging open. *What in God's name is he doing?*

Her heart thundered in her chest, its frightened tattoo

seeming to reverberate throughout the coach. Preston had shut the door behind him, but Bridget clearly heard him call to the highway raider.

"What do you want?"

His voice boomed loudly and authoritatively, no trace of fear audible to Bridget's disbelieving ears. Her heart lodged in her throat as she realized that Preston, without a weapon of his own, was confronting an armed robber. She would have commenced praying, but her senses were riveted to the sounds coming from outside the carriage.

The frightened horses were snorting and prancing, their edgy movements slightly jarring the carriage. The jingling of the loose reins grated harshly on Bridget's taut nerves, and she dug her nails painfully into her palms.

A faint moan from above indicated that the coachman had not, as yet, expired from his injury, and Bridget wondered how grave the man's wound might be. Would he die while she cowered here? With her cheek pressed against the cold floor, she felt utterly helpless and vulnerable. *Why, oh why, had Preston left the coach?*

As soon as the question formed in her thoughts, Bridget knew the reason. He had hoped to keep her safe by hiding her in the coach while he diverted the highwayman's attention. Thanks to Preston, at this point their assailant was not even aware of her presence.

Preston's thoughts sped one after the other as he stepped away from the carriage, his gaze affixed to the thief on horseback.

Although the man might only be intent on robbery, Bridget's beauty might prove too tempting to bypass. I dare not take the chance that he find her.

He warily eyed the masked man as he edged farther away from the coach.

Immediately Preston sensed that something about the bandit rang false. The highwayman's clothing was too fine, his boots freshly polished. The black cloak he wore concealed his form, making it impossible to determine his size, although Preston felt certain that he could overpower the man if only he could divest him of his weapon. Preston's gaze flew to the firearm, and his eyes narrowed speculatively. 'Twas no ordinary weapon the robber carried, but an expensive dueling pistol.

A spark of suspicion winged through his mind as he appraised the immaculately groomed roan skittishly pawing the dusty ground. The steed looked strangely familiar. . . .

"What happened to your henchman, Pitham?" Preston drawled, abruptly shattering the silence. "He failed to deliver the goods?"

The man started nervously, causing the horse to prance sideways.

"How did you know?" Lord Pitham returned accusingly, his nasally voice thick with surprise.

"Know what?" Preston asked. "That you had sent someone after me or that 'twas you masquerading as a highwayman? As for the latter, I recognized your mount. You purchased him at Tatt's last spring. And the blackguard you set on my trail proved to be a bumbling fool, not unlike his employer."

Pitham's beady eyes glared through the mask's openings.

"Who is the fool, Campton? You are the one staring into the barrel of my gun," he jeered.

Preston shrugged insouciantly. "Frankly, Pitham, I'm surprised that you were able to find me." Imperceptibly he edged farther away from the carriage.

"Hah," Pitham replied with a contemptuous laugh. "I knew that you would resurface. Your ship captain arrived in London, looking for you, full of stories regarding the unfortunate loss of your vessel. Although some feared you'd drowned, your devoted captain assured one and all that the resourceful Lord Campton would emerge unscathed.

"I had only to keep my ear to the ground, awaiting your miraculous return."

"And I have returned."

"Yes, more's the pity." Pitham shifted his weight in

the saddle. "You're simply too clever for your own good, Campton. You should have kept your nose out of my business, but no. You had to interfere."

"So what now?" Preston coolly inquired.

"Alas, the poor baron dies at the hands of a ruthless highwayman," Pitham mocked.

"You take a grave risk, Pitham."

"No more than the horse-breeding scam," he acidly retorted. "My life would have been ruined anyway once you exposed my swindling." He lifted one plump shoulder in an indifferent gesture. "Too bad for you, but it appears I must add murder to my list of sins."

Preston froze as Pitham lowered the pistol, preparing to aim. Only one thought flashed through his mind as he watched in trepidation the sun glinting off the polished weapon. *Bridget.*

In one brief second he reached inside his coat for the cylinder, forcefully hurling the piece of metal at Pitham's gun hand. At the same time another shiny metallic object flew through the air, joining the cylinder's assault.

"Aagh!" Pitham screeched, the gun dropping from his hand. The horse shied as he fell forward across the animal's neck, one hand clasped to the knife embedded in his shoulder.

Preston spun about to see Bridget materialize from behind the coach. Her face was deathly white as she held on to the carriage for support.

Leaping forward, Preston grabbed the loose reins hanging from Pitham's jittery mount. Ruthlessly wrenching the man from the saddle, he tossed him, groaning, to the ground.

"You son of a—" Preston bit back the angry words.

He quickly unleashed the reins and used them to bind Pitham's hands while the man whimpered and writhed helplessly, blood seeping from his wound.

None too gently, Preston rolled him onto his back, and with one swift tug, pulled the blade from Pitham's shoulder and tossed the knife away. The man cried out, then collapsed as he lost consciousness.

Unmoved by Pitham's pain, Preston completely forgot the villainous lord as he rushed over to Bridget.

"Bridget, my love, are you all right?" he rasped, gathering her into his arms.

She sank weakly against his chest, and Preston felt her nod feebly. He held her for a long moment until her quivering subsided.

"I didn't know you could throw a knife like that," he ventured.

"Neither did I," she shakily replied.

Preston smiled over her head, gazing into the distant horizon. "I guess I just got lucky?"

Bridget emitted a nervous half laugh. "I guess you did."

CHAPTER
23

Bridget's mouth fell open in amazement as their coach rounded a bend in the driveway and Sorrelby Hall came into view.

She had, of course, suspected that her cousin's home would be grand since Preston had informed her that the Forsters descended from one of the most distinguished and oldest lines in all of England. She had not, however, envisioned that Olivia lived in a palace.

Gray stone turrets ascended into the endless English sky, their peaks seeming to reach into the puffy clouds. The autumn sunshine glinted off the hundreds of mullioned windows gracing the manor's facade, and the rolling green lawn stretched as far as Bridget's eye could see.

"Impressive, is it not?"

Preston's question brought Bridget's head whirling around, and she smiled weakly into his handsome face.

"Faith, Preston . . . I—I had no idea," she stuttered, trying to keep the wan grin in place. "It's rather awe-inspiring."

She noted the sudden hardening of his aqua eyes as he asked on a gruff note, "Having regrets?"

"No! Never!" she ardently replied, placing her hand upon his arm. A more credible smile rose to her lips to accompany the warmth in her gaze.

She saw his features relax as he covered her small hand with his own large palm, and then he lowered his head to softly nip at her delicate ear.

Giggling, Bridget pushed him away as the carriage lurched to a stop in front of the wide stairway leading to the Sorrelby mansion.

"Preston, enough," she protested on a laugh when he insisted on returning for one more nibble on her earlobe.

He had just pulled away from nuzzling her neck when the footman opened the carriage door. Bridget shot Preston a warning glance, indicating that he was to be on his good behavior.

Preston answered her silent plea with a wicked grin, causing Bridget to roll her eyes helplessly.

"You, sir, are incorrigible," she whispered to the leering baron before accepting the footman's hand.

Stepping out of the coach, Bridget came to stand at the base of the stairs. She looked up at the intimidating edifice and took a shaky breath as she felt Preston place his hand along the small of her back.

The life-threatening encounter with Lord Pitham yesterday, followed by a frantic rush to locate a physician, combined with an extremely uncomfortable night passed in a nearby inn, had left Bridget understandably edgy. Although everything had been ultimately resolved—the coachman's wound tended and Pitham surrendered to the local constable—the events had taken a toll on Bridget's emotions. Was she prepared for this momentous meeting with her cousin?

"Ready?" Preston softly asked at her shoulder, unconsciously echoing her thoughts.

Expelling one more deep breath, Bridget bobbed her head, straightened her skirts, and proceeded up the stairway. Her ramrod straight figure gave no indication of the butterflies flitting around her stomach.

As they reached a pair of massive, carved oak doors, Bridget halted, squaring her slim shoulders. When Preston would have picked up the large brass knocker to announce their arrival, Bridget suddenly caught his hand.

"Wait!" she cried.

She looked up beseechingly into his puzzled expression and felt the color rise to her cheeks. She could not explain the sudden premonition that had crept up her spine, but the fine hairs at the back of her neck stood at attention, attesting to her sense of foreboding.

"I . . . I think I need a kiss for luck," she haltingly explained on a nervous laugh.

Preston's lips curved in pleased anticipation as he bent his head to hers. As his mouth sweetly caressed her own, Bridget forgot her worries, succumbing to the pleasure his kiss invariably produced. Mindlessly she laced her fingers through his silver-blond hair, taking strength from his sensual power.

Engrossed as they were, neither noticed the door swinging open as a trio of welcomers arrived upon the threshold.

"Damn me eyes!"

The hoarse shout arrested the pair, and suddenly Bridget felt Preston wrenched from her arms. The next thing she saw was a meaty fist powerfully connecting with Preston's jaw.

"Preston!" she cried out in horror as his tall frame fell backward beneath the unexpected assault. He was not flattened by the blow, but merely felled, and Bridget sank to her knees beside him. Leaning on one elbow, Preston massaged his ill-treated jaw while Bridget cooed words of comfort, quickly ascertaining that no bones had been broken.

Outraged, she leaped to her feet to confront his attacker. "How dare you? What—"

The words died in her throat as every bit of color instantly drained from her face. She staggered slightly, her vision blurring. *My God, my God* . . . Somebody grabbed at her elbow, and the warm, physical contact kept her from losing consciousness.

Shaking her head, she lifted her eyes back to the face of Preston's assailant.

"Da."

Barely whispered, Bridget felt as if the word floated eerily in the still air surrounding them, as if she were calling back the dead. If not for the echo in her ears, she would not have believed that she had even spoken.

There he stood. A little thinner, a little grayer than last she had seen him, but 'twas Da.

The hand at her elbow gripped her more tightly, and Bridget was grateful for the touch. It reassured her that she was still among the living, for at this moment she felt suspended between reality and fantasy—the fantasy that she had clung to these past four years. Da had finally come back to her.

"Bridget."

His very Irish husky voice ruptured the eloquent hush. He moved toward her, and Bridget literally collapsed into his strong arms.

"Oh, Da. Da," she sobbed, her fingers digging into his shirt as she wept unabashedly. Bridget felt the presence of other eyes but could not release her father for fear that, once away from her grasp, he would again disappear.

He softly crooned to her while she poured the tears of many years into his shirtfront.

After a few minutes, when Bridget was convinced that this was not merely another of her hope-filled dreams, she loosened her grip and peered into the blue eyes so similar to her own.

"I-I cannot believe it," she murmured, shaking her head in disbelief. "So much has happened—"

Abruptly the image of Preston, sprawled across the stairway to Sorrelby Hall, sprang to her mind, and she whirled about to find him quietly watching her from his prone position.

"Preston!" she cried before her father caught her arm as she prepared to spin away.

"Just a minute, lass," he roughly interrupted. "I want to know the meanin' of this."

Stunned, Bridget looked about, finally taking note of the attractive couple bearing witness to this scene. A gentleman, extremely tall—even taller than Preston—stood to the side of the doorway, his arm wrapped around the most beautiful woman that Bridget had ever laid eyes upon.

Copper-colored curls draped elegantly over the woman's shoulder as she watched Bridget's confusion with compassionate emerald eyes. To Bridget's reasoning, the woman was too beautiful to be real, and once again she wondered whether she were in the midst of a trance.

"Oh, my," the vision said, speaking past Bridget's shoulder to the form laid out on the threshold. "When I received your note, Preston, I had not thought that you and Bridget were traveling without a chaperon."

Patrick Flannery growled deep in his throat, and Bridget worriedly glanced toward her father before turning yet again to the prostrate Preston.

Everything was happening too fast for her to take it all in. Bridget brought a weary hand to her head in an effort to sort out her tumultuous emotions. Adding to her surprise, Preston serenely answered the redheaded woman as if he had not just been decked by a crushing right hook.

"Hallo, Olivia," he greeted from his ignominious position. "I *had* promised you an interesting tale, after all."

Overwhelmed, Bridget leaned into her father for support.

"Now, now, me dear," Patrick gruffly assured her, patting her shoulder. "Lord or not, he's not goin' to git away with this, or me name's not Patrick Flannery."

"But, Da—" she began to remonstrate.

"Perhaps," the dark-haired gentleman interrupted, "we should all move into the house."

As the troupe appeared to acquiesce to the proposal, Patrick released Bridget's arm, and she immediately dropped to her knees beside Preston.

She tenderly kissed his purpling jaw, and he sighed in mock exasperation. "I assume, wife, that this is yet another example of the good fortune you have brought me?"

"Wife?!" the threesome echoed in varying degrees of amazement.

Preston accepted the glass of wine with a wry smile, his other arm protectively encircling Bridget's tiny waist.

Colin Forster, the Earl of Sorrelby, had somehow managed to herd the flustered group into the drawing room before any more tears were shed or blood was lost. Thankfully, the father of the bride had yet to find his voice, and his thoughtful host had quickly thrust a tumbler of whiskey into the befuddled Irishman's hand.

Once all the parties had been furnished with a libation, however, chaos erupted as five different voices rushed into the silence.

"Da—"

"Olivia—"

"Bridget—"

"Now, now," Colin Forster's deep baritone overrode the cacophony. "Let us proceed in a logical manner." Drawing his wife to his side, he proposed, "Since there appears to be a great deal of ground to cover, Preston, why do you not begin with your . . . uh, marriage?"

"Certainly, old man," Preston smoothly replied, sipping nonchalantly at the aged claret. He squeezed Bridget's waist as he pulled her more closely to him on the divan. "It's really most straightforward. Bridget and I were wed five days ago in Scotland."

"Five days ago?" Olivia echoed accusingly. "You hinted at none of this in your letter!"

"At the time there was nothing to report. Our decision was made rather hastily," Preston added with a slight smile.

"What?!" Patrick roared, jumping from the tapestried chair, his hands already bunched into fists.

"Sit down, Da," Bridget hurriedly instructed, holding out her hand to forestall another attack. "It's not what you think. We didn't marry quickly because I—" She swallowed her words. "That is . . . there was no *need* to marry so swiftly."

Preston turned to look at his wife, arching a dubious blond brow. "That's not what you said to me, madam," he dryly teased.

Bridget sighed in vexation, glancing to her glowering father.

"Da, Preston doesn't mean . . . I mean nothing happened prior to our wedding."

Preston pinched Bridget's waist, and she shot him a fulminating look.

"Would you stop," she scolded. "You're going to make Da think that—well, you know."

His eyes twinkling, Preston peered into his wife's beet-red face. "I do apologize, my love. However, as I recall, you were the one who insisted we be wed immediately." Turning to the three other listeners, he explained with a shrug, "I had wanted to wait until Bridget had experienced her debut, but she was most insistent."

He grimaced as a tiny elbow found its way into his ribs.

"Just what are you sayin'?" Patrick belligerently demanded through narrowed eyes as he took his seat again.

From the corner of his eye Preston saw his wife's complexion take on an even more brilliant hue, and he chuckled softly. "Only, sir, that it was your daughter who proposed to me, not the other way around."

"Oh!" Olivia exclaimed from the hearth where she stood beside her chortling husband.

"I say, Pres, sounds as if you had a much easier time of it than I did," Colin commented, making no effort to conceal his amusement.

"Well, to be perfectly frank, old fellow, I am being rather gracious in describing it as a proposal."

"Preston!" Bridget breathed in embarrassment, sinking deeper into the sofa.

"Correct me if I misquote you love," Preston continued, his eyes sparkling merrily, "but weren't your words something like 'Preston Campton, if you don't marry me this afternoon, I'll never give you another moment's peace for the rest of your life'?"

"Oh, God," Bridget whispered to herself, closing her eyes.

"Decisive," Colin smilingly proclaimed, raising his glass in a salute. "I like that in a woman."

"Bridget Marie Flannery!" her father ejaculated, his expression clearly dismayed. "I dunna believe my ears!"

Raising her lids, Bridget cast Preston a threatening glare, causing his grin merely to widen, before answering her father.

"Da, Preston is deliberately misstating the situation. He had already told me that he was in love with me, and since I know the man is the most stubborn creature in all Creation, I had to threaten him to get him to see reason."

"But, really, Bridget," Preston chided, ruefully shaking his head, "dragging me from the inn before we'd even had our meal. A man hates to get married on an empty stomach."

"You dragged him?" Olivia asked incredulously, glancing at the petite figure curled against the uncommonly large Preston.

"I did *not* drag him," Bridget sharply contradicted. "My husband is purposely misleading you, and I vow that he shall pay dearly for this later."

She lowered her brows at Preston, who leaned over to whisper in her ear. "I shall enjoy making restitution this evening, my sweet."

As Bridget's countenance pinkened yet again, Colin Forster laughed out loud.

"Colin, really!" Olivia exclaimed. "They are just newly-weds."

A snort of displeasure emitted from Patrick's chair, and Olivia Forster hastened to pacify her guest.

"Patrick, despite the impression Preston gives at the moment, he is really a most upstanding gentleman. A baron, he has an estate in Winchester, a comfortable income, a most laudable reputation. Truly, sir, he has been considered a good catch."

"That may be," Patrick sourly retorted, "but I canna favor the idea of Bridget marryin' beneath herself."

"Da!" Bridget wailed, clearly agitated at her father's outrageous pronouncement. "You mustn't say such things!"

" 'Tis true whether you know it or not," Patrick declared with an emphatic bob of his dark head. "Your grandfather McClellan was a duke of the noblest clan in Ireland. And me own dear da was an earl," he stated proudly. With a mournful glare he added, "I dunna know what either of them woulda thought of their granddaughter marryin' a mere baron."

"Da, don't," Bridget pleaded, her concerned gaze flying around the room, wondering what everyone was thinking of her father's atrocious lies.

"Don't be embarrassed, Bridget," Olivia urged. "Your father tells the truth. I, too, descend from the McClellans, a name to be proud of."

"But . . . but that cannot be," Bridget argued, plainly stunned. "We come from Dunbriggan, a fishing village."

"Aye," Patrick concurred. "But your dear mother and I had not begun our lives so humbly. At the time I met Maire, our clans were feuding, so she and I decided to elope. We were shunned by both families. I wouldna regretted it but for what you missed, Bridget."

"Oh, Da!" Bridget exclaimed, feeling tears press hotly behind her eyelids. "I didn't miss anything. I had everything I wanted till . . ."

Patrick shook his head sadly. "I know. Till you lost your mum and then me. I'll never forgive meself, lass, for not bein' stronger after Maire died. You needed me and I failed you."

"No, Da, you didn't," Bridget protested, rising from the sofa to kneel next to her father's chair. "But, tell me, what happened to you?"

Patrick hung his head, the memory still shaming him. "I was a fool, lass. Too drunk to know what was happening, I was shanghaied by a group of sailors whose ship was short-handed. 'Twas a slaving ship, and when we finally sailed to the colonies, the captain sold me as a bonded man without any papers.

"Lucky for me, the fella who bought me was fair, 'though, of course, he didn't believe a word of me story." Patrick glanced up to Olivia and Colin standing at the hearth. "When the countess, here, started lookin' fer her family, she heard about me disappearin', and she and the earl hired a man to track me down. He found me and they bought me papers. They found me before they even knew ye existed, lass."

Bridget spun her head around to look gratefully at the couple as Patrick added, "I owe them my life, I do."

"How can we ever thank you for all that you've done?" Bridget whispered, forcing words past the sudden lump in her throat.

Colin smiled, dismissing his efforts with a shrug. "You might start by relating what you and Preston have been doing this past month," he suggested, his expression openly curious. "We had thought that Bridget was traveling with a companion, both due to arrive nearly four weeks ago. Patrick has been awaiting your arrival a week already."

Bridget flushed and she and Preston exchanged glances.

"Come here, wife," Preston beckoned with a sigh. "I fear my story of a naughty leprechaun might take us the entire afternoon."

EPILOGUE

"Champagne!"

Colin Forster's jubilant request could barely be heard by his servant due to the noisy hubbub following Lord Campton's pronouncement.

"A baby!" Olivia cried, clapping her hands in delight.

"A babe?" Patrick Flannery echoed, his expression a droll combination of shock and joy.

"Bridget, this is the most wonderful Christmas gift of all!" Olivia enthused, rushing across the room to embrace her blushing cousin. "How long have you known?"

"Only a few days. I wanted to be certain before telling Preston."

Preston brought his wife's hand to his lips. "Last night we exchanged gifts, and one of mine included a pair of teeny white booties." His wide smile clearly indicated his sentiment regarding the thoughtful present.

"Hadn't you suspected?" Colin asked of his friend, while juggling his own son, Reggie, in his arms.

"Frankly, no," Preston ruefully confessed. "I have been so preoccupied with Pitham's trial that I overlooked the telltale signs. Besides," he added, winking broadly, "I certainly would not have been able to judge by Bridget's increased appetite."

"Preston!" Bridget exclaimed, playfully snatching her hand from her husband's grasp.

"Honestly, Preston, I think it's a blessing that Bridget has such a healthy appetite," Olivia proclaimed with a decisive nod. "It's a pleasant change from all those anemic young Society misses who are forever fainting due to poor nutrition."

"Well, ye'll never have to worry about me Bridget on that score," Patrick concurred. "Even when just a wee one, the lass was a bottomless pit."

Bridget rolled her eyes, clearly dismayed by the topic of conversation. "Could we discuss the weather or Reggie's new tooth . . . anything except my eating habits?"

"I have an even better idea," Preston suggested, a slight toss of his head sending a silent message to Colin. "Let's finish exchanging our gifts."

"I had thought we had opened them all," Bridget stated, obviously perplexed. She failed to note Colin beckon to Olivia and Patrick as she turned to gaze expectantly into her husband's blue-green eyes.

Abruptly the soft click of the door closing caused Bridget to glance around. Everyone had disappeared save for herself and her beaming husband.

"Preston, what is this all about?" she demanded suspiciously.

Linking his hands behind her back, Preston drew her to him, a provocative twist to his lopsided smile.

"I have a surprise for you, my love." Still holding her close with one arm, he reached into his jacket with the other hand and withdrew a black velvet box.

Bridget's eyes widened in surprise. "You extravagant devil! What have you gone and done now?" she asked as Preston placed the box into her palm.

Tilting his blond head, Preston regarded her. "You know how I have teased you about bringing me nothing but bad luck?"

"How could I forget?" she sourly retorted.

"Well, I decided I needed to clarify that judgment."

Frowning with curiosity, Bridget opened the case. "Oh, Preston," she gasped. "It's absolutely beautiful!"

A diamond-studded gold pin, in the shape of a round pot, shone brightly from its satin bed.

"You, my precious leprechaun, have led me to all your treasures, and for that, I thank you."

As Preston's lips covered hers, Bridget knew in her heart that she, too, had found her pot of gold.